I0734993

OTHER WORKS BY ALASTAIR SHARP

There's a Way
Devil Whisperer
Crooked Wings
Spreading Wings
Up from the Bottom
The Book of Consequences
Taking Care

www.alastairsharp.com

ALONE

A Pandemic Novel

ALASTAIR SHARP

Alone
A Pandemic Novel

Paperback ISBN: 978-1-952982-30-9
Ebook ISBN: 978-1-952982-31-6

Published by Golden Ink Media Services   09/25/2020

Golden Ink Media Services
(302) 703-7235
support@goldeninkmediaservices@gmail.com

ALONE

Qui suis-je?
Who am I?

A voice cries out
In tears of loss
Bewilderment.

What was I
Before?
What shall I become?
Who knows?
The voice cries out.

The ripples of its cries
Eddy to the infinite beyond
And echo back
And back.

Alone in the wilderness
I cry.
To whom?
Who to?

Out of silence
She whispers:
Only you can know.
Only you.

ALONE

I had always wondered what it would be like to live all alone.

I am a social creature, always was.

When I was a kid and nothing was happening at home, I was an only child, and there was nothing to do, I would sometimes sit in the front window and watch the street go by because I didn't like being by myself. It was as if I didn't believe I was enough, just being me.

I was looking for something outside myself.

I was waiting for something to turn up.

I never found it, quite frankly.

I was always looking outside myself.

Maybe that's the point.

It could be that I was constantly looking in the wrong place.

I am sitting in the crenellated turret of a half-restored thirteenth century French château, drinking a hot cup of mint tea and looking way down into the valley below, where not a single vehicle moves on the Paris to Toulouse freeway.

I am alone.

I look out across the limestone hills, with their scrubby trees and their stony outcrops.

I am more alone than I have ever been in my life.

The signs of human activity, the power lines across a far hill, a cell phone tower in the distance, the serpentine bitumen of the freeway below, are all reminders, but not evidence, of human presence.

Look as I may, I see no person.

I am alone.

I found this exercise book in the château kitchen.

It's a kitchen from the middle ages, with a massive fireplace big enough for the denizens of the château to sit in for warmth in winter. It has a spit big enough to roast a whole beast. The stone floor, well worn, is probably the original. The kitchen table is heavy oak and could easily seat twenty.

This exercise book, brand new, never used, can be my companion, my soul mate, my means of coming to terms with where I am and who I am with.

Just me.

Luckily there is also a drawer of pens and pencils.

I will fill it up with my thoughts and memories because there is nothing else to do.

French exercise books have little squares to discipline the handwriting. Australian ones just have horizontal lines. This could be the difference between the two cultures.

The French like to keep everything in neat little boxes. The Australians aren't too sure what they are so they just go on living from day to day.

Et voilà.

An expat Australian commits himself in a French exercise book.

I can't imagine if anyone will ever read this, so I am writing it purely to pass the time but also as a personal exercise in self understanding, whatever that turns out to be.

I will try to write every day for at least half an hour, whatever comes up.

So here goes.

For the record: my name is Simon Teague. I am Australian and I turned forty last year.

Perhaps in the dim, unforeseeable future, this tattered exercise book will be found and studied.

Or not.

That depends on whether there will be anyone left.

Or is that too depressing a thought?

I suppose I should record how I got here.

I grew up in the most ordinary of circumstances in suburban Melbourne but I always secretly felt that I was being prepared for something momentous.

I lacked nothing essential as a child, but nor did we live in luxury. My parents were middling, middle class, middle of the road politically, mid-life stalled, middling.

My father worked in the public service, about halfway up the chain of command.

My mother had trained as a nurse but ended up being a conscientious housewife.

I did what kids like me did, but I never felt that anything I did was all that meaningful or extraordinary. Being an only child, I was doted on, worried about, over-medicated and sent to the dentist much too often. I went to ballroom dancing classes, boy scouts, tennis and swimming lessons. I tried a few musical instruments but musical I was not.

Although I have always been a social animal, I drifted from one friendship to another, but in none of them did I find what you might call mateship .

I was looking for something that just wasn't there. One after the other, each friendship dried up and became irrelevant. I don't even remember the names of most of the boys I spent time with. So many of the things we did made not much sense.

We used to dare each other to jump off the garage roof. We rode our bikes near the river and risked falling in. Nothing ever happened.

When I was in high school, again very little happened of any great importance.

I went through the motions, but it seemed rather pointless. I learned a bit of French. I can still remember the poems I had to learn for the oral exam. *J'ai ceuilli cette fleur pour toi sur la colline.* That was Victor Hugo giving a wild flower to a little girl. I don't think I learned anything more useful than that.

The only part of the school curriculum that engaged me was Drama. I auditioned for all the school productions starting as the youngest cast member, playing the paper boy in Our Town, six brilliantly-delivered lines with a passable American accent. My crowning glory, in my final year, was as a cruel Iago in Othello. I was good at cruelty it turns out and got an honourable mention in the interschool Drama festival. Not best actor but still, a little notoriety.

I can still recite some of the lines.

So after high school, instead of going to university like most of my confreres, and heading for the usual lifelong careers in regular society, I went to Drama school, where most graduates ended up as waiters or drove taxis.

Although I started out as a student actor, being an actor soon fell away. I wanted more than that. Just impersonating someone else for a while was fine, but I wanted to have more control over the whole spectacle.

By the end of second year, I was becoming a director. I realised that telling others how to act was more fulfilling than trying to do it myself. They had a course on directing and I was the most determined student they had.

It turns out I was rather good at it, at least enough people thought so to make me believe it.

I felt a bit like God, in a way. I could create something and command a group of willing humans to do my bidding. I could require them to have certain emotions, do certain actions, become whatever I wanted them to become.

There is a certain satisfying power to that. However, it is also fleeting and artificial. When the play is over, the actors go back to being themselves and I don't have any control over them. Transient power. I did know some theatre directors who tried to attain that kind of control over the people around them outside the plays, but I never got to that level.

Those who did that were almost always rather awful people whose company I did not enjoy.

Diedre Temple-Harmsworth decided I was the next bright young thing for her to nurture. She had a track record of picking up new talent, pushing them forward, using her theatre contacts from her own long and glorious life of performance to get them started and then shamelessly promoting them all over the place. She was the epitome of the *"Grande Dame"* of the theatre world.

She'd seen some of my student productions and worked to get me an arts fellowship, which allowed me to mount my own productions in a little theatre down a back lane. I was her protégé, being hauled off to cocktail parties where people with buckets of money were inveigled into supporting the arts. I was one of several bright young things in her coterie and at the time it all looked very promising.

I happily went along with all that for a few years, directing avant garde productions that shocked the critics, mystified way too many theatregoers, drew mediocre audiences and allowed me to sleep with some very sexy young things who thought I was a genius.

It's odd, sitting here now, utterly alone, that I once created a whole short theatre piece based on the one line, said over and over: I am alone. I am alone. I am alone.

I had an ensemble of student actors play out a suite of scenarios using only those lines.

In the program, I credited myself as the playwright.

I must have been prescient.

In reality though, after a few years of this, it all began to feel a bit hollow. I was going through the motions. I was being deliberately provocative, but for what? What was the point in doing all this? I felt, deep down, a total fake.

At the time I was living in a group house of creatives like myself. We were renaissance people, we told ourselves, brilliant across the spectrum of the arts and full of ourselves. None of us made any money but we thought we were the beginning of a new artistic wave, whatever that was.

Every now and then we would retire to the country hideaway of the mother of one of the girls. The mother was a potter who made grotesque asymmetric shapes out of clay and painted them with metal paint. Ugly to say the least. She was an aging hippie, always breathlessly introducing us to her latest skinny young lover. She was perpetually addled on something, vodka and lemon, grass, hash cookies or magic mushrooms.

It was the mushrooms that threw me out of the theatre.

We had all indulged, as we often did, in a huge omelette of Blue Meanies and onions. As the hit came on, I found myself running.

I was running away.

Running, when you are that stoned, is weird. You have no sense of your feet on the ground. I flew off down a hill before gravity took hold of me and I crashed into a clump of wattle bushes and lay there.

Then I went comatose. My body refused to do anything at all but my brain went bananas. I wrestled with all sorts of demons for hours. There was a part of me that knew I had to stay sane or I would never come back. I recognised these demons, in all their alluring forms, as being representations of me, myself or what I thought I was. They were demons fighting for dominance and I had to ward them off.

When it finally wore off, I felt I had won some kind of battle, but not the war. It was exhausting but I knew it was just the beginning. To win that war, I had to become a changed person.

It was dark by the time I could get my body to respond and I staggered back up the hill.

I had run much further than I thought and barely made it back.

I crashed onto an unoccupied bed and slept like a dead person.

When I woke, there was light everywhere and I knew I had to start everything all over again.

And I did.
Fast.

I went to see Deidre. We sat in her book-lined parlour with all its heavy velvet drapes and we drank Courvoisier VSOP in balloon-shaped glasses. I thanked her for all her patronage, and said I was going off to find myself.

She didn't seem to mind at all.

Instead she waxed lyrical about the romance of the young artist throwing everything to the wind, going off to find inspiration, but she also warned me to come back soon so as not to lose momentum.

I promised to stay in touch but I knew I was not coming back.

I left the group house, which was what happened all the time, bodies came and went. I told my parents that I was going travelling.

God bless my parents, they never really understood what I was all about but they were unendingly supportive. How many incomprehensible productions had they sat through? Now they expressed their worries about me going off somewhere with very little money and no plans.

Would I please stay in touch.

I promisesd I would.

I did, now and then.

The stones of this château are almost a metre thick. There is a timeless solidity to them that the silence seems to enhance. It was built back in the time when those with means had to fortify themselves against the potential for attack from those without means, or even more dangerous, those with more means who wanted to add to their wealth.

I'm told the crusader, Simon de Montfort, may have stayed here once.

I am the latest of a line of Simons, I suppose.

Maybe the end of the line.

The château is in the middle of nowhere.

It is roughly square with a strange protruberant rectangular side piece, that looks like an architectural afterthought. The turret is on the southside overlooking the valley which used to be, so I am told, very pretty with a small stream running through it. It used to be a popular fishing spot. Now the valley is cut in half by the four lane Paris to Toulouse freeway and the stream has disappeared underneath in concrete pipes.

The château has small inset windows, some still with the little squares of glass that were favoured in days gone by.

The stairs are made of stone to the first floor and oak from there up.

Other than the little local village, Saint Fé, the nearest town is Gourdon and that's half an hour away on windy one-lane roads. This area was called Quercy for centuries but now is part of the department called the Lot, after the river Lot that winds its leisurely way from east to west.

Why someone decided to build a château here on top of this hill is obscured in long and dubious history. The main reason is probably defensive. You can see in all directions and anyone who attacks it has to fight uphill. It's not a fortress but is built to protect itself.

Chloé Thomson de Beaurepaire, who now owns it, has tried to piece together the history but it's patchy. She says that she believes different Lords and their descendants held it for a few centuries at a time, then war and religion wrought their changes.

Chloé is American, married to a Frenchman, Alain de Beaurepaire and she has spent the fortune she made on Wall Street, in futures trading I think, to make this château more or less liveable. It's about half finished. The previous owners, an English family, had used it only in summer, so she installed the central heating, double glazed the major windows, put a cover over the swimming pool and heated it, gave almost every bedroom an ensuite bathroom, and brought in all the electrical appliances that Americans believe are essential to life. The solar panels are in a shed waiting to be assembled. The wind turbine lies white and flaccid in the long grass behind the shed waiting to become erect.

There are parts of the château that are as yet untouched, full of old stuff, gathering dust. There is a network of cellars underneath full of dust, cobwebs and probably ghosts.

Chloé is a goer. She never sits still and she talks a mile a minute. She is one of these people who I suspect thrive through life by just forging ahead and grabbing the good omens when they appear. She loves omens. She sold out of her hedge fund partnership, the way she tells it, because she had a dream that the markets were about to crash. She checked with her astrologer who confirmed the dream. She did this a month before the financial crisis in 2008.

She sat on her massive bundle of cash for two years, buying her house in Toulouse because Alain wanted to use it as his French base. She bought back into the stock market just before the resurgence began, after an i Ching reading that suggested immediate action, so she followed it. The stock market rose and rose, and she rode along with it for five years. Then a Tarot reading led her to cash out again. Although she missed the next few years as the market steadily went up and up, she felt she had been given everything she ever wanted and she swore that would be the end of her dealings on Wall Street.

However it is clear she can't resist, every now and then, rejoining the fray. When the pandemic started in China, she saw the potential for global financial disaster, confirmed by a South American shaman who she had sponsored to come to France. She immediately went off to New York to play, as only she knew how, leaving Clo in charge of the boys.

I am sure she set herself up to make another bundle, selling at near the top before the fall. I haven't heard, but as far as I know, she's still stuck in New York, although probably with more money than she knows what to do with.

Most likely the stock market has crashed incredibly, which had started before I left Toulouse, so she will most likely buy in again, because, knowing her, she won't be able to resist.

The stillness is incredible.

Nothing moves here that suggests the existence of humans.

There is no sound of machine, or human voice.

Only nature in all her voices announces the day with symphonic passages as the day waxes and then wanes, lullabies and pastorales as the sun passes overhead and heraldic climaxes at twilight.

I could have been a music critic.

The lead voices are the birds. Their choir has so many different notes and melodies. The littlest ones that chirp and make nests under the eaves of sheds are the sparrows. The great soloist is the blackbird who sings at the changes of light, morning and evening. The crows caw in French, so i suppose they are like French horns. Australian crows sound totally different. The chorus in support all day are the doves and pigeons, who coo and softly murmur almost continuously. There are unruly interruptions from the Pie who can cackle or click when they are not disposed to sing.

The music of the wind moves from the softest of whispers to the wild outbursts that make things rattle.

There's some iron loose on the roof of the shed where the electric car now sits uncharged and unchargeable. I ought to climb up and fix that roof. There are lots of little jobs to do.

There's a field mouse domiciled in the wood pile and I have been talking to it on and off. Actually I think all field mice look the same, so I could be talking to a different one each time we converse.

I have had no contact with another human for more days than I have been able to keep track of.

Although I love my morning coffee, even though I have to drink it black, the mint tea is great. Coffee is for mornings while mint tea is for afternoons.

Even though it is March and the late winter can be cold here, the mint is tough. The garden has enough mint to last a lifetime. I keep the big black kettle on the fire most of the day for the morning coffee and the mint tea whenever the desire comes on. The fire is also my only means of heat.

In the afternoons I climb the stone staircase with a steaming cup, three flights up to the turret, and watch the horizon, or the falcons, or the clouds.

Now there are no jetstreams anymore so the sky is wonderfully clear.

It was probably unwise to use the BMW to get out here in the first place. It's undeniably small, so there's not much room for what we should have thought to bring. Of course knowing what I now know I would have needed a fleet of trucks. Disasters have a habit of giving no warning.

This little box on wheels is called the BMW i13 and was promoted as better than the Tesla. At least it got me here and for the first day or two let me go up to Gourdon for supplies.

Thank God I bought more coffee.

When we first heard about this virus, this pandemic, we didn't give it much thought. It was happening far off in China and we were sure the government would monitor the situation and take care of it. Isn't that what governments are supposed to do? Then it began to spread. Clo had a phone conversation with her father who is a senior chemist with a big international pharmaceutical company in Paris and he told her that what was coming was very serious. He said they would be trying to create vaccines to deal with it as soon as they could. He told her not to worry. For a while we followed that advice, but then there was talk about people starting to get the virus and then people began to die from it. We were told it was incredibly dangerous, contagious and the only way to deal with it was to institute lockdowns.

Isolate was the word.

That was when we decided, why not take advantage of this and hide away in the château, til it all passes, or til Clo's father comes up with the antidote.

So we planned it, a nice isolated vacation in the country. I would go up, open up the château, and she was supposed to come up by train once she had handed the boys over to Alain.

I would pick her up at Gourdon station.

But it was too late.

They shut down the trains that day. They shut down the internet the next day, before we could work out how she could get here.

Of course I haven't heard anything since.

She's probably still there with the boys.

The only possibility which is getting more and more unlikely by the day, is she will walk up the track that leads to the château carrying a backpack, having walked all the way from Toulouse.

How long that would take I can't imagine.

Clo is not a long distance walker anyway.

No doubt she will have lots of stories to tell me when this is all over.

Back when we were in Toulouse, Clo had full use of the BMW for free, as part of her job, so I am in no place to complain. When I first got here I could plug it in and have plenty of juice. I could get up to Gourdon and back easily on one charge, but now the power's gone and the generator is out of diesel, I'm stuck.

It's a useless piece of precision-made German metal and rubber.

I could keep chickens in it I suppose.

Actually the chickens here seem very happy to run around all day and then go into their imitation of Prince Charles's medieval poultry palace. Chloé was a sucker for extravagant folly. She found the design in a Better Living magazine and had it copied by an elderly local carpenter. Lovely craftsmanship.

The closest neighbor, Jean-Claude, had taken good care of the chickens and so we are well supplied.

In terms of protein, the eggs are my lifeline.

When I left Australia I had no idea where I would go.

There was something exhilarating about the very act of going. I felt so happy to be leaving. There was a sense of shedding old burdens. I was going off not to be anything, not to do anything, not to impress anyone, not to add to my reputation.

I was just going.

I know the old cliché about going to find yourself, but quite frankly that's as good a description of what was pushing me.

Whatever it was that I was leaving did not satisfy the need. What I was going towards, I had no idea.

The image comes to mind of how snakes shed old skin in its entirety when they grow a new one underneath.

I was doing something like that.

That old facade had to go to make way for the new one.

Actually I think I was fed up with facades in general.

I needed to find the real snake.

I started with the cheapest ticket I could find which took me to Singapore.

It was not a place I deliberately chose. I didn't really mind where I was going. Nothing was pulling me towards itself.

I was leaving from somewhere, not going to somewhere.

It was the going that was the imperative.

I sat in the plane, this ridiculously flimsy thin tube of metal, hurtling above the earth, sitting next to someone I didn't know, and who didn't want to know me. We had momentary elbow contact from time to time and she had to get up when I needed the toilet. Other than that, we were not acquainted.

Far below, the endless red earth of central Australia slowly rolled away behind us. I had never been to the heart of the country, the red centre, and it looked as alien as if I were flying over Pluto. Was that my country down there? I felt no affinity for it. It was empty and barren. There was no sign of human existence.

Then as we circled over the waters of Singapore, there were dozens and dozens of ships sitting there. I could imagine that they had come from ports all over the world, carrying stuff, waiting to carry away more stuff.

Coming and going. Just like me.

I had the same sensation when we landed at Changi airport. There were hundreds of planes at the massive terminal, all with their noses in the troughs of the terminal building, like factory pigs. I thought of their tails as bird plumage, all the different colours and emblems. They too, once they had had their fill, would fly off to somewhere, carrying their loads of humans to be disgorged into another trough on another continent.

People going somewhere for a million different reasons.

Humans are busy folk.

It's strange to be thinking about that now.

The contrast between the crush of humanity that is Singapore and the empty sky of here.

Singapore smelt like the tropics, lush and wet. Once I had left the airconditioning and the French fashion duty free shops and stepped outside, the air was almost liquid. I had never breathed in air like that.

It was intoxicating because it was so different from the air I had breathed all my life.

Just breathing was a great new experience.

I went to the YHA hostel because it was cheap. Next to it, at that time, was a big open air food market that appeared in the carpark each evening and was gone again the following morning.

I sat at a rickety table with my newly acquired Singapore dollars and ordered a nasi goreng, which was the only thing on the flimsy cardboard menu I recognised.

Two girls came to sit nearby and I heard their Australian accents. We got talking. They were about to head off on the type of adventure that so many young Australians think they have to do before they go home, get married, have one and a half children, a mortgage and a dog.

They had bought themselves tickets on a bus going north along the east coast of Malaysia. It sounded like something to do and I had no other plans, so I went too.

I think they were quite relieved to have a male co-traveller.

They were young teachers who had just finished their required two years to pay off their scholarships. Now they were free and had savings, off they were going to find themselves, or something like that.

I suppose that's what almost all of us were doing, in our own stumbling way.

I was not particularly attracted to either of them. They were plain in a very natural way. They wore sensible clothes, had sensible haircuts and talked with that strange upward inflection at the ends of sentences, which is typical of certain Aussie women. Everything sounds like a question. They were smart, friendly and easy to travel with. Janey and Fiona had been good friends since early childhood, grew up close to each other and did almost everything together. I heard all about that as the bus rattled on and on. At first I wondered if they were a couple, because of the way they looked at each other and finished each other's sentences, but as I would soon find out, they were not. Nonetheless in every other way, they drew deeply on each other.

It was a good deep friendship, which I admired and which I envied.

As the bus wound its tortuous way through the jungle towards Kuantan, half way up the coast, we talked and talked. I learned all about their more or less joint childhoods, they had lived in the same suburb, gone to the same schools and played the same sports. They asked about my life and when I shared what I had done, I watched them being terribly impressed that they were travelling with a not exactly famous theatre director. They had vaguely heard of some of my productions, they had even been once to the little theatre that I used. I sensed that, if I had the inclination, I could add them to my list of adoring conquests.

There's a certain look they get.

The trick to living in this château, by myself, I have discovered, is daily discipline. Without that I would go nuts.

The one piece of modern technology that has not failed me is my Japanese solar watch It doesn't have an alarm but I have a rooster for that. To get me through my endless days, I stick to my discipline.

I have decided that the rooster is Boris. He has a certain Russian-ness about him, he struts like a cossack, and he is red. When he crows, I get up. I get up, as the old saying goes, at cock's crow .

Depending on the weather, I have a cold dunk in the dam or I heat water for a bucket wash in front of the fire. The swimming pool that I tried to turn into a fish farm is now toxic and unusable. I make breakfast with whatever the garden provides in season. I am so lucky that I like potimarron and I can eat potatos at every meal. There is coffee in abundance, but I am being careful not to use too much. I must husband my caffeine.

Before Chloé bought the château, the English family who had it as a summer retreat, had employed a local gardener who had planted acres of edibles. They just keep on giving and I am learning, by trial and error, about harvesting seeds and keeping them for the future.

After breakfast I meditate like I learned from my travels, it's a bit Buddhist and a bit yoga. Then I work. I find something to fix, or to dig up weeds or to cut down straggling bushes. There is always something to do and I make lists, to do lists, so I will never run out.

Then I make lunch, mostly I use eggs. Those dear feathered ladies have been totally reliable. And somehow without me knowing anything of animal husbandry, Boris keeps them in the family way and every now and then we have chickens. I am not a vegetarian but every time I bring myself to decapitate a male chicken and defeather and gut it I feel queasy.

Nonetheless I eat them.

Protein must be respected.

I take a nap almost every afternoon.

Then I go up to the turret with the mint teaa to watch the sky and the empty freeway. Nothing has passed on that freeway for I don't know how long.

This is when I write in this exercise book.

Turret, mint tea and memoir.

Then I walk the bounds. There is a circuit I do.

It's probably a couple of ks, and I like to imagine that I am playing the rôle of a medieval guard on the battlements, on the lookout. I don't expect to be attacked but I like to see what's what. I might see a rabbit or a fox. I might find chanterelles or cèpes, but my earlier experience with mushrooms makes me wary. I collect interesting stones or pieces of wood to decorate my abode.

As the sun begins to set, I chant the Buddhist hymn I learned in a temple in Thailand, I make some dinner and then read.. There are lots and lots of books in this château. There is one room which Chloé rightly called the library, full of all sorts of books. Boxes of them. A lot are in French and I make myself painstakingly work through them. The so-called French classics are hard to read because they use that French tense reserved for literature, Passé Simple, which is hard to grasp. I do like trying. Victor Hugo and I are now on speaking terms, beyond just the poems. Luckily the English family had stocked the library with what they liked to read in the summer, and left it all there when the financial crash sank their pleasure craft and they had to sell. I'm not so keen on endless vampire novels, but even they help to pass the time. I alternate between high literature in French and mental distraction in English.

Usually when the sun sets I go to bed. I have candles by the boxfull but I don't like to use them up.

That's my day.

It rarely varies.

The bus from Singapore took all day to reach Kuantan, a fishing and rice growing town halfway along the east coast of Malaysia. The bus stopped at endless two-bicycle towns. We could step out for a few minutes, while people got on and off, carrying chickens and steaming pots of cooked rice. We were stared at and talked about, and, in our turn, we looked at how the local people lived in their little fishing villages, each with its own small mosque and little wooden shops selling bamboo umbrellas and plastic utensils made in China.

The bus pulled into the middle of Kuantan in the late afternoon. It was drizzling rain and it was quite a walk from the bus terminal to the youth hostel with backpacks full of things that we would soon realise we did not need. We arrived soaking wet.

No-one else had booked in.

In the evening we were the sole patrons of a tiny restaurant next door, with a metal and thatch roof run by a Chinese lady who stood over us as we ate, saying "Mmai", which her son told us meant, in Hainanese, "Eat!".

We must have looked undernourished to her, white, skinny and anaemic.

That night, it started really raining. And raining and raining.

Within twenty-four hours, all roads out of the town were under water. We were marooned.

It's funny to think back to that time now.

Here I am much more marooned than we were then. And this marooning is solitary, very different. There the waters eventually went down and we could move on up the coast.

Here?

There are no floods to recede, I am on top of a hill.

It is a different kind of inundation.

The enemy is invisible and in reality, I don't really know what it is.

I do feel marooned and the apparent endlessness of it terrifies me, if I let it.

I am stuck and there is no way out that I can see.

I can't even be sure that what holds me here is just a virus, a pandemic.

Is there something else going on?

I have no way of knowing that.

The only way to find out would be to walk and walk and walk until I find something or I perish.

I won't do that.

What would be the point?

At least here, I am in the known . If I head off, where would I go, what would I find? It would be the unknown and I could be a lot worse off.

I long to have some kind of human contact.

I would like to talk to somebody, anybody.

I would like to feel human skin, to shake hands with someone, do the French kiss, "*Faire les bises*", one cheek or two or three, depending which region you are in. That kind of human interaction does something that nothing else can do.

Sometimes sitting up here in the turret, I pray to see a vehicle, a truck, a car, even a tractor, anything, go by below on the freeway.

Please God show me a helicopter.

Will this never end?

Although I have felt lonely in my life, on and off, I have never felt like this.

Can I stand it?

Can I bear just to get up every day, having slept alone, I eat alone, I work to keep myself from going crazy, then I eat some more and then I sit up here all alone and then I sleep again with the vain hope that tomorrow might be different.

It never is.

Will I ever get used to this?

One way I can quickly comfort myself is by going back into the past.

I suppose that's why people write memoirs.

Living in the past helps when the present is too daunting.

When Clo and I met Chloé, after we arrived in Toulouse, Chloé had just bought this château, Le Domaine de Buveny.

Clo was looking for something to do when she saw an ad for a nanny who speaks English. It was Chloé wanting someone to grapple with the boys, three of them under ten. I had my job as an English teacher already lined up, which was why we were in Toulouse in the first place, so it suited us quite well. Chloé has this rambling great place on the outskirts of Toulouse, they call a Maison Bourgeois. It has "*dependences*", meaning outbuildings intended in former days for the staff. She gave us one of them to live in so Clo was always on hand. At the time, Chloé was intensely focused on her new château project.

As she herself admitted, the château was a ridiculous money-gobbling monster, but Chloé was utterly besotted with the whole idea.

Her husband, Alain, born into a minor aristocratic family, de Beaurepaire, put up with it but only just. His family lost their own château after the war when there just wasn't the money to keep it going. He talks about it as being a burden on his family, and is happy that they don't have it any more.

Evidently his parents bore the scars of losing the last vestige of the family's glorious past and it had coloured his childhood in a way he would rather forget. The château in question, somehere in the Lot is just a ruin now, according to Alain, and beyond restoring. Chloé looked at it, couldn't believe the price, not much more than you would pay for a decent Citroën and was sorely tempted. It had been on the market for years and no-one showed any interest in it. She begged and pleaded but Alain forbad her to touch it. Too many ghosts, he said.

So Chloé began looking round for something close by. She wanted the family to have their own château again. She's thoroughly American but has pretensions of being part of a French dynasty. She speaks good French but can't lose the yankee accent. Her pronunciation of the letter r is totally New York. The velvety gallic r is beyond her.

Alain is a thoroughly modern Frenchman. He speaks impeccable English with a slight American twang, and is a wine merchant with a lucrative export trade running from France to Manhattan.

Utterly unlike the previous French generations, they have money coming out their ears.

It was funny for Clo and me, with not a rouble to spare between us, to have drifted into this circle. Clo and Chloé really hit it off and I went along for the ride. Alain wasn't around much, going back and forth across the Atlantic, organising consignments from all over France for his boutique on the upper east side. He sells bottles of prestige Bordeaux for thousands of dollars each.

Not knowing what has happened to the outside world, I wonder whether he still has a business at all.

Clo rather fancies herself as a bit of an interior designer, so she and Chloé spent hours deciding how this château would be brought back to life. I must admit I was rather intrigued myself. The theatre director in me was imagining how I would design it as a set for a film.

There is no doubt this château has atmosphere. You can feel the history emanating from the stone walls.

For the last year we have been coming and going as the work progressed. The plumbing has certainly improved and I loved the spa bath and the heated covered pool, till the power died.

I wonder if we will ever get to finish the project.

I caught a rabbit in a trap.

I found the traps in a shed and worked out by trial and error how they worked, without losing any fingers. I put a few out to see if they worked and put carrots in them. For the first few days, when I checked them, the carrots disappeared but no rabbits. Sometimes the traps had not even been sprung, just robbed.

Then one day there it was, not dead but badly broken by the cruel teeth of the metal trap.

I stood there when I came across it, stunned and wondering what to do. Then I looked up and I saw I had competition. A very large crow with its beady yellow eyes was staring at me and clearly laying claim to his dinner.

That rabbit is mine! I yelled at him and threw a stick. He cawed at me as he swooped off.

I had to break its neck, which I didn't like doing. It was warm and furry and its sad little eyes were full of terror. Anyway I steeled myself, put it out of its misery, skinned and guttted it and roasted it on the spit.

I did enjoy the benefit of the protein.

I am top of the food chain. I have no choice. Well I could become a vegetarian I suppose, but I think it's a bit late in life. I managed a meatless year in the monastery but they had great cooks and I never felt the need for meat.

Here I crave it.

I have reset the traps.

The monsoon in Malaysia comes on fast. I had not given any thought to weather forecasts and neither had the girls.

We woke up to torrents of water cascading off the iron roof of the youth hostel.

All around us the water rose as we watched.

No buses ran and we were stuck.

For the next week we were the only residents.

The manager was the son of the lady whose restaurant we would use exclusively. He spoke excellent English with something of an oxonian flavour to it. His mother's restaurant, with all its rustic charm, leaky roof and limited menu would become our sole source of sustenance for a long week. As long as we didn't mind rice with everything, we did well. Quite frankly I could have lived forever on her cooking, she spiced everything to perfection and the veggies were just a little *al dente* which I really like.

With nowhere to go and nothing to do, I became a sex counsellor.

It is not a rôle I trained for at all. My own sex life up to that point had been highly active but largely characterised as being unconscious, uncommitted athleticism with scant consideration for the wellbeing of whoever I was conjoined with at the time.

Now, in the middle of a flood, I was forced to reconsider what sex was and how to conduct it with care and attention. There is a saying that you only really get to understand something when you have to teach it to someone else.

It's odd to be thinking of that now. It is possible that sex, as I knew it, will never be part of my existence any more.

Quite honestly, sitting here, I have no inclination. Maybe I am having male menopause or something.

The girls were both virgins. Stuck together in the monsoon, we talked and talked about all sort of things and we got around to their dark secret. They had had boyfriends on and off but neither had ever got close to a sexual relationship with anyone beyond superficial petting. One of their aims on this trip was a determination to lose their virginity (such a quaint way of thinking about sex but they used that expression). They wanted to become sexually experienced and sophisticated. They had read all about it, seen plenty of films in which sex seemed to be such an important culmination. They had even studied some pornography.

At first we just talked. They asked me to describe my sex life. Strangely enough in the telling, it all sounded horribly exploitative. I exploited situations, sometimes shamelessly, and now and then I found myself being exploited. I had to admit that I had never really had a sustained relationship with anyone long enough to have a deep relationship that included physical sex as an enactment of love. I was describing transactional sex and it was almost embarrassing.

They were keen questioners. They wanted to know what my sexual partners liked, what they asked for, who had the most satisfying moves. They were very serious students.

Then it got a little tricky. As you can imagine, here I was the only available male. The manager was unashamedly gay, so he was not available (I actually had to make clear to him I was not myself that way inclined. He tended to lurk round the showers now and then).

They had obviously talked about this between themselves and they quite bluntly asked if I would be willing to teach them and enable them to achieve their goal. They wanted to become experts. It all seemed rather like some kind of lab. I can't say that I am all that knowledgeable about the female anatomy, especially those parts that are actively engaged in sex, but I did my best. It had no passion in it, in the usual sense, but there was their passionate desire to accomplish something, and in the end it was entertaining and certainly not unpleasant.

If I knew then what I know now, it would have been very different. Clo, being French, has enhanced my knowledge exponentially. She is the exact opposite of how those girls were back then. She knows what she wants and she knows how to make sure her partner satisfies her deeply.

Not to dwell on the details with Janey and Fiona, but I did my best. They wanted to explore and experience and we did all that. They didn't seem to have any qualms about watching each other and saying how they felt. Having grown up together they were very aware of each other's body and not afraid to be naked. They both had small breasts and narrow hips and didn't think of themselves as being physically attractive. It took me a little coaching to help them to go beyond physical nakedness to sexually provocative nakedness. That was new for them.

I felt a bit like I was back as a theatre director, doing a very sexy piece, only I was also the lead male character.

Clo would have laughed to see how I worked with them. She would have been a much better teacher than I was.

I did have to inform them that most pornography is really fake and that a lot of what they had seen was not obligatory for good sex. In fact I recommended not trying some of what they had seen, unless they were really drawn to it.

The whole thing was quite joyful, playful and in an odd way studious. They wanted to try everything, even a few things that I was not so keen on. They eliminated a few techniques by trial and error.

By the time the floodwaters had receded, both girls were new enthusiasts and sexually experienced enough to begin to have differential preferences and I had been sorely tested.

It seems so remote now.

Although there is everything I need to survive in this château, quite frankly I miss a few things.

The things I miss most, strangely enough, perched on a rocky hilltop, are the little things.

I would love a beer. There's a whole cellar in the château with dust-covered bottles of all kinds, reds, whites, rosés and all those weird apéritif drinks that every French department boasts of, like Ricard, Calvados, Lillet.

I open one of them from time to time but it's not the same. A warm afternoon with a cold beer, and maybe potato chips would be heaven. I've got the potatoes but no idea how to make them crisp. And anyway, as they say, drinking alcohol on your own is depressing.

I do miss French bread of course.

And cheese. France is the king of cheese. When I first got here I couldn't believe the range. There are thousands of varieties to choose from, aisles of cheese in the supermarkets, incredible huge rounds of unpasteurised goat cheeses in Sunday markets and all those creamy cheesy things from right round here, like Rocamadour. I brought some with me, bought some more on my visits to Gourdon while the car had juice, but they have all been and gone.

Ah what a delight it would be to have fresh bread and strong cheese.

I do miss music. In the phone I had lots of Leonard Cohen which seemed to be the perfect accompaniment for isolation. But once the phone died, the music went with it. I was no longer able to indulge in the Tower of Song .

I do sing to myself, all sorts of things, but I would love to have someone else to back me up.

The wine cellar has quite good acoustics which adds tonality to my baritone renditions of negro spirituals. Sometimes I feel like a motherless child .

I can't sustain it very long.

The one thing I don't miss is TV. I know that everywhere beyond my hill, there must be all sorts of terrible things taking place. I don't know what they are and I don't really think it would help me if I did.

I am learning to live with the philosophy of ignorance is bliss .

What happens from here on will happen and I will deal with it, when it makes itself known.

Once the monsoon waters had gone down enough, the buses started to run again.

We said goodbye to the manager of the hostel and his mother who we had become very fond of, promised to stay in touch and we headed north.

We stopped in Kuala Terengganu for a couple of nights, renting a beachfront hut for ridiculously few ringgit per night and eating fish, fresh out of the water, sold and cooked by the fishermen who caught them. My two newly sexually awakened companions happily continued their education and I was beginning to feel that I could do with a break.

We moved on up the coast after a few days to Kota Bharu on the northern-most end of the east coast of Malaysia.

We got a lift with a young American Peace Corps guy who was working as a teacher in the local high school.

When we arrived, he invited us to stay with him and also to visit his school.

It was the only high school in the state, teaching in English using a curriculum from Cambridge University. We were introduced to the Principal, who was a surprisingly young man with quite an Australian accent.

It turns out he had trained in Perth and played good cricket.

"I can bowl the best googly in Kelantan," I remember him boasting while showing me his wrist action.

He got very excited when he learned that the girls were both teachers. He asked if they would be interested in joining his staff. I watched them exchange looks. The Peace Corps guy, his name was Phil, told them they would love it.

He sang the praises of the school, the diligence of the students and the fabulous countryside of Kelantan. The local beaches are fabulous, he told them, especially Pantai Cinta Berahi, the Beach of Passionate Love.

They smiled at each other and were sold.

Was I interested? The Principal felt he had to ask me, I suppose, but he was a bit half-hearted.

I told him, I really didn't feel qualified.

He didn't seem to mind.

I smile when I think of our time in Kota Bharu.

I had a good time there, a world so different from where I had lived, and it was tempting to stay.

It is an exotic part of the world. The weather, the lush forest, the warm and friendly people, the relaxed pace of life.

It has its oddities. It is a very religious place, where ninety percent of the people are Muslims. They have religious police, who, if they catch an unmarried couple together unsupervised, make them marry each other.

Non-Muslims however are another story. They can do what they like, because they are non-believers and destined to go to Hell anyway.

This especially applied to all the expats, Europeans, Americans and Aussies who worked or played in Kota Bharu.

There was one overriding activity, other than a lot of dope.

The name of the beach suggests why.

We, all three, moved into the wonderfully expansive and ludicrously cheap village house that Phil rented from a Chinese shopkeeper, whose son was in his class.

His house was brand new, up on stilts except for the cemented back area which housed the squat toilet, the bucket bath and the gas rings which constituted the kitchen. He had dozens of fruitful banana trees, where you could lean out of the glassless windows and help yourself.

The girls began to prepare to teach. Janey was a science teacher, Fiona taught mathematics. The school couldn't believe their luck as those two disciplines were the hardest to fill.

They had a couple of days to study the curriculum, before getting started, but in the spirit of the local expats, as they began to integrate, I saw that they had their eyes on Phil as their next private teacher for their ongoing education.

It was very sweet that they asked if I minded.

Quite frankly, I was relieved. I gave them my blessings but at the same time I felt I needed to get a little space from the prospective *ménage à trois*.

One day sitting in a bamboo hut that served as a shop by the road near the school, I was enjoying a steaming bowl of the local Laksa, thick noodles with shrimp, when a large bald European man wearing nothing but the local costume of sarong, walked in. The young man who had cooked the dish and had served me went over to him and put his hands together in a very reverential greeting. The older man stroked his face lovingly, then noticing me, came over.

"English?" he asked.

"Australian."

"I meant language not domicile", he said. He had a strong Irish lilt to his voice.

He ordered his Laksa fluently in the local dialect and sat down opposite me without being invited.

"Haji Daud bin Moussa", he said, which I did not understand at all, till he added: "Is my name."

"You sound Irish to me."

"That I will not dispute."

Then he, unprompted, told me his story. He was indeed Irish, born to an aristocratic family who owned multiple castles and estates in County Cork. Although he had now inherited one of them, he had turned his back on everything Irish, converted to Islam and was determined to live in Kota Bharu forever. The income from the castle and its farm would keep him living in comfort for the rest of his days.

I admired his good fortune.

"No" he said, "all is destiny my son. Mektoub, as they say, All is written."

In my turn I gave a short version of my own destiny.

"Teague!" he hooted. "You're a son of Ireland."

I am more than a bit hazy about our family tree, but I gave him the benefit of the doubt.

He said, as a fellow countryman, he should take me under his wing.

By the end of lunch he had invited me to stay at his house.

It suited me perfectly.

And he paid for the lunch.

His house was magnificent.

It was a vast wooden building on stilts with polished wooden floors, wooden slatted shutters instead of windows and high ceilings with gently turning fans. Around the house was a lush garden filled with tropical fruit trees and vibrant coloured flowers. The most surprising part of the house though, was his staff. He had a dozen young slim Malay boys who he said he was sponsoring to go to school. They came from inland villages and stayed with him for free in return for doing chores.

As it turned out they did a little more than that.

Indeed the morals of Khota Bharu were unusual. It seemed that nobody minded that this Irishman had all these toy boys at his disposal. He didn't hide it at all.

I gently let him know that I wasn't that way inclined and he didn't push it.

Once we had cleared that up, we would sit on his wide verandah during the regular afternoon rains and talk. I began to really enjoy his company. He liked to be called Daud, although his boys called him *"Tuan"*, which means sir.

"To name a thing or a person is to make it real", he told me.

When I asked him about his name, he told me how even when he was a boy he could not relate to his given name, "My Christian name", he said with a sneer. "I was one of a million Patricks. Like potatoes in a sack."

I assumed he had taken a new name when he converted to Islam.

"I did indeed. Much as I despise the Catholics of Ireland and all the dreadful things they did to us, I did enjoy the old testament. Wild stories there, my boy. So I chose the Arabic versions of some of my favourite characters, King David and our old friend Moses."

He told me endless stories about Ireland, his family history, how he converted to Islam (he said it was for love and I did not really want to hear the intricate details about that), his trip to Mecca, which allowed him to add Haji to his name, and how he felt he was now a man of the soil of Kelantan.

"Planted here till I go to heaven."

He did try to interest me in Islam, talking about the virtues of a spiritually focussed life, inviting me to come to the Mosque across the road, but I didn't feel the pull.

I told him I was a Methodist and he laughed.

"You'll never get into Heaven with that label."

I think of him often, now as I sit in my own castle, far away and a very different world.

I wonder what would have happened if, like he did, I had thrown everything to the winds and converted to Islam and lived in a Malay village.

I am glad I didn't.

I wonder how he is doing now.

Finding the dead farmer and his wife was a difficult day.

As part of my daily discipline, I would walk the bounds of what I thought was the property of Le Domaine de Buveny. I always passed close to the next farm house before veering off along a low stone wall that was probably hundreds of years old.

In previous visits with Chloé we had met him, Jean-Claude, who was in his eighties. His wife was Eveline and made jars and jars of fabulous confiture. Whenever we visited them we would stagger home with a box of conserves, pickles and home made sausage. They were salt-of-the-earth French with the soil deeply ingrained in their souls. They were childen of "La terre," the land.

The day I arrived, I saw them from a distance. He was on his old red tractor and she was in their yard. I had waved and I had meant to go and say Bonjour, but somehow never got round to it.

Chloé has been paying them a small monthly sum to be the caretakers of the château. He would keep an eye on the garden and husband the chickens and Boris, so that whenever Chloé or her friends come up, there were farm eggs ready.

I hadn't seen them again since I got here, and I assumed that they thought they didn't need to come up any more, if I was there.

They are very discreet.

Then everything went quiet.
Too quiet.
I didn't hear his tractor or see smoke from their chimney.
Finally on my afternoon beating of the bounds, I took a detour to see them.
There was a definite sense of lifelessness around their house. Usually there are chickens and ducks wandering about, cats sunning themselves and Jean-Claude on his tractor, to which he seems almost permanently attached. Usually I would find Eveline in the garden or the kitchen, her twin domains.
I looked around and saw nothing.
It was weird, eerie.
I could feel it.
I knocked on the door and when nothing happened, I pushed it open and called, as one does in French: "Il y a quel qu'un? Anyone home?"
After no response, I took a step inside the kitchen.
They were dead.
He had died in his chair by the fire, which had long died out. He still had his boots on and was reclining in the chair, with his head thrown back and his mouth wide open.

She was slumped at the kitchen table, her head on her arms as if she had fallen asleep. There was half a bottle of red wine open and a wasp had drowned in it.

I made one last sad little verbal attempt to wake them, but I knew they were gone.

I had never seen a dead body.

I have gone to a few funerals in my life. Four to be exact, two grandfathers and two grandmothers. My father's parents lived quite close and I saw them often but they were not much fun to be with, they seemed kind of wooden to a kid. I only ever saw them when we went as a family. The only good thing about grandparent visits was that my Grandma cooked fabulous Sunday roast lunches with gravy.

My grandfather died of a heart attack the year he retired. His wife went a year later. Their funerals were almost identical, boring and somehow missing any kind of emotion. My father was suitably solemn but that was about it. I remember wanting to ask questions about death and dying but my parents were not willing to talk about it.

I never saw their bodies, just the coffins.

My maternal grandparents lived in the country and we didn't see them much. My mother's father had been wounded in the war and spent his days in a rocking chair on his verandah. I always felt he was half dead the few times I saw him. My mother's mother seemed to be perpetually worried about everything.

I just wasn't that interested in any of my forebears.

I regret that now.

They might have been a lot more interesting if I had taken the time or made the effort.

Anyway they're gone now.

So the bodies of Jean-Claude and Eveline were my first experience of witnessing human death.

My first impulse was to run. But I stopped myself because I sensed that most likely I was the only person who would see them.

I had a responsibility.

The question was what to do?

On the one hand, I should do something for them. I couldn't just leave them like that to become some kind of macabre art work. On the other hand, I was very aware, seeing there was a total shutdown all over France and that the virus was spreading everywhere, they could be infectious.

I stayed frozen at the doorway and made sure I didn't touch anything.

It was impossible to know if they had died of the virus or something else.

I stared at them for the longest time, hoping that maybe the whole thing was some kind of hallucination and they would just spring back to life.

That wore off and I went outside very carefully and thought about what to do.

Under normal circumstances you would simply call the relevent authorities and they would take care of it. Now, as far as I could tell, I was the local authority by virtue of being the only human being around.

There was no-one to call.

I knew I was being called upon.

They should be buried, but if they had the virus I might get it by touching anything in their house.

In the end I realised the only way I could safely and honourably give them their final resting place was by cremation.

Hopefully their Catholic souls would forgive me. Assuming that souls have religion. Can you have a Catholic soul? Maybe it's only people who have to have a religion and their souls are freer than that. Anyway, the only way I could think to do it would be to burn their house down round them as a funeral pyre, like I had seen in India along the Ganges. Not houses of course, but in India they make a big pile of wood and the bodies go in the middle.

I don't even know if Jean-Claude and Eveline were Catholics. Certainly there were no signs of religious affiliation in the house. They tended towards family photos on the walls and porcelain dolls on all the horizontal surfaces.

I thought about taking some of the things in their house that could be useful.

Then again would I catch the virus if I touched anything?

I decided to take the risk.

I made myself a face mask out of a scarf and I put on some old overalls that I found in a shed, along with some big gumboots and gardening gloves. Then I cut the bottom off a very large plastic bottle, big enough to fit over my head.

Then looking like some kind of garbage-heap deep-sea diver I clumped down the track, with some big plastic bags and ventured into the house.

Just before I left Toulouse, there had been official bulletins about disinfecting things. Everybody was urged to wash their hands all the time, wash the veggies bought at the supermarket, wear gloves when pushing a supermarket trolley and all that. So anything I planned to take from Jean-Claude's house I should consider as potentially lethal. Tip-toeing, as best I could in gumboots, I edged around their stiff bodies. They smelled rather awful and I was close to throwing up into my face mask.

They had been dead for a while.

I felt a bit like a thief as I collected quite a stockpile of edibles in tins and jars. Eveline was good at making pickles and chutney. I would have a lifetime supply. They had some coffee, not my favourite brand but coffee is coffee. I go for Italian but they preferred supermarket house brand. There were other supplies that I took : flour, salt, sugar and all that sort of staple and useful stuff. I filled the plastic bags and used some boxes that were in their back porch. There was no beer, which was a disappointment. I found some useful tools, some kitchen utensils, disinfectant and cleaning fluids, that might come in handy, and boxes of matches and candles. They had a gas cooker with a big and heavy bottle and I took that.

I carried it all outside, ready for a thorough disinfecting.

I looked at all their family mementos, sepia photos from earlier generations and objects of decoration, little dogs, crocheted miniatures and a few sporting trophies from a very long time ago. Evidently Jean-Claude was a minor champion at Boule, or Pétanque as they sometimes call it. I found a set of *boule*s, six silver balls in a box, and decided they might provide me with some amusement, although throwing silver balls onto gravel without an opponent is not as satisfying. I learned to play when I was in Versailles when some of my language school colleagues were dedicated Boulistes and played every lunchtime. It has a wonderfully unpredictable element to it because Pétanque is always played on ground where there are stones or tree roots to provide unexpected twists and turns. A bit like life in general really. You are trying to get as close to the little white jack, the *cochon* , as you can, but if there is a stone, then your beautiful trajectory can turn into a careen to the sidelines.

Looking at all this stuff, I felt like I was in a museum of the life of Jean-Claude and Eveline.

There was so much of it.

In reality, none of it meant anything to me and I could see no purpose in hauling it up to the château to add to all the stuff that was already there. I was confronting the quintessential uselessness of stuff.

I came to the conclusion that, maybe like the pharoahs being interred with all their belongings in the Egyptian pyramids, all this should go up in flames with their owners.

It actually seemed to be disrespectful to take anything that was personally theirs.

Other than their personal mementos, there was so much in the house. They were hoarders. A lot of what they kept was not in good condition and there were multiples of things that no-one would want. Three old fridges in their back workroom would be a good example. I have no interest in rosey cheeked porcelain dolls either.

I felt a bit overwhelmed, what to take and what to leave. I thought about books, till I remembered that the château had plenty. More books than I could ever read.

They had hundreds of old French cds and videos, Charles Aznavour and friends. Seeing I had no power, they were unplayable. Fleetingly, I thought about furniture, but do I really need furniture? Apart from anything else, most of their pieces were way too heavy. The French word for furniture is meubles which means moveable. These did not qualify.

I gave it all up.

Anything I took would have to be practically useful and carry-able.

And in reality, I couldn't conceive of what my future might be, so how much of all this was worth bothering with was an open question.

I poked around in his outbuildings.

He had a diesel tank, half full and other containers of chemicals in his sheds which could be useful, but I would explore those at a later date. Diesel meant I might be able to run the generator. There was always the thought that I might still be here in winter and I know that it snows here. So I might really benefit from having enough fuel to run the generator.

Then there were the cars. He had three of them.

One was a white van, called a Jumpy. The French do choose odd names for their vehicles. The second was an old Citroën, a DS which they call La Déesse , the Goddess. The last one was a really decrepit Deux Chevaux, that quintessentially French car with a torn canvas roof hatch, emblematic of the nineteen fifties. It looked like it had not moved for quite a while by the cobwebs all round it.

I was used to thinking that having a car was necessary for a good life. So here were some cars and I thought, well I have wheels, if I want. It was a bit scary to think I could simply drive somewhere and find out what had happened to the world.

I left them there for later. I could come back and explore as long as I didn't burn down his sheds by mistake when I fired the house.

Once I felt I had raided their supplies as much as would be useful, dozens of jars of fig jam and pickled cucumbers could last for years, I pulled the boxes well away from the house.

Gingerly I piled flammable things round their two bodies, paper and wood, to make sure they burned really well. Then I began to pour two-stroke fuel onto the wooden floors and the furniture and the walls. The house is made of stone and I hoped that everything would burn inside that stone like an oven.

I found myself thinking of this whole scene as being somehow cinematic, like I was the set designer for a horror film, like Joan of Arc burning at the stake, or medieval witches.

When it was all ready, I stood in the middle of the kitchen with the two bodies and I apologised to Jean-Claude and Eveline, asking them to forgive me if I was doing anything that displeased them.

Who knows, maybe their spirits were circling above.

I had read that the dead can be attached to their bodies for a while before they float off. The Buddhists have a whole set of rituals that last for forty days. Unfortunately I never learned what that was.

In reality I had no idea about how to conduct a one-man funeral, so I recited one of the Buddhist hymns I had learned from my stay in the monastery in Chiang Rai. I vaguely remembered it had to do with the fragility and fleeting nature of life, so it felt appropriate. I had no idea what Catholics do for their departed except the last rites and had no idea what they were.

Why I kept thinking they were Catholics, I don't know. I didn't see any religious symbols in the house.

Then I lit a match, threw it onto the fuel and nearly set myself on fire. The place exploded into flames and I backed away, beating burning ashes off my overalls.

I stood back outside and watched it. The smoke rose, black and acrid, high into the still air, twisting away, and I imagined their souls being carried up and off in the smoke.

Au revoir Jean-Claude, adieu Eveline.

It took more than an hour.

The thought crossed my mind as I watched the black pall rise higher and higher, if there was someone else living on some far hill who saw the smoke, they might get excited, thinking they were not alone and come to see what had caused the fire.

The smoke rose and rose into the still, clear air and nothing came of it.

Watching the smoke billowing up, I remembered the ceremony that the Shaman from Ecuador had conducted in the garden outside the château last November.

His name was Kundi, I think.

Chloé had sponsored him to come to France to do cleansing ceremonies in the houses of her wealthy circle. Chloé's freinds were ladies who believed in evil spirits tormenting old houses. It was a convenient and fashionable way to explain their troubles. Just get a shaman to cleanse your house and your husband will start paying attention to you again.

Kundi was a very sweet, shy man. His face was heavily wrinkled but when he smiled, he seemed to be able to quadruple his wrinkles. He had no English, so he travelled with his grandson, who sported a ponytail to his waist and spoke excellent English with a strange almost cockney accent. He told me he learned English by watching Monty Python videos.

The ceremony included lots of alcohol being spat on the participants, and whacking semi-naked participants with tree branches. The finale was a fire ceremony in which Kundi said the evil spirits who had inhabited this château were being invited to leave. He didn't say what they were but Chloé was very pleased to have a spiritually cleansed château. God knows what sort of nasty things happened in the middle ages, although this château does not have a dungeon, or as the French put it : *Donjon*. I didn't have much interest or belief in evil spirits, but the ceremony was pretty powerful and Clo and I both felt really stoned afterwards. It was about the same as a mushrooms trip.

I'm not sure what the connection is, other than smoke.

As the house was rapidly reduced to ashes, I didn't feel sad at all. I didn't know Jean-Claude and Eveline all that well. We'd had a few conversations. My level of French was such that, if I really concentrated, I could follow his rambling stories told in his twangy local accent, where vin became ving and pain became paing . At least I learned some of the local history. His family had lived in that house unchanged for generations, the only major change being the indoor plumbing. During the French revolution, there had been skirmishes in the district and there were bodies from that time buried in an old cemetery at the bottom of the hill where our track leaves the road. The Germans did some very nasty things to the locals during the second world war. Jean-Claude was a kid at that time and saw some of it. He admitted that, as his family stayed neutral, they did not join the resistance, and probably did better than many other families during the war. He said his father always believed that the only way to live well was to keep your head down and your sheds locked.

I withdrew from the smouldering ruins and went back to the château.

I took off my protective outfit and thought about burning it, till I realised that the boots and the overalls were valuable. I would have to disinfect them. I left them outside.

I needed some time to be quiet and somehow detox myself, before I began detoxing my stolen goods.

I opened a bottle of Crémant, which is Bordeaux's version of Champagne, by way of a wake.

I drank too much, saluting the souls of my neighbors, and fell asleep in the kitchen. Crémant doesn't keep once it's opened, so I felt I shouldn't waste it.

I got wasted instead.

If I had died, I would have looked like the corpse of Eveline at the kitchen table.

I woke up the next morning with a nasty head.

When I went back to their house, I was pleased to see it was no more than a bed of ashes inside the stone walls.

There was a gentle breeze and the ashes swirled in soft circles.

I could imagine the souls of Jean-Claude and Eveline like those ashes, soft and free to float.

The roof had completely caved in, so now just the stone walls and the chimney remain as testament to the departed.

They stand like headstones.

I thought about making some kind of plaque but maybe there is no need.

It is quite possible that no-one will ever come to see what happened.

Luckily none of the sheds had caught fire.

I wondered about their chickens and ducks, but when I went out there, the fence had been broken and I guess a fox or wild dogs had helped themselves. Feathers and beaks lay here and there, but nothing salvageable. They also had a pig but he, or she, had decided to leave and that fence too was breached.

They had cats too but I didn't see them.

Cats are independent and they are probably happily living wild lives catching pigeons.

I thought long and hard about the cars. The Jumpy looked like the most recently used one, so it should run. I hunted for keys. It was after quite a while of hunting that I realised I had probably burnt all the car keys in the house. A car without keys, unless you are a successful car thief, is just a piece of junk.

Never having been remotely interested in mechanics, I had no idea how you jump start a car. How do you jump start a Jumpy?

In a way it was a relief. I didn't have to face the prospect of driving into the unknown.

Otherwise the sheds were a trove of useful stuff.

Rooting round and finding treasure would become a regular adventure as part of my daily walk.

I spent a couple of weeks living with Haji Daud in Kota Bharu and they were a time of peaceful reflection.

He was a philosopher at heart and he loved to consider the nature of the universe as a deep mystery to be solved in two ways at once. Your mind has to find satisfaction, he said, quite often, But your soul has to find repose.

In many ways I think he taught me how to consider my own life from both those perspectives and I am very grateful to him for that.

Nonetheless I felt a sense of the need to continue my journey. What sort of journey, I had no idea, but I had a feeling that if I stayed in Kota Bharu much longer, I would become just another piece of the landscape with no satisfaction or repose.

I didn't want to stagnate.

He nodded when I shared this.

"Take to the road my son. You are a pilgrim, because you don't recognise your kind of Mecca yet. Go find the holy grail."

I said goodbye to Janey and Fiona, who seemed to be thriving both in the school and with their extra-curricular activities. They had both expanded their experience very much in the spirit of the local beach, gleefully sharing their newest exploits.

Quite frankly they were both beginning to look much prettier and quite sexy. I quietly congratulated myself on having done some good work there.

We had an almost tearful farewell and we promised to stay in touch.

I headed for the Thai border.

The local bus left me at Sungei Kolok and I walked towards the bridge into Thailand. There was a little booth on either side of the bridge. On the Malaysian side, a very bored older officer glanced idly at my passport and nodded me through. I said *"Terima Kasih"*, thank you, in my best Bahasa Malayu, which made him smile, and walked across to the other side where a young Thai man in a very tight uniform checked my passport, stamped it and asked me if I was looking for sex.

I know Thailand does have that reputation but I was surprised about how up front it was. I told him I was fine from that point of view and asked about the train to Bangkok.

He had a reasonable amount of English and as I was the only person crossing the bridge, we got talking. He wanted to know where I was from and what work I did, then I asked him about his life. He'd had aspirations to go to university and become a businessman but his family was very poor and he had to work to support his parents. He was bored in this job but it paid more than any other jobs he could find.

It was a quiet day, so he invited me to lunch in a wooden hut next to his booth.

Here a young girl who he said was his sister, was cooking tiny fish on a fry pan which she served to us with big bowls of steaming rice. She smiled very sweetly and the young man, who told me his name was Ban, said that she was very good at sex and very cheap. I politely smiled back and told her she was very beautiful but that I wasn't in the mood for sex. She seemed rather disappointed, but I am sure only from a financial perspective not my physical charms.

There is only one train that connects from the border to a much bigger town further north, so I had hours to kill. In the end I succumbed to her pleading, which was pitiful, and gave her some money. I wasn't expecting anything in return but she insisted that she should do what she was paid to do. She was very sweet about it but it didn't add anything to my knowledge of the subject. Instead it made me feel sad for her.

I suspect in most countries I could have been arrested because of her age.

At the end of the afternoon, I thanked Ban and his sister for their generous hospitality and took my backpack off to the station.

The train to Bangkok stopped at interminable stations and took a night and a morning to get there. I tried sleeping but the carriage kept filling and emptying as the night went on and I had to keep a good grip on my backpack. I would nod off with my arms round the backpack and wake up to find an old lady staring at me while clutching a bamboo basket with a chicken it. Then I would nod off again and wake up to find someone gently stroking the hair on my forearm. This was a young boy who was fascinated that I had hairy arms. His dad watched carefully from across the aisle.

When eventually we got to Bangkok, as I plunged into the human melee that is the forecourt of the Krung Thep station, I was exhausted.

A young spruiker grabbed my backpack and I staggered off after him down a back alley to a dingy hotel where I changed money at a terrible rate, not having been fully awake to recognise the rort. I paid off the spruiker and staggered up some rickety stairs and crashed onto a bedbug-ridden mattress, in a room not much bigger than a cupboard.

When I woke up, having no idea where I was or what time it was, my body was covered in bites and the room smelled awful. I checked to see that my valuables were still intact in my money belt which had created a thick red welt across my stomach. I had a bucket wash in a bathroom at the end of the corridor that had not been cleaned for quite some time, then went downstairs. The old man at the desk asked if I'd had a good sleep and I lied.

He asked me if I wanted a woman and I said I didn't think it was a good idea before breakfast. He smiled and in his broken English assured me he could get many different kinds of woman at any time. Very cheap. Or a nice young boy if I preferred.

I assured him I would keep that in mind and went off to find myself a slighly more salubrious hotel, with cleaner linen and no offers of sex.

I went back to the station and watched where European travellers were going and found a hotel entirely patronised by Westerners.

It was double the price of the other hotel but had a pool and was basically sanitary. It seemed a bit zenophobic to only hang out with foreigners but I got lots of tips about what to see, where to get good dope and where to buy black market whisky. There seemed to be a certain hedonistic kind of traveller culture there, which was fascinating, but I was not drawn to it. More than a few of the residents had become more or less permanent.

Instead I just walked around by myself getting to feel what Thais were like. The noise and bustle of the city intimidated me, but little by little I ventured further way from the hotel.

I spent a couple of days wandering about the city which the locals call it Krung Thep, the City of Angels, going to the obligatory temples and floating markets, but it all seemed unreal, almost artificial, and I felt disconnected from everything. I don't think I met any angels, although I was often accosted in doorways by very pretty young girls who did look angelic.

I sat at a little tea shop one morning drinking noodle soup when a young monk came and sat with me. He wanted to practise his English. He was very softly spoken and had a gentle smile. There was something about him that made me feel relaxed.

He asked me the usual questions and I gave the obligatory rendition of my life and country of origin, speaking slowly and carefully. He watched me closely, sometimes mouthing the words I was using, to practise them.

At some point we got into religion, of which I had no real deep experience at all. Sunday School really doesn't count.

He was very concerned that I did not have a living awarenss of divinity in my life. Looking at me very seriosuly he said that every soul needed to connect to the universe and the divine.

I had no reason to disagree with him.

That's how I got to live in a monastery on a hill overlooking Chiang Rai in the north of Thailand. They welcome anyone and there is no expectation that you have to follow the Buddhist faith.

I had no other plans, so when he told me about the monastery where he had studied, I took it as the most useful indication of next steps.

He stayed with me, as I collected my backpack, paid my dues and walked to the station. He waited till I was about to board the train, then he sang a little song that he said was a prayer that I might find the true path. Then he put his hands together in that wonderfully choreographed movement of reverence that seems to exist all over Asia and waved as the train pulled away.

I sat in the train, as it chugged its way through endless rice fields, feeling very grateful to that young monk.

After the long slow train and then the bumpy local bus ride, I wandered into another world, hanging on to a dim idea that maybe spending time in a monastic environment might give me some insight into who or what I was supposed to be.

Maybe whatever little discipline I now have comes from that time.

I am sure it does.

Up until then my life had very little discipline to it.

The life of a monastery is scheduled to the clock.

Bells ring, monks follow the time-honoured rituals of their chosen path and the world turns on its axis.

There is such certainty to it all.

Now and then there are special days and big ceremonials, but on most days the routine is the same. You rise, you bathe, you pray, you chant, you drink tea, you work, you eat, you rest, you work some more, you pray, you chant, you go to sleep. You can also play volleyball.

The temple was my favourite place.

It was square with a high domed centre over a two metre high golden Buddha. In each of the four cardinal directions there was a door with a porchway with guardian statues of lion dogs on each side. One of my early chores was to sand down all eight of them, which took weeks, and then repaint them with waterproof bright yellow paint. I had a fellow worker in the form of Franz, a very overweight Austrian who told me that he had worked as a barge captain on the Danube till his lover, evidently a very good-looking young slavic boy, called Dik, committed suicide into the river. This shocked Franz so much, he abandoned ship that day, left the country and came to Thailand. Every morning he would sit in the temple and weep. He would ask the soul of Dik, why he had gone. He wept for an hour every day and asked for foregiveness. Then he would join me in sanding and painting. People who came and went in the monastery would sometimes get us confused, Australia and Austria. We would quote that T-shirt that they sell in Vienna which says : No kangaroos in Austria. Franz and I became good friends.

I wonder what became of him.

One day he was gone, saying nothing to anyone.

The temple was the centre of all activity in the monastery, both physically and spiritually. It sat at the highest point of the hill and we would gather there four times a day for chanting, prayers and meditation. I had never meditated before and it took me a long while to get a sense of what it was. The head of the monastery appointed a young monk to be my teacher and in his distinctly limited English he instructed me in the basics.

"Mantra." he said. "Repeat. No thoughts. Peace."

So I did my best. I practised saying the mantra that he gave me till he was satisfied I could say it properly. Then he kept straightening my back when I sat, and that seemed to be the end of his task.

Even now, sometimes as I meditate, I imagine him straightening my back and I sit more upright.

Every morning I would dutifully attempt to follow his instructions. I could repeat the mantra for thirty seconds or so before my mind kicked in. Half the time, at first I would sneak a look at everyone around me, all sitting very still, very upright, and I would wonder what they were really doing.

Then one day, an early misty morning, cool and still, when I sat down for meditation, I repeated the mantra maybe twice and suddenly flipped off into another world. I have had experiences like that with mushrooms or hash, but here I was on nothing but a cup of morning tea. I found myself floating, I was a free being, I had no sense of having or even needing a body. Above me there were other beings floating and smiling. I felt I knew who they were but I couldn't quite get it. I felt happier than I had ever felt. There was a sense of: "Ah this is what I am supposed to be doing."

I came out of that meditation with a deep desire to live like that.

Of course, the human body is a body and it has its own limitations, so I felt trapped in it. It's a heavy piece of meat to cart around. I began longing to meditate more deeply, to float bodiless more often. The sensation was never quite the same again but it was enough to have given me a glimpse of what was possible.

I have meditated, more or less, every day since. I even had the temerity to teach Clo. Actually I think she is better at it than I am. She has visions quite often when I just work at getting detached from useless thoughts.

Once the pandemic established itself in France, and everywhere else for that matter and things started to close down, Clo and I decided we would hide out at the Domaine for the duration.

There was talk of closing everything down and confining everyone to home. We didn't fancy the idea of being stuck in a dependence in Chloé's garden.

We thought it would last maybe a week or two, or maybe a bit more, but certainly it wouldn't last once summer kicked in. We had read the plague books, like Albert Camus and Marquez and it seemed like we knew how to deal with it. Plagues, so they say, don't like warm weather, so it would soon be gone..

So we thought we would go somewhere sheltered, enjoy the peace and quiet and wait patiently. This château ticks all those boxes.

Alain was oddly blasé about the whole virus thing and he said that was fine with him. He wasn't so keen on having us around anyway.

The boys were in school and he had another woman who came to help out. I have a sneaking suspicion this woman did other services for Alain as well, but I can't be sure. Well, I can be pretty certain, just by the way they looked at each other.

Sensing that a lockdown was on the cards, I decided to go early to set up with the plan that Clo would follow me in a couple of days by train, as soon as she could hand over the care of the boys.

She never made it.

There is a part of me that misses her terribly.

When we met in London, ten years ago now, we slowly, bit by bit, began to recognise that what each of us was looking for seemed to be clearly evident in the other, or more exactly, there was more of what we were seeking in the other, than we had found up to that point.

Soul mates?

Who knows?

I'm not really sure I know what that means anyway. She brought out something in me that I never knew was there and I think without knowing how, I did the same for her.

When we were together, there was a wholeness that I came to delight in and to trust.

I really miss it.

She had become a part of me and without that part I didn't feel whole.

I think loneliness has always lurked in the background of my consciousness. The fear of being alone has substance that includes the fear of being abandoned or betrayed. If I have no-one to be with, then who will take care of me?

I think it is something as infantile as that.

But it is there, no doubt about it.

I do not like being alone.

I do not like not having Clo here.

I do not like not knowing what has happened to her.

I do not like the horrible thought that I will never see her again.

I do not like.....
Then I catch myself.
This is not doing me any good.
I don't think I have ever had depression as such, but when I start to tell myself that I am lonely, then that's as close as I get.
I know depression kills people.
Thank God I learned a little something about controlling my mind when I was in the monastery.

I spent a year in that monastery.
It sat high on a hill above the town and in the early morning it seemed to sit on a sea of morning mist, serene and detached.
This château has something of the same aspect. It can sit on clouds trapped in the valley.
The gardens of the monastery were very different from here. Everything was lush and subtropical with peacocks and small roe deer roaming freely in the gardens. In the morning the sound of bells would ring across the countryside from one monastery to another.
There was a timelessness to life there where minutes and hours melted away, so that I lost track of days, weeks, months. I dropped into a natural harmonious rhythm of monastic life.
I followed the practices, tried to understand the teachings, loved the company of monks and seekers from all over the world, listened to endless stories of lives lived but not fully understood and ate vegetarian.
I could have lived like that forever.
I wrote letters to my parents extolling the virtues of monastic life and they wrote back worried, carefully expressed epistles about my suspended career. My father was of the opinion that if you didn't make it by the time you were thirty, it was too late. In the monastery I was beginning to discover a new definition for how to make it . I doubt he would ever be able to grasp what I meant.

Now that spring is really in full bloom here in the Lot, everything is growing fast.

I think it must be April by now.

The days are getting longer. Whatever was planted last year in the garden is coming up all over the place.

I am going to get really busy.

Up to now I have been living mostly on what was stored in the grenier , the food store, pumpkin, potatos, turnips and all that sort of thing. Luckily I like all that and I make soup and stew and I'm happy.

There is some flour and there are baking bowls, so I am doing my best, but the only source of heating is the fire and I get burnt offerings more often than not.

There's a shed full of tools, so I will get going.

The ride-on mower and the rotary hoe are very fancy but useless because I don't think I have the right fuel. There are cans of what I think is fuel, but I might use the wrong thing and cause a fire. It has to be sweat and blood, good old manual labour.

Maybe I will find a goat somewhere to keep the grass down.

All the stuff I brought back from the ashen ruins of Jean-Claude's house will come in handy. The tins of food, the jars of jam and pickle, the tools, the tins of lubricant and white spirit will all have a use I am sure.

I did very thorough disinfecting and, as far as I can tell, I am none the worse for it and it's all clean. The diesel fuel is there, if I ever get the courage to try to start up the generator again, but I am beginning to feel that life can go on perfectly well without electricity, so why bother.

I rescued quite a few rolls of toilet paper.

Of course sometimes I wonder what has happened to the outside world.

Did everyone die except me?

That is too terrifying a thought.

As I drove out of Toulouse, I listened to the radio, as best I could, they talk fast and use jargon I don't get, I sensed how widespread this virus was and the word pandemic was now the word of the day. I knew Australia had applied strict lockdown rules already and closed the borders. Australia is good at that, being an island. Lots of diseases that have plagued the rest of the world never got a foothold because of the vigorous controls of entry. However, I had to wonder, were my parents alright? They were now in the critical age group and lived in a village for active retirees. I had spoken to them a week before I left Toulouse and they were full of life.

I wonder how they are now?

And Clo? Is she OK?

It is hard not knowing.

Because there has been no traffic on the freeway at the bottom of the hill, running empty from Toulouse to Paris, I can tell that whatever lockdown was imposed the day after I left, is still going on. No trucks from Spain heading for Belgium. No aircraft fly, although the first couple of days I was here, I heard helicopters, but not any more.

The only form of traffic I have seen was a herd of deer one morning, tearing across the top of the hill being chased by a pack of dogs. They disappeared but it brought to mind a few jobs for me to do. If there were deer, then I need to make sure the fences round the vegetable gardens are tight and strong. If there are wild packs of dogs, I have to be ready to defend myself.

There is a gun. It's a single barrel rifle and there is a box of cartridges.

I have never used a gun and I would probably be an awful shot but it's still good to know it's there.

In northern Thailand, I very quickly lost track of the days in the monastery, until one day the head monk told me that after one year, the *dharma* (the right way to behave) required that I go out into the world to share my wisdom.

That came as a bit of a shock to me as I had no sense of having gained any wisdom at all.

Nonetheless he was insistent.

When I asked for some guidance on where I should go, he said he felt my journey should be to India.

When I asked him why, he shrugged and said: "What I see comes as a gift from the universe. We must respect such communication. To resist is to push against an irresistible force."

I couldn't argue with that.

Who would I be arguing with?

I had a very heartfelt last day and every moment of the daily routine seemed so precious. It was as if I was experiencing everything about the monastery for the first time. How heavenly the chanting was, how delicious the tea, how friendly the smiles of the monks.

I was going to miss all of it.

As I waited for the bus to the train station, many of the monks came out to say goodbye. They all put their hands together in prayer and wished me a fruitful journey and that I might find the right path to Nirvana.

I felt a lot of love for them as they waved me off. They had been such simple and warm companions.

I was quite a different person, I realised, as I sat for the long hours in the train going south. It may not have seemed to be exactly wisdom, but I had gained some kind of acceptance of myself which is a good step forward.

Was I closer to Nirvana?

I had no idea.

I had no other plans so, in order to follow the suggestion, or was it a command, to go to India, I went down to Bangkok, I went back to the same non-bedbug-ridden hotel feeling oddly repelled by the hedonism of its residents and shopped around for a ticket.

There was a remarkably cheap flight from Bangkok to Calcutta.

The flight was with Air India and the plane smelt of curry.

My fellow passengers were either elderly Indian couples or young Europeans like me, many with beards and long hair, the men anyway.

It was a short flight over Burma and the Bay of Bengal.

The guy sitting next to me was German, He told me, as we took off, that he was carrying a load of heroin in his belly in tiny plastic bags. Why he told me this I have no idea. If you were going to smuggle anything, why would you tell anyone?

Pretty soon I realised he was not altogether there and he could well be carrying imaginary cargo. Or he could be carrying real heroin but be so stoned as to not be able to hold his tongue. I had no idea. He talked nonstop the whole way. He also seemed not to have had a bath for quite a while.

It was a relief to get out of the plane.

Smells are interesting input.

Rather like landing in Singapore more than a year earlier, it was the air in Calcutta that struck me. After the smells of the plane, here were so many new smells, perfumes, odours to take in.

I felt very excited just smelling it.

While I waited for bus that runs from the airport to the city, I saw my fellow passenger, the German guy, being picked up by a big black BMW. Maybe he was telling the truth after all. I decided that the car had to be either Mafia or the police.

I caught the rickety red bus along with all the other Europeans. The Indians all seemed to take taxis. Half the bus was filled with backpacks stacked high.

I had asked several of the passengers where was a good place to stay and they all agreed that the Sikh hotels were the best.

I followed two young Swedes, who said they had been given a good address. We weaved our way through narrow back streets with little shops selling all sorts of pots and pans, to a small and scrupulously clean little place with tiny rooms facing into a central courtyard.

It was unbelievably cheap.

I spent a few days wandering around the city of Kalikat, which is how they say it in Bengal.

I loved it.

There seemed to be music everywhere. If you overlooked the constant need to avoid stepping on homeless families sleeping on the pavements, it was a vibrant and pulsating place.

The lung of the city is the Medan, a big open space in the middle.

There were goats and crows everywhere.

Again, based on the advice of other travellers, I went to small Sikh restaurants where they said the water was pure enough to drink. I never got sick so they must have been right.

In one of them I sat opposite an older woman with white hair dressed in a white Indian sari. She was Polish. She told me that she had been to India many times and was about to go to Varanasi to see her Guru. She told me that her Guru, who was a woman, was the most accomplished Tantric Yoga teacher in India.

I told her I had no real idea about yoga and that I wasn't really sure why I was in India at all. I told her about the command I had received from the Buddhist temple.

She looked at me long and seriously.

"Then it is surely destiny that you and I sit here. You must come with me."

So I took that as a sign.

She knew exactly how to buy train tickets, second class, how to pay a porter to get us good seats, and how to yell at people who tried to take them.

She was fearless and I meekly followed along behind.

The train took a day and a night to get there, stopping many times during which Olga, my guide, would buy hot food from the vendors who passed under the windows at each station with steaming pots on their heads. I was more or less terrified that we might be eating fried typhoid or something, but she assured me that as it was cooked it would be fine and she was right.

As the train rattled noisily along, often following the Ganges, Olga told me about the form of yoga that she practised. I had not heard of Tantra Yoga up till then.

It was only after I had been in the ashram that I realised she was using euphemisms to describe what was practised.

She talked about meditation and yoga postures and the awakening of divine energy and it all sounded very uplifting. She said it was essential to find the right teacher and to obey exactly what they taught.

I was looking forward to learning about it.

She said that I had already done the first important steps by being in the monastery in Thailand.

Now, she told me, I would develop rapidly and achieve high consciousness.

It sounded impressive.

When we finally got to Varanasi, or Benares as some people call it, she told me to stay guarding the luggage, my backpack and her Louis Vuitton suitcase, while she found a porter. She was back in minutes with the skinniest stick of a man who threw both pieces of luggage effortlessly up in the air and balanced them on his head. Then we plunged into a churning sea of human bodies, following the bobbing suitcases.

As the throng thinned out we caught up to him, slowing down as he climbed up a steep winding lane. It was miraculous that such a skeletal body could carry that much weight, that far, at that speed. For his gargantuan efforts, he got a couple of rupees at the gate of the ashram and seemed most grateful.

Inside the gate was a cobble-stoned courtyard surrounded by a rambling old building made of stone, several stories high and covered in creepers.

We were greeted by a most beautiful young Indian girl in a gold and white sari. She had amazingly white teeth and dark dangerously seductive eyes.

I was more than a bit exhausted from the train journey and running after the porter, but she really woke me up.

Olga smiled at me.

"Indira." she said with a knowing look. "Very beautiful"

As Indira booked me in, I inhaled. She smelled exquisitely of sandalwood.

"For how long will you be staying?" she asked with her sexy Indian inflections.

I wanted to say: "Forever," but I muttered "Three days."

A small Indian boy dressed in a white cotton suit showed me to a dorm room where two other men had left their belongings, then I went downstairs to join Olga for what she said was the late afternoon chant.

We stood in a little white stone temple with an imposing statue of a goddess with a black face, red tongue extended and a garland of skulls. This was a very different deity from the Buddha in Chiang Rai.

"Kali," whispered Olga, and put her head on the floor in reverence.

I obediently did the same.

The floor was made of grey marble and was wonderfuly cool.

Other people joined us, a few Europeans and some Indians, and then a crackly recording of chanting came over the loud speakers and a man, who I assumed was a priest, came in wearing only a white lungi and white stripes of ash all over his body. He stood very erect and waved a lamp in front of the statue. The words of the chant repeated themselves many times, so after a while, I got the hang of it and joined in.

I had no idea what we were chanting about.

It wasn't much different from the Thai chanting.

When it all finished, everyone bowed again, and Olga took me off to the dining hall, an open pavilion with long grass mats spread out on the floor.

We ate rice and veggies with our fingers along with dahl soup.

I looked around for Indira but I did not see her.

"Tomorrow," whispered Olga.

By the end of dinner, I was drooping and happily crashed onto the hard wooden bed in the dorm and passed out.

I was woken, while it was still dark, by someone blowing a conch shell in the doorway.

I sat bolt upright and I saw that the other two men in the dorm did the same.

They were both Europeans, so I asked them what happened next.

One put his fingers to his lips to show it was meant to be silence then beckoned me to follow him.

He took me to a wash house.

There was a row of cold water showers and the residents of the ashram were standing under them, lathering themselves with one big cake of soap that was handed down the line. What I did not expect was that all the residents, male and female, were there and all had shed or were shedding their clothes.

My guide took off his clothes and put them in a pile on a bench and motioned for me to do the same. I'm not too embarrassed to be naked, drama school had quickly fixed that, but this was a bit of a shock.

Olga, who had a lot more very white flesh than I had realised, gave me a cheery wave as she stood under one of the showers.

Then I saw Indira.

She walked into the wash area wearing a simple white smock which she neatly lifted up over her head. She was superbly naked. She gave me a lovely smile, and I quickly got under the cold water to hide what was about to betray my appreciation for her.

At the end of the shower we were handed little white towels to dry off and then we dressed again.

As far as I could tell, no-one else found any of this unusual.

There was more chanting in the temple in front of Kali whose name was repeated many times.

Then in the dining hall we had chapatis and chai for breakfast.

Olga sat next to me whispering about what would be happening for the day.

There was a pavilion behind the building where hatha yoga mats were laid out.

"For yoga no clothes," said Olga.

So once again, totally naked, we sat on yoga mats waiting for the teacher. It was a mixed group of bodies, old and young, male and female, Western and Indian, skinny and pudgy. I tried as hard as I could not to focus on the bodies around me.

That was until the teacher came in.

It was Indira, again she shed her smock with such a simple fluid movement.

I could not look at her.

She began to speak in a soft voice givng instructions and then demonstrating the postures.

I tried to follow what she was saying.

I tried to get my body to do what she was doing.

She saw me struggling and she came over.

She ran her hand along my back to help me to extend my spine, but instead the electric shock of her cool hand caressing my body made something else extend.

I lost it.

I freaked out.

I was terrified that everyone would see that I had an erection.

I shot out of the pavilion, without remembering to take my clothes.

I went up to the dorm and frantically found other clothes to put on. I was sweating like crazy.

I sat there on the hard wooden bed feeling wretched.

Olga came in and brought me my clothes quite a while later and sat on the end of the bed.

"You did not expect this?" she asked.

I shook my head.

"It scares you?"

I nodded.

"You will get used to it."

"I don't think so," I managed.

"It's just the body."

"I can't," I said.

"Then perhaps you are not as ready as I thought."

Well that was that.

I packed my backpack, thanked Olga for taking care of me and slipped away.

I didn't even ask for a refund of the three days I had paid for. It wasn't much.

I wandered miserably with my backpack, fending off porters wanting to carry it, till I found a little hotel down by the river. I booked in, feeling wretched and weak and lost.

I lay on a simple hard bed for the rest of the morning, staring at the slow ceiling fan, with my mind drowning in self-loathing. Then finally to try to regain some kind of inner calm, I went out to the river, and found my way to the ghats where they were burning dead bodies.

What is it about bodies?

We live in them for a certain time, then they drop off and we burn them, at least in India.

On the other hand we are fiercely attracted to what bodies do. And even more troublesome, we are fiercely attracted to certain other people's bodies.

I thought about that quite a lot.

I felt inclined to curse the burden of having a body and all its shortcomings.

I was saved by the young man who ran the little hotel.

"You should do yoga," he said.

I asked if it meant taking your clothes off and he laughed, "No, no, no."

He knew where I had spent my first night in Varanasi.

So that was how I learned to do yoga postures, clad.

The teacher was an older man, Ramanuja, who was amazingly flexible.

I did two sessions with him every day and he was very gentle with me.

Very slowly, session by session, I began to feel better about my body again.

Ramanuja said, and I always remember this, "The body is a temple."

He had a little spiel about how to treat the body as holy, what to put in it, how to keep it pure, and who is the deity in this temple.

"It is God who dwells there" was the last sentence, always.

He gave this short speech almost every day.

His classes were small and had a passing parade of locals, but mostly it was Europeans, either tourists just being curious or more genuine seekers who had come to Varanasi on their own pilgrimage.

Ramanuja spoke excellent but stilted English with very correct grammar.

When I complimented him on it, he said "Oxford."

I asked if he had studied there and he said "No, no. Oxford dictionary."

I liked the idea that doing yoga was a kind of pilgrimage to the temple of my own body.

I began to appreciate how my body began to open and stretch itself little by little.

And now, here in this château, doing yoga every day, it still does.

There is no end to what the body can do, if you give it the incentive and you have the discipline.

Doing a bit of yoga every day keeps me feeling good about having a body as well as making me remember about the temple and who dwells in it.

I stayed several weeks in Varanasi, doing yoga and wandering along the river. I found lots of different temples to visit, some with naked Sadhus, others with holy men covered in nothing but ashes or mud. Somehow, though, their naked bodies did not have the same effect as Indira.

I never ventured back to the Kali ashram and I did not see Olga again.

At last I began to feel like I was not getting anywhere, so I caught the train back to Calcutta, managing to negotiate my way without any guide.

All the way back I felt a bit lost and empty.

What had been the point of coming to Varanasi?

Why was it necesssary for me to go to the Kali Ashram?

Had I missed something important?

Was I just too chicken, too scared?

Was I, as Olga said, not ready?

I got back to Calcutta and went back to the same little Sikh hotel.

The next morning, sitting in the simple little concrete room of the smae Sikh hotel, I did some yoga stretches and then sat for meditation.

I invoked the atmosphere of the monastery in Chiang Rai.

I wanted to expunge all images of the Kali Ashram from my system.

I asked for a sign, where should I go, what should I do?

It was a long and deep meditation and I came out feeling much better.

There had been no inner revelation but I was happy to wait for the sign.

I went to breakfast in the Sikh cafe round the corner and was enjoying a hot chai when a Sikh man came over to me.

"You are looking for a ticket to London," he said, as a statement, not a question.

"Maybe," I managed.

"Yes yes, I have it very cheap. You will leave tomorrow."

And that's how I got to London.

It was indeed a very cheap ticket with Pakistan Airways, which meant I had a long and hot and sticky layover in Karachi sitting on a hard plastic chair in the transit lounge where there was nothing to eat or drink and all the children seemed to have major colds or stomach flu. The airconditioner seemed to be there to make a noise but did nothing to cool the air.

You get what you pay for.

Every time I think back to my time in India, I wonder what would have happened if I had had the courage to stay.

I never met the Guru of the Kali Ashram.

What would have happened if I had?

Would I now be a highly evolved being like Olga suggested, naked and enlightened?

Now that I have read quite a bit about Tantra, I realise that I was not ready at all.

Sometimes I fantasise about how it might have been if Indira had become my Tantra teacher, but that's all it is, a fantasy.

I am pretty certain it was not my path to enlightenment.

I will never know.

As I am now, in this château, I try to think about what I gained from being in India.

On the one hand I learned about Yoga, but other than that, I cannot make it out.

Why did I go?

What did the Head Monk see that made him sure I should go there?

I devote some of my meditation time trying to get a sense of it.

It is probably a waste of good meditation time.

I do wonder if maybe the point of all that nakedness was to rid me of my preoccupation with the body, but I didn't stay long enough to find out.

You could say that the body is nothing more than the vehicle that carries us through each incarnation and is of no intrinsic value in itself, or you could say, like Ramanuja, that the body is a temple and should be worshipped.

I suppose I am somewhere in the middle.

Truly speaking, being here makes no more sense than being in the Kali Ashram.

The same questions are still swirling about.

Maybe being here is the opportunity to do what I couldn't do there.

But what is that?

London was cold, grey, smelly, dank.

And that was just the airport.

I had to work hard not to curse the Sikh salesman.

However, once I had changed the small amount of many I had left, I took the tube to Victoria Station.

My backpack, sitting on my lap, smelled like India.

I told myself that once again I should wait for an indication from the universe about where I should go.

It turned out to be right there on the platform at Victoria Station.

It was a girl from the Ukraine who fell over my backpack. I picked her up and in a way, I picked her up.

Lydia was cute, newly arrived and as lost as me.

She had the address of a hostel up an alley behind a fish and chip shop. By the time we had walked the few blocks we had become rather good friends.

She had a wonderfully lowered eyelash way of looking at me and every now and then, as she spoke, she would stroke my arm. I felt quite intoxicated by her.

Was she the next Indira?

We found the hostel and met a young French woman who was the manager.

Her name was Clotilde, Clo for short.

It was early in the afternoon and there was no-one about.

After we had checked in and the manager had shown us to our respective dorm rooms, Lydia came to mine and said she had something she wanted to share. Her look was full of meaning.

As soon as we entered her dorm room, she began to tear my clothes off. She devoured my body like a hungry lioness. There was an urgency that was electrifying. Then she stood back, watching my face as she took her clothes off..

This time I did not hold back.

She was a voracious lover and I certainly learned some new information that the Australian girls would have delighted in.

By the time we were both exhausted, others began to come in the hostel and we had to behave ourselves.

I was beginning to wonder excitedly where this would all lead. There was a feeling that somehow what I had not managed in India might be offered to me again.

I promised myself to be more courageous.

The next morning when I looked around to see if Lydia wanted to join me for breakfast, the manager, smiled sweetly and told me that Lydia had checked out early and left no forwarding address.

I was devastated.

I sat dejectedly in a crowded cafe near the station full of young men in suits and women talking into cell phones.

I felt like an alien.

I wandered around in the smoggy morning air trying to understand what that little episode was all about.

Who was Lydia? What did she represent?

I spent the whole day feeling very morose and abandoned.

I dragged myself back to the hostel.

Clo was there and she saw that I was miserable.

She made me a cup of tea and we sat in the tiny lobby of the hostel and I told her a little of where I had been travelling.

She was a good listener, and as I talked my mood changed.

She was a very attractive young lady.

When I first got up here to the château, I unpacked the BMW, what little it could carry and set myself up.

Clo and I had been here often enough to be fairly familiar with how it all worked, turning on the power and the water, at least before they both failed.

While l waited for her to call, I dropped into a steady routine and I was looking forward to an idyllic, almost monastic life, but with Clo.

Other than my trips to Gourdon when the car still had power, I had not left the château.

What was the point?

Where would I go?

It took me a while to recognise that having a car had been something I took for granted.

When I didn't have it anymore, when there was no more power and I had no means of transport, at first I felt annoyed, while assuming that at some point the power would come back on again and I'd go back to the way it was before.

When it began to look like I was seriously stuck, that was different. I had to deal with feeling like a prisoner but without walls or barbed wire.

There were days when I raged about my situation.

How did this happen to me?

Who did this to me?

Whose fault is this?

All that kind of mindless raging.

Then I would calm down and convince myself to believe that it would soon sort itself out.

I had to convince myself that Clo would turn up and the virus scare would be over and we would be able to tell our grandchildren all about it fifty years from now.

So that didn't happen.

The days went on carless, leaving me stranded on top of a rocky hill in the Lot.

Some days I was content with that.

Life is easy here, I have plenty to eat, a nice view.

Then there were the other days.

It's strange how mood swings work, they can ruin a whole day or last thirty seconds.

Maybe one of the outcomes of this experience will be that I am better at understanding the power my mind has and that, to live well and happy, I have to keep an eye on it and redirect it when it threatens to undermine me.

I need to mind my mind.

It was probably ten days or maybe more, after the power went out, before I ventured as far as the bottom of the hill on foot. The track descending from the château meets the road at the bottom, which then runs along beside the freeway.

When I got down there, passing Jean-Claude's sheds, nothing moved.

It was depressing to be standing at what used to be the starting point for outings.

Now it was the face of the unknown.

I was about to go back when I noticed movement on the far side of the road.

I crossed the road to where there were some trees.

Beyond them was another farm with a farm house on a hill, probably as old as Jean-Claude's. I had no inclination to go near it and no desire to deal with any more dead bodies.

The movement I saw turned out to be a cow.

I don't know much about cows but this one was all by herself with an udder that looked like it was going to burst.

I picked some very sweet grass and held it over the fence and she came up. She was obviously very used to people but had not been milked in days. She had a huge belly, jutting out on one side which I thought was a bit strange. She came up and she nibbled at the grass. I got some more and she seemed to really like that. At the end of the fence, there was a gate with a chain holding it closed but no lock. I went into the field and she came over to me. She had a halter round her neck and she let me stroke her wonderfully soft skin. I took hold of the halter and walked a few steps. She seemed very willing to come with me.

I led her through the gate and she came willingly. Together we walked gently back up the hill to the château.

If the farmer was dead, or had gone away, which seemed possible, seeing she hadn't been milked for days, then maybe I had a responsibility to do something about it.

She was so placid.

I put her into a fenced area that had been built for the English family's dogs. She wouldn't be using the kennel. There was knee-high spring growth grass so she loved it.

I found a rope in one of the sheds and attached it to the halter so I could tie her to the fence and then I had a go at milking. I had never done it before. In fact my only experience of teats had been on humans. Nonetheless I tried and I did manage to get it going. I think she was at overflow point so she was very content to let me try. After quite a while my fingers were sore but I had a couple of cupfuls of fresh milk. It had been years since I drank straight milk, but now I could enjoy a genuine *café au lait*.

I let her free and thanked the universe for its generous gift.

Now I had a supply of liquid calcium, a living lawn mower and a source of fresh manure.

My first date with Clo was fish and chips downstairs. The batter was awful but she was fascinating. There was something about the way she held herself, the way she would look at me, slightly side-on as if she was trying to see inside me. I loved her French accent, although her English was pretty good. She had an engaging way of probing, which prompted me to say things about myself I would never have wanted to say on a first date. She wangled the story of Lydia out of me, which was a bit embarrassing. Evidently she had been in the hostel and we had not been very quiet. I asked her if she knew why Lydia had gone and she just smiled. Sometimes, she said, with her eyebrows raised, our paths will cross for just one moment and then, *voilà, c'est tout*, that is all there is.

I was beginning to hope that our crossed paths, Clo's and mine, would last a bit longer.

The site of that first date was not the most romantic of spots, as we sat on grubby plastic chairs amid the clatter of what was mostly a take-away joint run by olive- skinned men who could have been Greeks, or maybe Palestinians. It was hard to tell.

That was all background.

Just sitting with Clo that first night is memorable for her willingness to listen, her attentiveness and her warm eyes. It didn't matter to me where we were, because her company was totally absorbing.

She was radiant, she had a glow about her.

When she smiled it was genuine because her eyes smiled as her face smiled.

Now and then she would touch my arm and her touch was both electrifying and gentle.

That night as I slept in a dorm with several other travellers from all over the globe, I couldn't stop thinking about her.

We met for breakfast, and then lunch, and we have been together ever since.

From that first plate of fish and chips onwards, I craved her company.

Little by little I began to sense who she was. She revealed just a little of herself, layer by layer and I loved the discovery of her. She was deep and each time, there was something new.

I loved it.

And quickly I knew that I loved her.

At last I felt a sense of what being together with someone might mean. I began to accept that she could know me, read me, understand me and I could do the same for her.

I had never had that in my life.

On rainy days I go into the undeveloped parts of the château. The back half of the ground floor was probably farm workspace, and maybe even used for housing animals in winter.

There is a collection of rooms full of unsorted stuff in endless boxes, so I began to root around to see what I could find. I came across a trove of old photos of this château in a box of frames.

The one that fascinates me the most, I think maybe was taken in the late nineteen thirties. There's a little Renault car out the front of the château and a tractor with tiny front wheels. There's an oldish man standing beside the car with a beret on, so I assume he is French. He is looking into the camera without a smile. Next to him stands a boy of about ten with as serious a look as his father. I am assuming that is their relationship. There are chickens and a pig in the background and several horse-carts lying at angles off to one side. There is nothing on the back of the photo so I know no more about who they might be than I can glean from looking at it. What is interesting is that when I go back to it, I keep seeing more things. It's like a puzzle revealing more of itself, bit by bit.

I didn't see the woman in the background at first, because she is in the shade of a tree. She is young and has long hair let down and she is laughing at something that I can't see. She is wearing a white blouse and a long skirt.

Who is she?

What was she doing there?

Why is she laughing?

Looking at it, I imagine I can enter that photo and be in this château back at that time.

It gets quite real sometimes, like a daydream.

How different life must have been.

I have just added veterinary midwifery to my list of newly developed skills. Actually not too much skill but it would look interesting in my CV.

The reason the cow was lopsided was that she was about to give birth. That also explained why her udder was so full, I suppose.

I woke up to her mooing and when I went out to see what was happening, there was a head sticking out of her rear end. She was standing still with her legs wide apart pushing and mooing, with her back arched. Of course I had no idea what to do, so I simply talked to her, encouraging her and telling her it was all going well. That's the extent of my midwifery skills.

Then out he came.

A skinny and slimy little thing plopped out, all in one go, onto the ground and then with some nudging from his mother, he staggered to his rickety legs. She gave him a good tongue bath and then guided him to the udder and within minutes he was drinking from his mother's teats. That really is what teats are for. He does a good head butt to get the flow going.

It took a while for the afterbirth to be ejected and I wondered if I should do something about that. I didn't need to. She knew what to do. As soon as it was all there, she ate it.

I think I have a boy calf, so at some point, I might have my own bull, if this isolation goes on long enough.

By the time I hit London, I was running out of money, having spent most of what I had left on the airfare. I tried various places with Help Wanted signs and scored cash under the counter work in a bar for a week, just round the corner from the hostel, washing glasses and getting my bottom pinched by the Lebanese owner. It had distinct limitations.

Clo and I had begun to really enjoy each other's company but living in the claustrophobic environment of inner London, in the confines of the very basic accommodation offered by the hostel, was constricting.

My meditations, when I could never be sure who was in the room, were woeful.

The contrast with the monastery was a bit too much for me. I told Clo that I thought I should go somewhere less frenetic, hoping that maybe she might be ready to move on herself.

She was.

She said she was really ready to give up the hostel management. So we agreed to look for something better, particularly as my bottom was not responding well.

As it turned out, Clo, who is very good at networking, heard of an offer to house sit.

She had a friend who organised high-end house sitting and had an emergency vacancy. The manager of one of her most important houses had just been arrested for running a methamphetamine lab in the greenhouse.

Could we start right away?

We could.

The next day, Clo quit, I said goodbye to my Lebanese boss from a careful distance and we very happily took the train out of London.

Our new abode was on a country estate in Surrey. It was the classic English country setting, as you might imagine in a Jane Eyre novel or one of those films about aristocratic families a hundred years ago. It was luxurious in staid English taste, with Chintz and velvet everywhere in the parlour and the sitting room, huge framed pictures of forebears and somewhat old fashioned plumbing upstairs.

We were picked up by the managing agent who was a tiny Welsh woman with thick rimmed glasses. She gave us a breathless rundown of what we would be required to do in an accent that was pure Wales. Clo said she barely understood a word, but we both nodded as she rattled on. She gave us a sheaf of notes and left us to it.

We would be paid a tiny sum to live in and look after the estate, but we really didn't care.

The lady who owned the estate had a hereditary title, being the granddaughter of a Lord. We always had to refer to her as Her ladyship .

The estate was very quiet because she preferred to live in Malaga in Spain most of the time. She had been a budding opera singer before her fortuitous marriage to an older man who didn't last long but left her a fortune. Although she was not exactly a young woman any more, she had met a Spanish man a few years earlier who persuaded her that she could still be famous, if he managed her. I suspect he was more impressed with her bank balance than her vocal cords. He was also very handsome as evident in a picture of them together in the main parlour.

Our job consisted mostly of supervising the gardeners, both of whom were Lithuanian boys with scant English but were very knowledgeable about shrubs. We were responsible for calling and directing the tradesmen who seemed to be endlessly tinkering with the plumbing and the electrics, and hosting one dear old fellow, her nephew several times removed, who would come every weekend on the morning train from London, sit out on the patio, do the Times crossword and smoke cigars. He would go back to London on the Sunday night train. He had very specific food requirements. His favourite item was toasted Cheshire cheese with pickled onions. He didn't talk much but we got quite fond of him.

We had use of a little old green Morris Estate car for transport, going off for shopping to the little picturesque local village and outings now and then to ivy-covered pubs for English beer.

Life in Surrey was quite idyllic.

Although Clo and I had a very physical relationship right from the start, we did not sleep together till then, but in the sedately English second bedroom with all its embroidered cushions and satin sheets, I fell more and more in love with Clo.

When we weren't doing minor chores, which never took very long, we would walk and for us both we fell in love, not just with each other, but also with the English countryside. There were long, almost manicured walking paths, occasionally requiring careful steps around horse manure, that took us along hedge-rowed fields, past duck ponds and manor houses, classic houses in Tudor style and thatched cottages with rabbit hutches.

It was all so English.

Of course episodes like that in life can't last long, or they lose their lustre.

Her ladyship was suddenly forced to come rushing back from Malaga, after her accountant was arrested and charged with serious fraud. It turned out she was his prime victim, and as he had been bilking her for years, she could no longer afford us or her Spanish promoter.

From the moment she swept in, we endured several days of absolute chaos in which the poor lady looked more and more demented. She neglected her appearance, which up until then had been impeccable. She wore nothing but her dressing gown and slippers, and her hair was a haystack. She tended to crash around the house shouting at everyone, both those present in the house and on the phone with her quite powerful soprano vocal cords in full flow. This went on day and night.

As quick as we could, we slipped away.

I never heard the outcome of all that but I imagine it was not pretty.

It is strange that certain people constantly attract trouble to themselves.

Luckily, while we were living in Surrey, Clo had been talking regularly to her favourite aunt who she adored and who adored her.

Her aunt Antoinette had already asked if Clo would come back to France to look after her. She was ailing rapidly with some kind of auto immune disease. She lived alone on the outskirts of Versailles.

It was the perfect next step.

We caught the bus to Dover and went on one of those Hovercraft ferries that seem to glide on mist, as we scooted across the Channel.

Versailles is a fascinating place with a glittering history and a vibrant community. This is where I learnt to speak French, study a bit of French history and become an English teacher.

Tante, as I always called her, was a very sweet lady, quite formal in her manners but with a secretly wicked sense of humour. She became my French teacher, patient but exacting. She was forever rolling her eyes at my Australian accent even if I could do a reasonable rrr like the French. I was miserable at conjugations. Clo and I always spoke English together, so up to then I had almost no French. If you fall in love with someone in a certain language that's the language you always want to use together. Ours was an anglophonic love affair.

It is strange to say was .

We never finished our relationship and in many ways I felt we were just beginning, even though we have been together for more than ten years.

I shouldn't say was because we still have a relationship, a good one, even if we are not in the same place. I make myself remember that so I do not lose hope that at some point we will pick up where we left off. We will have some great stories to tell each other and we will go on from there.

I have to hold on to that.

In Versailles, we lived with Tante for a year, in her *"Manoir"* as she called it. It was several hundred years old and had been the home of her family for several generations. We had a bedroom under the eaves of the slate-roofed mansion and had an iron bathtub big enough for both of us at once with lion feet and copper taps. The house had formal parlours and a sweeping stone staircase in the centre of the foyer. She had to employ one woman solely to come and clean all the chandeliers once a week.

The garden was quite formal with topiaried shrubs, all overshadowed by oaks that were heritage listed, le patrimoine , and several hundred years old. Tante claimed they were planted before Napoleon came to power.

Tante did not need all that much care in reality but she did adore having company.

While she gently faded away, my French improved rapidly. She and I would spend one hour every morning in her meticulously-kept drawing room and she would torture me through the conjugations and the rules of French grammar, with all the exceptions. We would discuss the news of the day and I got to understand a little of the byzantine workings of French politics. She felt that France would have done much better if they had kept their royals, rather like the English. She had liked the rather royal demeanour of Charles de Gaulle but not necessarily his policies. She had a radical streak in her. She told me stories of her youth, especially what she got up to during the 1968 uprising in Paris with Danny le Rouge. Although she was quite formal and mannered, she had a way of alluding to things that was wonderfully suggestive. I delighted in her company and to this day I am very grateful for having known her.

Just remembering her makes me smile.

I got a job in town with a crowd who ran a language school and they loved the fact that they had someone who spoke English but was neither English nor American. Being an Aussie in France is a *"porte ouverte."* Everyone loves us. We represent the last wild frontier with so many dangerous creatures. They have all seen the documentaries where crocodiles eat German tourists. And we can beat the All Blacks at rugby, at least sometimes. Any time I would allude to my country of birth they would say : "Oh, I always wanted to go there, but it is so far away, so expensive and soooo dangerous." In shops I always got good service because of my origins.

Tante faded away slowly before our eyes and she was quite matter of fact about it. She had never married, although she had several affaires , which she told me about in rather colourful detail. She had inherited enough to live well without a spouse and she just seemed to prefer men who were already married to someone else. Maybe she just liked variety. Or the frisson of clandestine rendezvous.

She planned her demise with precision. We knew exactly how she wanted her funeral to be run and who was to be invited. She wrote her Will with a local notaire. Clo was to be her sole beneficiary. The French laws of inheritence are very complex but she worked it out. As Clo is the only member of her generation, she is an only child, like me, she is the obvious benefactrice.

My French lessons went on, even when she could no longer get out of bed. I think they were mutually beneficial, especially at the end when I was a welcome distraction.

As well as looking after Tante, Clo found work in town, managing a shop that sold lingerie. The French are very particular about that and the range is prodigious. Clo adores all that sort of thing and it meant that Clo herself had a wonderful collection of very sexy underwear. She was gifted with a body that lends itself to being seen in very little and I loved seeing her so adorned, or rather unadorned.

Clo ticked all the boxes in my list of the qualities that I would like to have in a partner.

Not only was she wonderfully physically attractive, small and shapely, superbly formed, but she had a quick mind, a quirky sense of humour and a warm heart.

She had everything as far as I was concerned. She could be quite bossy, but that's not too high a price to pay for everything else.

I do miss her incredibly. What fun we would be having inventing our country lifestyle.

I so need someone to share with.

Now that the skies above the château are warming into full Spring, my days are filled with gardening and collecting things that I find growing wild. There must have been a number of other dwellings around the château at some point and all of them would have had potagers veggie plots. And flower beds. I find wild leeks growing in the long grass. I pick irises and wild roses and fill vases with them. There are all sorts of berries growing that promise summer bounty.

I have set the rabbit traps and every now and then I get one. I always apologise to it and thank it for giving me sustenance.

There is no shortage of things to eat and things to admire.

I am very aware of the abundance around me.

I might fall into lapses of loneliness, but very often I am just full of gratitude for how I am taken care of.

If only Clo had made it, everything would be perfect.

I do enjoy the company of my cow, who I am happily calling Ma Vache . I think she is a Limousine, a wide-boned blonde variety, that come from around Limoges. She is wonderfully placid, loves a good neck rub and is happy to be milked without being tied up. I don't take much, a cup or two does it for me. I now drink one cup of milk and one coffee, *un grand crème*, per day. The rest of the milk goes into her son, who I have been calling Mon Veau which is French for my calf. He is totally tame and tends to follow me around a lot. He is very playful and every now and then has a fit of youthful exuberance and dances up and down, then races round the field. What I will do with him when he gets big, I have no idea, assuming this all goes on that long. Maybe I can train him to pull a cart and I will have transport, but where I would want to go I can't imagine. I suppose I could cut a hole in the fence at the bottom of the hill and we could go up and down the freeway for a hoot. It's a pity to have a such a well-made freeway totally unutilised.

When Chloé bought this property, they were just building the freeway, so it is brand new. Before that, this château was really miles from anything. Even now, to use the freeway, you have to drive a long way, close to Gourdon, to the nearest Sortie to get on it. Sometimes when I am sitting up in the turret with my mint tea, I imagine the surprise the earliest residents would have if they could see what was built at the bottom of their hill.

The pages are beginning to fill in this exercise book.

It's like having someone to talk to, someone who listens without interrupting.

The topic of conversation varies from day to day and helps to keep me sane.

Sometimes I have nothing to say.

Now and then I read over some of the pages.

Sometimes I like it, sometimes I think I am just way too self-indulgent.

But here I am writing this.

I met Clo's family after we moved to Versailles.

She had talked about them, on and off, and I knew that she had felt she needed to make distance from them to feel she could live her own life. They had pushed her to go to university which she did for a short while, heading in the direction of business, heavily influenced by her father. She said she lasted two years till she had an affair with one of her teachers. He turned out to be manic depressive and nearly killed her, so she says. Anyway after a near disaster when he threw himself into the Seine and had to be rescued by the water police, she knew she had to escape.

That's when she went to London and for quite a while refused to communicate with anyone except Tante.

She finally relented enough to allow her mother to talk to her once a month on the condition that her mother did not beg her to come back to France, get married or have a baby. If her mother started to cry she would hang up.

When we moved to France, to take care of Tante, Clo's mother was ecstatic. Then when she was introduced to me, she was cautiously optimistic that Clo's life was getting a bit back to normal. When she found out that I had worked in the theatre, she considered that I was an artist, like her. I rather liked her, but she always seemed to be living in something of a fantasy world.

Her parents live in Paris in a very modern apartment that has been created out of an old warehouse. You wouldn't even know it existed from the street. It is quite a flash part of the city, not far from Montmartre. There is a narrow entrance gate which you need a code to be able to open, then you walk under an old building and suddenly you find yourself in a wide open sunny courtyard with big olive trees in pots. There is an underground carpark, which is a great luxury in Paris and all the apartments, I think there were ten, are built into the structure of what must have been a huge warehouse. The sawtooth roof all made of glass is still there.

Clo's family is unusual. Her father is a research chemist with a large international pharmacy company. He is a great believer in modern medicine being able to cure anything. He is a voluble talker and tends to dominate any conversation with the power of his voice and convictions. Like so many French people, he talks over whoever he is talking with. He is not easy to be with.

Her mother is a violinist and plays in a baroque quartette. She looks like someone born in the wrong era. It is as if she plays that music so that she can live in the era where she belongs. She dresses to suit, not only just when she plays but all the time.

The other two members of the family are adopted. They are both Colombian boys, brothers whose parents died in an earthquake. They are very shy boys and both have musical talent, although much to the annoyance of Clo's mother, they tend to prefer Rap or heavy metal. One plays keyboard and the other almost every instrument known to man. I actually think they are brilliant, but Clo's mother mourns the absence of serious music in their repertoire.

I was introduced to them all on the occasion of Clo's father's fiftieth birthday. The apartment was packed with all sorts of folk from his world and a sprinkling of other family members. Tante did not come. She wasn't well enough and in reality she and Clo's father detest each other.

Clo's mother proudly introduced me to all sorts of people, almost all of whom wanted to speak to me in their best English, some of it being more or less incomprehensible. Most of them were scientists of one kind or another. I think it was something of a relief that she could introduce her daughter's companion as someone she liked.

Her Mother came out several times to see her sister in Versailles, but she tended to dissolve into tears much too quickly for Tante's liking.

I love watching the sky.

The cranes fly north in the spring and I hear them calling to each other as their wide V-shaped formations find thermals and they spiral upwards before moving on. I imagine them saying to each other : Keep going Fred, you're doing good! Keep going!

Every now and then the lead crane will turn and the whole flock will circle because they have found a warm thermal updraft. Round and round they go, until they get maximum altitude and then away goes the V again. The whole thing is magical to watch, each bird flying in the wake of the bird in front and how the lead changes from time to time. The lead bird gets no assistance so tires more quickly than the others. How do they know to do this?

The other birds that know how to use updrafts are the different kinds of raptors, wide-winged birds of different sizes circling, floating motionless in the updrafts, often in pairs, till something catches their eye then dropping swiftly, wings folded back and in, to pick up lunch. Pity the poor bunny who ventures out for a nibble when the raptors are circling. Some of the smaller ones, I think they might be falcons, are able to hover in place, with their wings moving quite fast, before diving earthwards.

After Tante died, the money and her house went to Clo. I had grown very fond of Tante and I think it was mutual.

Her funeral was , more than anything else, a festival of flowers. She had ordered them all herself and had engaged a floral decorator for the event. Even when she could barely talk any more, she still had the floral decorator come to discuss the arrangements. Clo presided over the event and I hovered in the background. Tante had chosen who would be there, mostly ladies of much the same vintage. Most of them were very impressed with the floral display and said they were planning the same kind of thing for themselves. Tante had reminded them all that they would all be gone soon, so they were all quite prepared. There were no tears. She had been adamant about that.

Tante had given up religion, she said, when the young priest she had fallen in love with, when she was quite young, told her that celibacy was the only way to get into heaven. She said, with a sly smile, that even though he believed in being celibate, he still liked to put his hands under her skirt, but that was all.

She said the whole thing put her off religion and she decided that if God did exist, then she was happy to wait till she died to find out.

We lived in her afterglow for a while, till all the formalities had been completed.

While we continued to live in Tante's house, I had to do something about my passport. Clo and I became Pacsé, which means informally married. It is a way to get legal status. It also represented for both of us a commitment. Sort of like married but not getting married.

I liked what it did to us.

Somehow I felt that I was entering into a new phase of us as a couple. Clo said she felt the same. She had had lots of boyfriends along the way but mostly they were short-lived and most had not lived up to her expectations. She shared a couple of horror stories of men who had dark secrets, like criminal backgrounds or violent inclinations. He said if all Australians were like me, she should have emigrated there long ago. I took it as a compliment.

So once I was legally connected, I was eligible for a *carte de sejour*, a permanent resident card.

To get there, I attended the course on French culture, had my interview to see how compatible I was with French life, did the health check to make sure I was not importing tuberculosis, and took the written test on my understanding of French culture. Most of it seemed aimed at Muslims, to make sure they learned that it is illegal to have more than one wife and that women can have their own bank accounts.

My application wandered through the corridors of the French bureaucratic system for quite some time, about nine months as I recall, and then one day, Voilà! as they say, there it was. With all the concomitant benefits, except being able to vote, I could happily live in France for ten years.

By then we had spent a year in Versailles, and although I had studied quite a bit of French history, I had never set foot in its famous palace and had no desire to. Seeing hordes of Chinese tourists trooping along, following their flag-carrying guides, made me totally disinclined. It's a monstrosity anyway, a hideous flamboyance to amuse the Sun King, while the peasants starved.

After a while, it seemed time to move on. Without Tante's presence, it was pointless continuing to stay there.

We both felt it.

Clo had always wanted to live in the Pays Basque, that part of France that in so many ways is not French. It's Basque, proudly and loudly. Half of the Basque people live in France and half in Spain, the Spanish half were tagged as terrorists because of ETA who blew things up in the name of claiming independence. They've given it up these days, although now and then a cache of weapons is discovered. Maybe if the virus kills off millions of Spaniards, then the Spanish Basque, if they have survived, will declare themselves a country and try to annex their French brethren.

Moving out of the house took some effort.

We set about selling the property and all its contents. It's more complicated than I imagined.

Clo is not a patient person when it comes to bureaucracy and the business of finishing all this nearly ruined our relationship. She kept yelling at me to help but I couldn't understand what on earth all these documents were talking about. We had to engage an expert to check if there were termites, another one to give the house an energy rating, and a third one to signify that it was not in danger of being flooded. I could see why one in four French people work in the bureacracy.

Luckily there are people who will buy the entire contents of your house. We got several to come and do a quote. Evidently some of the furniture was pretty impressive, which led to something of a bidding war between two old men, who knew each other and evidently hated each other. By accident we had them at the house on the same day. It could have turned ugly, till I came up with a sort of drama game I knew from my drama school days. Each piece of furniture was discussed and we played a sort of trading game. If you take that piece, then I take this piece. I acted as the umpire and in the end we got rid of almost everything. They both had matching Renault white vans which they filled several times over. I had to supervise because there were arguments as to who had bidded for what. In the end I put labels on everything.

It was both a relief and sad to have the house empty.

The last night we were there, we slept on the floor.

Selling the house itself was easier, because one's of Tante's dear friends had a son who was a Notaire, a lawyer, what in Australia we would call a solicitor. In America the word means someone who begs or solicits.

Anyway, in France, Notaires are allowed to sell houses. He was good and had a buyer within weeks.

The paper work went on for a while, with signatures and tax stamps and levies to be paid.

We survived all this.

When all the bureaucracy was done, I said goodbye to my French students, who were always trying to learn how to pronounce g'day with an Aussie accent, and we headed south.

The train flew across the French countryside, at blurring speed, paused for breath in Bordeaux and then whizzed off again through the pine forests of the Lande towards the Spanish border.

We looked around for a romantic *pied à terre* . We avoided the big towns, Bayonne and Biaritz, and discovered a little cottage for rent on a hill overlooking the little boat harbour of Saint-Jean-de-Luz. It was a picture-perfect stone building with stucco walls and climbing roses. On the front deck you could sit under vines and watch the fishing boats come and go below.

For six months, while we ran through Tante's money, we dined in the little fish restaurants of the town, went for long walks amongst the sheep, and learned to sing folk songs in Euskadi, the Basque language. It was all very pleasant, my French improved, Clo and I enjoyed each other's company, and time passed.

Saint-Jean-de-Luz has two kinds of beach front, the surf of the Atlantic and the still water of a bay that leads to the harbour. We developed the daily habit of walking down the hill for coffee and croissants on the harbour wall, watching the fishing boats come in from the night's haul, and then going round to the sandy beach of the bay and swimming out to the buoys. Our afternoons were made up of me giving English classes and Clo indulging in the Thalasso, the health spa. Quite a chunk of Tante's money went into essential oil massages and downward facing dog exercises.

The stone walls of this château are symbols of solidity. Whatever may have happened within them, the walls have watched detached. There are signs of events around them, maybe some bullet marks on one wall, some etched graffiti on another, but the walls are solid.

The layout of the château seems to have centered around the kitchen and the defence. The turret is above the core of the château while the kitchen occupies a large part of the ground floor. It looks like in times past there was a large social area beyond the kitchen, but at some point someone decided to break it up with interior walls. I will sometimes sit in the kitchen which has the best feel to it, and imagine all the generations of French families who sat there.

Back when it was built as a fortified redoubt, some of them would have been chevaliers. One of the sheds certainly looks like it would have been stables in another era.

The horsepowerless BMW sits there now.

The longer I stay here, the more meditation becomes a cornerstone of my daily existence.

I sit every day and I love that time.

There is a little room that I think might have been a chapel at some point. It has a small arched stained glass window with little red and blue diagonal squares. The room is tucked under the stairs at one end of the building and is only big enough for at most six people to sit in. When I found it, it was being used as a closet. The ceiling is quite low and is made of oiled wood and comes to a point above the window because of the stairs winding up above it. I found a wonderfully soft big purple cushion upstairs and I have that propped against the wall. I couldn't believe my luck the first time Chloé brought us here when she showed me her statue of the Buddha, a bronze round-bellied version about a foot high. I think he is probably Chinese, given the size of his belly. The Thai versions are tall and slim with high domed bronze or gold headdresses. Chloé's was hidden on a shelf surrounded by other found objects from her worldly travels. She knew I had spent time in a Buddhist monastery so she thought I would be interested in it.

Now I have rescued him from his worldly surroundings and installed him on a small table, draped in a white woollen blanket, under the window.

He presides over my meditations almost as if he is a living breathing supervisor.

When I come in, I bow, like I used to do in the temple in Thailand and we go from there.

I usually start with some yoga which always helps me to focus.

There are times when I transcend this human body and float into a state of disembodiment which is as close to ecstasy as I have ever been.

It is fine to discuss what is the body, but to leave it behind is something of a relief.

On other days, I sit there and scratch my arse, till the time is up.

I have a kitchen timer which is clockwork, so it doesn't need batteries. I set it for an hour. Sometimes I curse it for breaking a wonderful transcendence and at other times I feel like shouting at it: Hurry up and go off!

No two days are the same in meditation.

There are some back areas of the cellar with all sorts of stuff in it that I am just beginning to explore. I found another box of old photos, fading sepia shots of picnics and farm workers from long ago. Someone must have been a keen photographer a long time ago. Poring over the new collection I had the same sensation, that every time I would look at a photo I would see something new. And there she was, the same young woman, hair down, laughing. But just as in the first photo, she was obscured, hard to see. She was sitting on a rug with some children, but there was a blotch on the photo that made her difficult to detect, but it was her.

Once I saw her, I was certain.

She fascinated me.

We ended up in Toulouse because we were running out of money. The same group who had the language school in Versailles also had one in Biarritz, not far from Saint-Jean-de-Luz. They were happy to re-employ me, but after a few months they were forced to close because the rent was far too high.

Biarritz is an expensive place. At the same time they had just lost their English teacher in Toulouse. They were willing to pay me to go, and to pay for Clo as well, if I would be in charge of their English department.

We had done the best of what the Basque had to offer so off we went.

Then Clo met Chloé and here I am.

Why am I writing in this exercise book?

When I read back over some of the stuff, I think, what is the point?

It is like asking the seminal question: what is the point of anything?

Maybe if Clo had made it, things would be different.

It is very important not to get miserable.

But then I cheer myself up by spending a glorious sunny spring day in the garden, digging and weeding and planting seeds of things that could turn out to be, well, almost anything. I have found jars of seeds with labels, beans of various kinds, all in French, but other jars with no labels but I am planting them anyway. Will I be here to harvest whatever they become? It makes me think of the stories of forestry workers who plant acorns knowing that they will never see the fully grown oak trees but they plant them for the generations to come. I will have to start doing battle with grubs and bugs and insects that like eating veggies. I have no idea what you do about that, but in the shed I can see various containers of chemicals.

Do I want to go all organic? I will have to think about it.

I let the chickens and Boris loose in the garden so they can eat the bugs. I vaguely remember that's how they get rid of bugs in Vietnam, with ducks. It might work with Boris and his cohorts.

My efforts at fish farming did not go well. I thought I would use the swimming pool as a fish pond and then eat the fish. I had seen little fish in the creek on the other side of the hill, away from the freeway. I took a colander down there and caught a few, carried them back in a bucket and put them in the pool. A large white herron ate the lot the next day.

I think the pool might be full of chlorine anyway.

There was a time, just after we arrived in Toulouse, when Clo thought she was pregnant. We had never broached the subject of creating a new generation and it took us by surprise. Did I want to be a father? What kind of father would I be? Did Clo want to be the bearer of a totally dependent little person, who would require her attention for the next, at least, twenty years? Neither of us had a clear answer to any of those questions. We talked and talked. Did we want this child to be French or Australian? Did we have a gender preference? What langauge would it speak? What would we call it? Where would we live? Would we have to become rooted to one spot and buy a house and a car and a washing machine? And then suddenly the whole thing was moot. False alarm. Her gynaecologist told her it was probably a false positive test.

However it did something to us.

Up until then we had just been living for ourselves, doing whatever felt good, with no sense of a future. It brought up the deep questions of being-ness. What is the purpose of being born? I had just turned forty. She was two years behind. Did she want to have childen, and if so, she had to do it soon. We never really arrived at a decent conclusion to all these questions. We actually agreed that we would talk some more about all that in the solitude of the Domaine when she got here.

And now?

Here I am sitting in a château and she is..... I can't even imagine where she is.

Is she stuck in the Maison Bourgeois, being driven crazy by three house-bound French boys and Alain and his lady friend?

Does she miss me?

Is she looking for a way to get out?

Or did the whole of Toulouse get wiped out? Dead bodies littered everywhere, corpses like Jean-Claude and Eveline, no-one left to bury the dead?

When I start to think that way, which I do try to avoid, I begin that downward spiral. Why are there no planes flying?

Why is the freeway deserted?

Where is everyone?

Sometimes I get into a state of despair. Then I have to make a big effort to choose my thoughts. The Buddhists are very keen on that and if nothing else, from my year in the monastery, I at least understand the principle even if I struggle to put it into practice.

The solution when this comes on and it is still daylight, is to go and milk Ma Vache or dig in the veggie garden. Doing things is always a good distraction.

Sometimes I will just run around the field with Mon Veau who is always up for a gambol.

Being on top of a hill, the highest of a group of hills, the château withstands days of strong wind.

I love the wind.

I love to wake up to the sound of the leaves in the newly green oaks thrashing away in the power of fast moving air. It is amazing to consider that's all wind is, moving air and yet look at what it can do.

If our wind turbine had been erected in time, I would have endless electric power. But even without that, just watching what it does is a wonderful gift in itself.

One day an iron sheet came loose off one of the sheds and flew across the garden and sliced a branch off the pear tree. It would have taken my head off if I had been there. Powerful force, our friend the wind.

When I was in the monastery in Thailand I used to watch the village kids flyng their kites.

I had never done it. So I decided, with all this wind, why not?

There were piles of newspaper in the shed, no end of sticks, and there was duct tape in the workshop. The garden shed had reels and reels of string used, I imagine, for the runner beans. Anyway I had all the ingredients.

I made the classic diamond shaped kite with copies of the Sud Ouest newspaper, with a tail made out of knotted rags.

I ran around the field with Mon Veau running after me, trying to launch it.

It took a while till I discovered that the art of flying a kite is to let it go. When I did that, giving it much more string to lift up, then away it went to the fullest extent of the string I had allowed. It dipped and swooped up and I felt a sense of its freedom.

I wanted to be as free as that kite.

I found myself laughing joyfully and Mon Veau thought it was great fun too. He danced around me, picking up on my enthusiasm.

Then I tripped over him, and he and I fell in a heap and I lost my grip on the end of the string.

My kite flew off, now completely free and is probably somewhere over the Loire Valley by now.

Although I have no idea what day it is, it must be just about Easter.

Tante, my best source of French culture, taught me about the traditional story told to French kids at Easter, or Pâques as they call it. According to this story, all the church bells in France fly off on Good Friday to have an audience with the Pope. That's why you don't hear church bells between Good

Friday and Easter Sunday. The Pope gives them lots of hard boiled eggs (probably chocolate eggs these days. These days I suspect that the Pope subcontracts to Lindt) and the bells fly back on Easter Sunday dropping the eggs in the gardens as they go. So on that morning, as soon as the kids hear the church bells, they all race outside and hunt for Easter eggs. That doesn't explain why the supermarkets are full of Nestlé Easter eggs from the beginning of February.

Anyway I don't hear any church bells and I haven't since I got here. I could pretend it is an endless Easter Saturday. On the other hand, quite possibly all the bells got the virus and died in their bellfries. The nearest church is Saint Fé and although in the past, if the wind was right, you could hear the hours and the half hours, now there is nothing coming from there.

Eggs on the other hand, I have plenty.

Just to make life interesting, I vary how I cook them. I have experimented with putting different herbs in omelettes and some are really good. I have no idea what they are and I always hope I am not about to poison myself with some friendly-looking deadly nightshade. Basically I assume that if Ma Vache will eat a herb then it must be OK.

The other thing about eggs of course is that chickens come from them.

Setting aside the conundrum of which comes first, I am wondering about how to make sure I will have the possibility of replenishing the flock. If I eat one of them every now and then, I must also replace them.

How do you do that?

Maybe I should just leave some eggs and see if they turn into anything.

I have decided to use a magic marker to leave some eggs in straw nests and see what happens.

The girls give me more than I can eat anyway.

Easter, when I grew up, was all about going to church. My parents went to church on Sundays with monotonous regularity. They are Methodists.

I went till I was about 12 and then one day I realised that it was very boring and that I really had no interest in going. I discussed this with my bewildered parents and they tried to persuade me that I should go because God would not be happy with me if I didn't go.

I did not believe a word of that and from then on I decided that God was pretty much irrelevant. If God was unhappy about it, he never mentioned it to me, so I think he thought I was irrelevant too.

My decision hurt my parents as parents rather than as practioners of the faiths. I don't think they had much missionary zeal, they were just disappointed that I wouldn't do what they did. I never sensed in either of them a deep love of God or anything like a spiritual commitment. They went because that's what you do if you are a Methodist. That was their method.

I quite liked Sunday School when I was little. They told interesting stories. I always wanted to meet someone like Jesus, but I never did. He sounded like an interesting person to talk to.

The fact that he lived so long ago meant it was just a good story. I had my doubts about whether most of the stories were true. It didn't bother me much if they weren't because I like fiction.

When I think back to how earnest some of the Sunday School teachers were, I am sure they were convinced it was all the gospel truth.

Now it is Easter once again, or sometime around now and what does it mean?

I found out somewhere along the line that Christianity just picked up an old pagan Spring festival and reworked it, kind of like Disney did with Winnie the Pooh.

I think even the coloured eggs are pre-Christian relics.

Good Christians are a bit hard to find. I have only met one or two who really believed in a heartfelt real relationship with God through Jesus.

My favourite Christian was a Franciscan monk who worked with street kids in Naples in Italy. I met Brother Arturo in the monastery in Thailand. I was fascinated when I found out what he did for a living, so to speak.

We would sit under the awning of our dormitory building in the hot afternoons during siesta time. He told me that from his perspective, God had called him to be a Christian monk when he was a teenager living in a wealthy part of Naples. His family were aristocrats who owned a castle high up above the city. He grew up with all the privileges of wealth, like their second house on Capri, and his father's garage full of vintage Maseratis, but he felt hollow inside. He told me all this in his wonderfully thick Italian accent.

He was seventeen, when he had a vision of Saint Francis in Assisi during a school visit. Saint Francis had appeared in a bright shining light, he said, and told him he was born to be a monk and he should serve the poor. It was so powerful he said that he left school right away, to the horror of his family who expected him to study law, and he joined the Franciscans.

The trouble was, and his voice would become low, almost conspiratorial, as he spoke, he had no experience of the love of God or Jesus. All he had was the command of Saint Francis.

Then one day, when he was still in Assisi studying, he met a Buddhist monk from this monastery. They talked about God and he realised that God, as described by Christianity, was only one of so many different ways you could experience him. Brother Arturo said the monk was the first person he had ever met who seemed to have a real living relationship with God. What really fascinated Arturo was that the monk would sit and meditate in the Basilica of Saint Francis and have deep experiences of his version of God, not the one for which the Basilica was built.

This was so impressive to Arturo that once he had been ordained as a Franciscan monk and started to do his work with the poor in Naples, he had applied to go on a spiritual retreat, which evidently the monks are supposed to do once a year. They let him go to Chiang Rai, which was very brave of them. And there, he said, in this Buddhist monastery, he discovered what it meant to be a Christian.

He said, sitting in meditation in the temple, he would have ecstatic moments of oneness with Jesus.

Arturo said that to him, for the first time in his life, Jesus was alive and full of love, and had been waiting so patiently for Arturo to wake up.

He said he had a vision one day where Jesus told him that he was so happy that Arturo was coming to his monastery.

Jesus regarded the Chiang Rai monastery as his, just like the Buddha regarded Assisi.

So now Arturo goes back to the monastery every year for a three-week spiritual check-in with Jesus and he is one of the happiest people I have ever met.

I wonder where he is now.

It has been raining all day, so I have not gone outside much. Sitting up here in the turret with my mint tea, in the late afternoon, gazing out across the rain-shrouded hills, I was feeling very at peace with myself.

Then suddenly I saw movement on the freeway.

I jumped up, spilled my tea, and peered down into the rain.

What was it?

What was moving down there?

It was moving quite slowly but big enough to be something significant.

I put on a parka that was hanging on the hooks by the back door. There's a whole motley collection of coats from who knows how many visitors.

I took off down the hill.

About halfway down there is a small clearing with a rock that gives a reasonable view of the road below. Stopping there, I peered through the rain to try to work out what it was.

Sangliers.

A troupe of some twenty wild pigs on the freeway! They were all bunched up together, big ones and little ones.

The disappointment that I felt in that moment was as heavy as anything I can remember.

I could barely summon the energy to climb back up the hill, hang up the parka and crawl into bed.

The sadness that swept over me was like drowning.

When I woke up, sitting in the dark of a rainsoaked night, I realised that I had been living in hope and that a group of wild pigs had just killed it.

Hope is a dangerous bedfellow.

There has to be a better way.

But you live for another day.

Somehow, something gives a little pleasure and the little sparks of joy that begin to glimmer can easily be fanned into a warm glowing return to equilibrium.

It could be as simple as discovering that a little, very fluffy sparrow has made its way into the chapel and is sitting by the Buddha as if she has come to pray.

I remember that Tante used to tell me that she believed whenever there was a bird in the house, it brought good luck. So with this acceptance that a symbol of grace had been offered, I sat to meditate.

My meditation was peaceful and still, and when I came back from some far off warm and cosy place, the little bird had flown.

Where it went I don't know. I couldn't, in that moment, remember if I had left a window or a door open.

It didn't matter. The bird had come, done her bit and quietly departed.

I got up feeling good.

Pigs on a freeway were just a humorous footnote.

I lit the fire, made morning tea and cooked a potato omelette.

I went out to say *Bonjour* to Ma Vache, who was waiting at the edge of the field and drew down a cup of milk.

Mon Veau was very happy to see me and wanted a neck rub. He doesn't have any horns but he loves a rub where they would be if he had them.

Then I visited the hens and Boris and they ran around and clucked happily into the veggie garden when I let them in. I have discovered the very first of the strawberries, tiny little ones but very sweet.

In all this I revelled in a sense of plenitude.

How lucky I am to have all this.

Sometimes when I sit up here in the turret and gaze out over the hills, I wonder about the nature of my existence.

Is it possible that I am all there is left of the human race?

On one hand that's a really scary thought. It brings up those long held fears of being alone. I makes me miss the people I enjoyed being with. It makes me regret the things that I did and the many things I should have done but never got around to.

On the other hand it has a kind of ego-ish bravado to it. If I am the only one left, then I am no longer answerable to anyone.

No-one cares what I do.

There is no-one to curb my excesses, there is no supervisor peering over my shoulder, and there is no parental control.

Or I could think of my namesake.

I am King Simon.

I reign supreme.

I am the Emperor of all I survey.

I am God.

Well, that depends of course on how I choose to define God. I recall at some point someone, somewhere was selling a T-shirt that said : I was an atheist until I realised that I was God. There could be something to that.

I don't remember what Indian scripture it was that someone shared with me, at some time, that described the beginning of the universe like this: God, in all his glorious isolation had an impulse. He said to himself: Let me become many.

So he did. Out of his own will, he created this universe and he rather liked it.

The only problem was that in the creation of the universe, he lost a sense of himself. He forgot that all things were made from his own being. He got trapped into the thought of himself as being small and limited.

Now and then, though, as one of the instances of that limitation, he wakes up to himself and remembers : Oh yes, I am God.

Then that lucky entity re-enters the state of Godhood, merging back into one-ness again.

I think that would be a very good thing to achieve. It's all very well to jokingly say to myself: I am God. It would be something altogether better if had the deep experience, beyond questioning, that I was indeed God.

There is another way to look at it? As an Australian, I learned something of the Australian Aboriginal spiritual beliefs, the most evocative of which was that they believed that they all come from the earth and return to it. In each place, the local tribe would venerate a mountain or a river with the understanding that it was the mother of their creation. When they died, they merged back into the land from which they had emerged. It made a lot of sense to me.

Now I sit here in the middle of France, not that far from where the Neanderthal cave drawings were discovered. Those people were about the same vintage as the earliest Australian Aborigines.

I imagine how it would feel to look at the hills around me, as being where I sprang from as a human and to which I will return.

Trouble is I was born in a city. These hills, bare and rugged as they are, are not the soil from which I sprang.

Nonetheless, when I am gazing out at these hills I sense that there is plenty of sacredness around here.

A few hills away is Rocamadour, a pilgrimage site in the early days of what would one day be France. If you were a nobleman and you commited a sin, then, if you walked from the place where you committed the sin to Rocamadour, you were forgiven. On the other hand, peasants who sinned lost their heads right away.

So the place has a long history. Even before Chrisitian times, it had prehistoric residents.

Rocamadour is a vertical town, clinging to the side of a cliff with medieval churches all clustered together half way up.

Chloé took us there the first time we came up here.

It is a tourist site, with endless souvenir shops perched over precipitous drops, selling T-shirts and coffee mugs with profiles of the village. The three churches, hewed into the rock and jutting out on ledges, have relics from the original saint Saint Amadour and there is a small black Madonna statue that is believed to have been carved by the saint himself.

I can't say that I had any sense of sacredness when we went there.

Maybe it was the discomfort of elbowing our way through hordes of German and Dutch summer visitors, staggering up the endless stairs or, instead of inhaling the sacred atmosphere of any of the churches, it was being blinded by endless flashes from cell phones.

Nobody prayed, everyone snapped.

I had the feeling the tourists were collecting their memories in their phones, not in their souls.

If I had the courage to venture out beyond my hill, I could walk there in a couple of hours.

My fear is that I would find death.

Dead tourists littering the streets, rigor mortis sculpted priests kneeling before altars and dead attendant baristas in the restaurants. Imagining the whole scenario of corpses, at the top and the bottom and all the way up, littering all those stairs, I could picture it like a Dürer etching of Hell.

On the other hand why would I want to go there?

I will think about it.

On another rainy day I spent the morning rooting around in the château to see what was hidden in dark corners and in forgotten cupboards.

All sorts of stuff, some of which made no sense to me. It must have made sense to someone.

If, in some dim distant future, there are remnants of humanity left, will I ever get to meet them?

If not, at least I can live in the history of this place and all its hints and revelations about what it was and who lived here.

It is a bit like trying to solve a mystery.

There are some things that really do strike me.

The young woman in the two photos haunts me.

I imagine asking her: Who are you? Why were you here? Do you have anything to tell me, anything that you learned by being born at that time and living in this château?

I assumed she must have lived here, although she could have been a visitor.

I prefer to think of her as having lived her whole life here.

I carried some of the most promising boxes up to the kitchen and read documents mostly written in long hand, as best I could.

I didn't understand a lot of it and I can't say I learned anything. I am sure I misunderstood most of what I was trying to read.

Then there she was.

It was a small cardboard folder, a simple booklet, about the size of a modern passport. In it was a tiny sepia photo of her. I am certain it is her. It has the date 1936. She was eighteen. She was born on November 12, 1918, one day after the Germans surrendered at the end of the First World War. She was born in Sarlat, which is about half an hour's drive from here. This booklet, issued by the hospital in Sarlat, is her licence to be a nurse, *Une infirmière* .

I just checked that in my trusted source. Thank you Monsieur Larousse, your dog-eared, long out-of-date dictionary is my constant companion.

Her name is Adèle Dieulefait.

I think you can translate that surname as God did it. or God the fact.

Am I reading too much into the name?

So she was a nurse and if she was alive today she would be 94 years old.

She is very beautiful in this tiny faded photo, not much bigger than a postage stamp.

She looks right into the camera, very serious but with a slight, very slight smile. I can imagine her sitting in a photographic studio where the camera man is shrouded in a black cloth and his camera is the size of a shoe box and he holds up one of the old fashioned flares in one hand.

She probably had to sit very still.

I put away the boxes I had been rooting around in and took this little booklet to the chapel. Where the little bird had sat, I placed it, so I can see it before I begin my meditation.
Why?
I don't really know, but there is something about her.
So now when I go in every morning, after I bow to the Buddha, I find myself saying Bonjour Adèle , and then I sit with my eyes closed and whatever meditation is on offer shows itself.

It was perhaps the third day of doing this when she came into my meditation.
It was vague, ethereal. I sensed, as much as saw her, more a presence than an image, but I knew who it was.
It didn't last long but it made my heart race.
I came out of meditation feeling such incredible energy.
The rest of my day, I couldn't shake the feeling that I was not quite as alone as I thought.

For the next few mornings there was nothing and I began to feel disappointed.
I think expectation is the arch enemy of good meditation.

Then on another rainy afternoon I did some more digging in cupboards, and I found a scrap book with newspaper clippings from Le Sud Ouest, going back to the end of the Second World War. It was interesting to see what was considered news back then. A lot of it was agricultural.
Then there she was again. She was standing with a group of men beside an ambulance, in her nurse's uniform. The article was dated the 12th of November 1949, her birthday. However, the photo came from the early days of the war. The article that went with the photo, however, was a revelation and a shock.

It talked about the decision to dedicate a memorial to Adèle Dieulefait, in recognition of her heroic actions during the war, as part of the Resistance, *Les Maquis* .

She had been part of a team that treated wounded resistance fighters and hid them from the occupation forces and also from the Vichy. There had been a safe house, and I think, if I understood correctly, that house was on or very near this property. In 1944 someone had betrayed them to the Germans and they raided the safe house and she was caught. There were several wounded fighters in the house and they were executed on the spot. The house was destroyed with explosives and she was taken away. She was held in a cell for some days and, according to this article, she was interrogated and probably tortured as the SS tried to get her to betray the members of her team. The article described her heroism as she refused to say anything.

She was shot against the church wall in the tiny local village of Saint Fé.

This is where, according to the article, they were proposing to build the memorial. I have driven through the little village, which is not much more than a *Lieu Dit* which means a place called, and there is not much to it.

I have never driven slowly enough to notice a memorial, but according to the article, it was going to be put at the spot where she was executed.

I could walk there from here in probably less than half an hour.

I lifted the article very carefully off the page. The château has all sorts of picture frames with old photos and some not very good art work. I found one the right size, got rid of the faded copy of Monet's lilies, and cleaned the fly specks off the glass. Now she sits with her nurse's booklet in the chapel.

From then on she has been here, as if somehow I woke her up from a long sleep on some other plane of consciousness.

Maybe she has been waiting for me.

The Buddhists believe in reincarnation, like the Dalai Lama being born life after life. I don't disbelieve in it, but up till now, I have had no sense of it in myself. I don't even remember anything of this life for the first three or four years of it, let alone anything earlier than that, certainly not any past life. Maybe the human capacity to forget drops the veil on all that.

But now there is something lurking deep down inside me that says: Maybe we have been together before. Was I, in a previous incarnation, part of her crew? Am I one of the men in her ambulance photo? Is she now coming back for some unfinished business?

It is so tempting to imagine, because her presence is so strong.

Adèle is now part of my life.

Am I being unfaithful?

While I miss Clo and I wish like crazy that she had made it out here, she seems remote to me, a vibrant memory, a tangible sensory recall, a physical loss. At night, sleeping alone, I crave to be able to turn over and touch her skin. But it is always with a sense of loss, not presence.

This new presence is undeniable.

Adèle is here.

I can feel her, almost as if she is in the air, and in meditation, now and then I can see her.

Is she a ghost?

She feels very benign, so I have no sense of being haunted.

Ghosts get a bad reputation, probably all the fault of Halloween.

This one, if that is what she is, is not negative at all.

There are various ruins of old buildings dotted around the property, and I am wondering which one was the safe house that the Germans blew up.

I have walked past lots of them and not felt anything, but now I am pulled to go and find it.

In my meditation I ask her to show me.

There is no immediate energetic shift, but I live in hope she got the message.

Mon Veau has taken to going with me on my walks.

He behaves more like a dog than a young bull. Sometimes he trots along beside me and then bounds off into the grass to find something juicy to eat.

Sometimes he will playfully butt me in the rear when he comes back. I don't mind that too much because he's just a calf, but he will be a big bull one day and he could wipe me out.

I wouldn't want to end my incarnation lying out in the field with shattered bones.

Mon Veau trotted happily along as I visited most of the ruined houses I had seen before, but I didn't feel anything.

Then after a couple of days of wandering about I went back to the creek where I had harvested the fish. I had not explored the other side of the creek and I wasn't even sure if it was still part of the château grounds.

Mon Veau hesitated when I waded across, but then he decided he liked the creek and jumped in and splashed about with great delight. I can only imagine what the fingerlings, the little fish, thought of that.

He seemed to like it there, so I sat down to watch him.

And there she was. I could feel her close and I knew she was telling me where the house was. Behind where I was sitting was a thick bramble of blackberries, *Les Mûres* .

I knew with a sudden certainty that this must be the place. I closed my eyes and she was very present, not visible, but there.

And with my eyes closed, I did have the sensation : I know this.

Eventually Mon Veau got tired of the creek and came over and playfully butted me and I lost my connection.

Nonetheless, it felt like an intimation of a certainty and I was content to accept it as the first step.

I got up and looked at the brambles. There was going to be quite some work to do, if I was ever going to penetrate that lot.

As we began to walk back to the château, a very new idea began to form. It seemed to me that there was a reason I was here, apparently stuck, marooned and isolated. Instead of seeing myself as victim, suffering for no good reason, there was some kind of design behind all this.

I was supposed to be here.

This was part of something old, much older than just my puny little forty year old self.

I was coming back. There was something unfinished with me and Adèle and that was why I was here.

At the same time, why we needed to have a viral pandemic to get me here, remains a total mystery.

It is hard to justify the deaths and suffering of millions of people, just so I could have a mystical reunion with a long dead nurse.

Of course I could also be entertaining a total fantasy.

If I am meant to discover what this is all about, then she will have to help.

My meditations now have a new aspect. I come in and I bow to the Buddha. Then I look at the two photos of Adèle and I say Bonjour. Then as I sit with my eyes closed I consciously let go, so that whatever is to be offered to me in this meditation can come, without me interfering with it.

I have come to accept that Adèle is a conveyer of information, when she feels like it. She is fickle.

The slight smile that I see in the little sepia photo suggests she has a bit of a sense of humour. She's playing hide and seek with me.

Sometimes, there is just the soft velvet darkness of innerness which is wonderful all by itself.

Then there are the times when we are off into other worlds, some of which I understand, feeling a certain recognition, but for others I have no idea. She is not always evident but I tend to associate her with them.

Whether she herself appears or not, she is conveying what I need to receive. At least that's how I am choosing to ride along with it.

I have seen visions, I suppose they are visions of Versailles, but not modern Versailles as I knew it, and even something that I think was earlier in French history, medieval Toulouse maybe?

If this is all her work, she is something of an historian.

At the end of that kind of meditation I sit and try to understand, as deeply as I can, what I just received.

It's probably about half and half, where some of it seems to make sense and some makes no sense at all.

All these fleeting images of places and people have me wondering. If Adèle and I did in fact meet each other during the Second World War, then maybe that was not the only time? Maybe she is letting me see some of the other instances?

It could be something like the twisting double stranded helix of DNA, intertwined lives, crossing and crisscrossing every now and then.

It is all a bit of a fantasy, but with nothing to lose I go with it.

There is no-one peering over my shoulder supervising, critiquing my thoughts, no-one to accuse me of losing my mind, so I can do what I like.

I have the infinite luxury of indulging in weird notions and romantic nonsense if I want.

There is nothing to stop me.

And while I can see how potent all this is, I just have to be careful that what I choose to invoke does not bring me down.

But the opposite has happened.

What a change this has made to how I feel and think.

I can say to myself: I am not alone.

And yet I am alone.

I can say both and neither contradicts the other.

Nothing has changed outwardly, but now that alone-ness feels not just bearable but powerful. It is as if a door has opened in my sense of myself such that I don't miss anything, or lack anything.

I am just here and that's fine.

And because I am alone, I can allow this to happen.

If Clo were here, I don't think it would.

The one thing that bothers me, just a little, is Clo.

Because what has caused this new euphoria is the presence of someone, although not physically, there is a subtle sense of betrayal of Clo.

When I was with Clo, I never felt lonely. She always made me feel at ease and welcome. I loved her company, the touch of her skin, the music of her French accent, the scent of her body.

Up to now, because she has not been here, I have felt wretchedly lonely.

There is a part of me that tells me that I ought to be able to feel sufficient within myself without any outside help. But up to this point, I have had no idea how.

Maybe from now on I can learn that.

And maybe I will have help.

I suppose it depends on what I consider to be outside .

In between gardening and other things that I have persuaded myself need to be done, I have time on my hands.

My daily discipline keeps me focused but there is still plenty of free time. I have been thinking about the house hidden in the blackberries. The more I thought about it and even recognising how much work it would take, the more I felt drawn to it.

So now I have decided it would be my form of memorial to Adèle if I clean out the brambles to unearth the destroyed safe house.

I am certain it is there.

The idea of a memorial had been in my mind since I read the article in the Sud Ouest. I had let go of the thought of walking to Saint Fé.

What would be the point of that?

I would stand before the memorial erected by the locals, assuming it is still there, and then what?

On the other hand, like other places around here, Saint Fé might now be a memorial to all the current and now dead Saint Féans, dead not by German gunfire, but by a virus that spares no-one, except me. I might be walking into a little village of corpses.

It would be safer and somehow more appropriate for me to create my own memorial.

Armed with an axe, a pick, a machete, clippers and gardening gloves I went back. Mon Veau got into the water and danced about for a while, before wading ashore and nosing about in the bushes.

Blackberry brambles are nasty. You have to approach them with respect and chip away at them little by little. After about an hour of this, I had carved out something of a corridor into the centre of the bramble.

It was there.

I found the stones of the house, all in a tumble, but clearly the building blocks distinctive of the local architecture.

I left it that first day, feeling exhilarated that I had found what I was so certain would be there.

The next day I went back.

And the day after that.

It took me a number of days, doing maybe an hour a day, till I had it clear enough to reveal the size and shape of the house.

That was when it became clear that the Germans had blown it up but not burned it. There were little shards of broken green bottle glass that would have melted if it had burned and there were some now rotten beams lying at angles against walls.

I became an amateur archeologist and started sifting carefully through the rubble.

For quite a while there was nothing of any importance, that I could tell. There was cutlery, broken china, a few rusted tools and misshapen kitchen utensils, tortured into shapes that invoked the hideousness of the act that hit them.

Then I landed on a little treasure trove.

The floor, in what must have been the kitchen, was made of flag stones. You could see the worn-down part of the doorway where, probably for centuries, farmers had clomped in and out in their work boots. I traced along the edge of the stone floor to see where the walls would have been, and then I discovered that one of the stones in a corner was loose.

Out of curiosity I prised it open to reveal a hollow space underneath. A small pile of objects had been stashed in it.

There was a jar of old french francs, several hunting knives and a small square tin box. All this had been hidden away and the Germans must have missed it.

Maybe they didn't really search the house too much.

Having read the story of what happened, I could imagine them rushing in, guns drawn, catching the Maquis by surprise and shooting them dead, where they were. Why they didn't shoot Adèle, I suppose, was because they decided she would fold easily under a little pressure and could be persuaded to betray her comrades.

Maybe they had other notions about what you do to a female resistance fighter.

I did wonder if I was inadvertently standing amongst the shattered bodies of assassinated Frenchmen, but I saw no bones.

I carried the contents of the stash outside.

The francs are no longer recognised as currency and anyway, maybe, seeing what has happened to the world, currency itself no longer exists.

The knives were not weapons for fighting so much as hunters' knives.

Then there was the box with its lid tightly rusted on. I sat with it in the sun and I closed my eyes.

I felt a restraint about trying to open it, as if it were a sacred object and that I needed permission. I wanted to feel right about it before attacking its resistance. I was looking for some kind of sign.

Mon Veau was the messenger. He was bored and wanted to go home, so he butted me very gently from behind.

OK, I thought, that's the message and I got up, collected my tools and carried the contents of the stash back to the château.

The box would have needed a screwdriver to get it open anyway.

I put everything in the chapel with the photos, the little booklet and the framed news clipping. It felt like I was building a shrine with relics.

France has hundreds of such places, little churches with the bones of the hand of a long dead saint, a few threads of the cloth that some saint wore for her martyrdom, or their shoes.

My shrine was for Adèle, who I don't think would have qualified as a saint.

And yet, what makes a saint?

The Catholics have their very specific miracle-based criteria, while the Methodists tend not to bother with saints at all. I know India has living saints and I have read some of their books. In India anyone can be a saint, sort of by popular recognition. Some holy person gets a following and they are regarded as a saint. I saw some of their ashrams in Varanasi.

Well Adèle has a following of one, so maybe I am starting a new movement, which will only ever have a membership of one.

Saint Adèle?

I doubt she was very saintly.

I keep putting it off.

Not yet, not yet.

The box sits there for days and I feel no impulsion to open it. Or is it no permission? Maybe it scares me.

Or am I relishing the mystery, afraid of disappointment, that it has nothing in it but dead cockroaches?

While I milk Ma Vache, pick my rapidly proliferating strawberries, or lie in the lush long grass with Mon Veau, watching clouds, the contents of the box are always in the back of my mind.

I have been back to the ruins of the safe house, chopping away more of the brambles and digging around inside. I have found more bits and pieces but nothing to shed any further light on who was there.

However even the little things can tell stories. There are bullet casings between some of the flagstones and I found a small handgun hidden in the remnants of a wall. I have checked every stone to see if it moves and that's how I found it.

Whose bullets were they?

Whose gun was it?

How come they didn't get to use it?

I have begun to clean up the inside, carrying away piles of rubble and weeds.

I think in the end I would like to see the bare stones revealed, so that the house that once was, is now preserved as the explosive aftermath.

I keep checking to be sure there are no human remains in it.

All the little objects that I collect, I will place on a kind of altar, perhaps in the middle, where the sun will strike it, a symbol of bringing light to a dark past.

As I toil away on the brambles and disinterring the basic stonework, I wonder about the Germans.

Who were they?

How did they feel, bursting into this old stone farmhouse with their guns, and shooting Frenchmen on sight?

Did they feel a sense of duty, to country or leader, or did they just do what they were told, hoping it would all soon be over and they could go home to their children?

Did they enjoy doing that?

Were they in fact Germans or were they Frenchmen who sided with the Germans. Talking to Jean-Claude, I discovered that there was a kind of French police called Milice. He spat when he told me about those collaborators and said they were a disgrace to their homeland. Traitors to La France. At least I think that's what he said. He had been drinking at the end of a long hot summer's day and his accent, already tricky, was getting more and more slurred.

As I begin to create my memorial to Adèle I have a fantasy that in some far distant time, when all this has long gone, a new civilisation will arise and they will come across this memorial, like the discoveries of ancient pyramids in the Mayan jungle and experts will argue and academics will write dissertations about what kind of religion it was.

Who was the deity of this temple?

What rituals were performed here? Maybe I am the priest of this temple, destined to humbly serve it, till my dying day, forever alone in my dedication.

The stuff of fantasy.

In the ancient, pre-Christian temples of Rome, they used to sacrifice bulls on high holy days, so Mon Veau had better behave himself!

By the length of the days and the gathering afternoon heat, it must be May by now. The little white flowers called Muguet that the French give to each other on May the first are popping up in the overgrown gardens by the château walls. I think the Sun King started that tradition. Sadly, as I am the only Sun King here, I have no princess to bestow them upon.

Princess Clo, may I present you with this bunch of muguet as a token of my undying love. I bet she would like that.

There are daffodils and jonquils everywhere, little white bell-shaped flowers and bright yellow forsythia, and lots of other very pretty things that I don't recognise.

I pick flowers and put them on the altar of the chapel.

I must have been a priest in one of my past lives, because it makes me very happy to do all this.

And still the box sits there.

Until she tells me it's time.

She came in a dream, a very graphic and disturbing dream. In this dream there is violence everywhere, the sound of guns.

In this dream, I am a small person, a small boy, running and running. I hold the hand of a little girl, smaller than me, who cannot run fast. There is something about one of her legs.

Behind us, there is the sound of explosions, getting closer and closer. We fall to the ground and I cover her to protect her. She says, very distinctly: "I have left you the ring." And then everything goes black.

I wake up in a sweat. I lie there feeling like I have been physically twisted and torn. My breath is short and agonised.

It takes a long time to get back to a state of quiet.

"I left you the ring," she said.

So I opened the box.

At first I thought there was no ring, just envelopes, yellowed and blotchy. I opened them as carefully as I could because they were brittle and flimsy. In each was just one folded sheet with handwritten French. It was going to take quite some work for me to decipher them.

And then at the bottom, the last one had a very short note and a fine plain gold ring wrapped in a scrap of silk. The note said : Mon Jacques je t'aime. Attends-moi. Dans l'avenir je sera encore dans tes bras. Ton Adèle My Jacques I love you. Wait for me. In the future I will again be in your arms. Your Adèle.

I sat with the ring in the palm of my right hand and I began to cry.

I am not a crier, never was.

But here the tears, the long held back tears, the unreleased grief, poured out of me. I sat there weeping, rocking backwards and forwards and unashamedly cried my heart out.

As I finally subsided, I dropped inside myself to as deep a place as I have ever gone. In that place I did not exist in any form and yet I was conscious, more conscious than a human can be.

I was conscious of an endless field of energy around me, expanding out, infinitely out. I was at the centre of the vortex of that energy. I was all powerful, I knew that I had been given an insight into the nature of all things, the knowledge that contains all knowledge.

And I was filled with love.

I radiated love.

I drank in the air of love around me.

How long I was in that state I have no idea, but slowly, ever so slowly, everything began to soften and fade, as if I was being gently caressed back from sleep by a benign hand.

At last I opened my eyes.

The ring was on the fourth finger of my left hand.

I have never worn a ring.

I have never gone in for bodily adornments of any kind. I have no tattoos, no piercings.

This ring felt like it had always been there and fitted absolutely snug. It was certainly not going to come off easily, because I tested it.

How it got on there, well, who knows.

I reverently put the tin back on the altar.

As far as I was concerned that tin was a holy relic.

I would treat it and its contents with the utmost respect.

I spend more and more time in the chapel and less in the garden.

The memorial is going to have to wait.

There is something I have to arrive at, and I can only get there by staying in the chapel and sitting, and sitting, and sitting.

There are moments where I can return to that incredibly deep place, but never for very long.

If my mind kicks in and says Ah there it is! , it's gone.

I must learn to be more and more disciplined.

I must discipline my mind. It is as delicate as walking on a tight rope, without thoughts.

Hold the balance.

Breathe.

At other times, absolutely nothing and I can't stand it, I have to jump up and go out.

However, even when meditation is not helping, the presence of Adèle is constant.

And not just in meditation.

Often, in becoming sleepy at night, she's around the bed and I can almost see her. Sometimes out in the field, it is as if she is just behind me, almost like she is in the photos, there but not there.

And yet I don't know any more about her than I did before. I have this thin little gold ring on my finger, the finger where normally a wedding ring is worn.

Was I Jacques?

I don't know.

I want her to tell me more.

I held back a little before I decided to try to read the contents of the other envelopes in the box.

When I touched the first one, I felt nervous. There was something about them that was sacred and commanded respect. The envelopes were dry and in danger of disintegrating in my hand.

I very carefully opened the first one and ever so gently unfolded the one sheet that was inside.

It was written with a naïve kind of handwriting almost like you would imagine a child to write. The script was quite large and carefully formed. It is the brother of Jacques, who signs himself Clément. He sends his love to his Mother and to

Jacques his brother. Maybe he is only a teenager and is not used to writing much.

I held it in my hand and tried to imagine him, young, innocent and terrified.

I put the letter with all the other objects around the Buddha.

I needed to give myself space before opening the next one.

After meditation a day later, I opened the second envelope. The hand is much surer and flowing. It is harder to decipher but I got the main gist of it. He signs it Georges. He salutes his two adored children, Christoph and Elise. He tells them to be strong and asks them to look after their mother.

I carefully folded the letter and put it back. I wondered whether Christoph and Elise are still alive. Obviously they never got this letter, but did they know what became of their father?

I closed my eyes and tried to imagine him. There was a feeling of masculine strength, but nothng more. I felt tears running down my cheeks as I thought about him.

Inwardly, I blessed his soul. What it must have been like to have lived at that time with the constant threat of violent death. Every French person had to choose what side they were on and what was important to them. They would live or die according to that choice.

The third letter is signed, as far as I could make out by Yves. His writing is indecipherable. Maybe there is a certain style of handwriting peculiar to France.

Although I have no clue what he wants to say, I bless him nonetheless.

When I opened the last one I couldn't even decipher the signature, but I sense it is another man.

I am sure that they are all letters of farewell to loved ones, in case something happens.

I am most likely a witness to the last thoughts of the resistance fighters in the safe house, who perhaps knew their days were numbered.

I can imagine them hunched round a table in the safe house kitchen with a single candle burning, writing these notes to those they loved, knowing that at any moment they could be dead. Maybe there was only one pen and they shared it, one after the other.

Did they read their letters to each other before they sealed them in the tin?

At least someone got to read, as best I could, their final messages.

After the last envelope, I sat for meditation with the intention that their souls be at peace.

I found myself in deep and powerful meditation.

I asked that the souls of Adèle and Clément, George and Yves and the other one, whoever he was, be released from anything that holds them back from being at peace.

Who was I asking?

I don't know.

When I came out of that meditation, I picked up the framed article from the Sud Ouest. The picture of the ambulance had a caption underneath naming the people in the photo. I had not taken the time to read it. Standing next to Adèle was Jacques Gougnard.

Was that the same Jacques?

Was it me?

I had no feeling of that, just the thought.

He was taller than Adèle by a good head and had broad shoulders. He looked older than her, maybe in his thirties. He had a thick black moustache and a strong forehead. In many ways he looked like what I imagine a resistance fighter would look like. He was built like a farmer, as around here I imagine at that time everyone was. I instinctively liked him. It was only when I used a small magnifying glass that I could see his hand on her hip. He had to be the same Jacques.

The other names of the men in the photo were not any of the letter writers.

I would have to rely on my imagination for what they might have looked like.

In a strange way, I now don't feel lonely at all.

It is as if I have invited all these souls to come and join me.

We are one happy little company.

These souls and the two cattle and Boris and his chickens, we are a whole community.

How could I possibly feel lonely.

And then along came George.

That's what I thought he said when I first saw him and asked: What's your name? and he bleated what sounded like Geoooooorge.

He's a goat.

I think he is quite old, white with a black blotch on his right flank, a beard and quite long horns. He moves a bit stiffly so he may have been hurt somehow. He just turned up one morning, bleating.

I think he's lonely, because he seems to like our company and he's welcome, except when I forget to close the veggie garden gate and he rips into the young shoots that I am hoping will be my summer sustenance. I have since secured the gate much better. He and Mon Veau have a wary relationship, but I am sure with time they will get used to each other.

Mon Veau is growing fast. He is still very friendly and loves to walk with me, but I am aware of how strong he is becoming.

When he was born he came up to my hips on his skinny little legs, now he is all beef and nearly as tall as my shoulders.

I wonder how many other domestic animals there are out there, abandoned by their humans and feeling lonely. I could end up with quite a menagerie.

And if this pandemic has wiped out the whole human population, there must be millions of them, horses, cows, sheep, dogs and cats, guinea pigs, camels.

Then again they might all be doing fine, liberated from their human constraints.

Some of the seeds that I planted back in the early spring, soon after I got here, are beginning to reveal themselves.

Some were labelled so I knew what I ought to be getting but others were just seeds in jars. Now I am beginning to see what could be various sorts of pumpkin, although it is too early to know what sort. There are what I think must be radishes and maybe members of the cabbage and cauliflower family. I am not all that knowledgeable about plants so they could be anything.

With a bit of luck I will have a plentiful supply both for the summer and to store for the winter.

Will I still be here in the winter?

I have no idea what chemicals to use against pests but the chickens and Boris seem to be doing a pretty good job with bug protection, although I see little white moths attacking tender young shoots. Maybe I need a tame owl or something for that.

There are owls around because I hear them at night, with their gentle hoo-hooing echoing across the valley. There must be quite a few because the closer calls are answered from further away.

I haven't seen one yet.

There are some berry vines beginning to bear fruit too. I have raspberries and what I think might be blueberries and already I am competing with the birds for them, specially the blackbirds, the Merle. Maybe I should build a scarecrow.

There's a fig tree that is just beginning to form hundreds of figs but it will be a long time before they are ripe. Same with the pear trees, two of them, some kind of peach, I think, and an apple tree that is very old with a gnarled trunk but lots of blossom, so it should be good. There is a sense of abundance that is very joyful. Often I find myself wandering about talking to the fruitful trees and thanking them for what they are going to be offering.

Talking to trees is a new experience.

I have decided that it must be about May the 8th by now. Whether it really is or not I don't have a clue, but I know that in France it is a *Jour Férié* , a holiday to honour the end of the Second World War. May the 8th 1945. So in honour of that day, I will officially open the memorial to Adèle Dieulefait and her comrades, in the safe house across the creek. Mon Veau is invited and so is George if he so wishes. He doesn't walk with me like Mon Veau, and Ma Vache just prefers the grass by the château.

The safe house is all cleaned up.

The brambles have all gone. I piled them all up and poured some of the precious two stoke mixture on it to help it burn. They crackled and spat but within half an hour there was just a little patch of ash left. It felt right to incinerate what was obscuring the safe house. Its protective work was done and it needed to be obliterated.

To my delight I have found wild irises coming up where the brambles were. They must be as delighted as me, getting to come up unimpeded after all these years.

I have dragged several stones into the middle of what was, I think, the kitchen, because there are the remains of a fire place on one side. On these stones, I have placed the jar of francs, the hunting knives, the bullet cases and the gun. I have surrounded these relics with smaller stones to protect them.

I have brought a vase of glass thick enough to withstand the weather and picked roses from around the château walls. I vaguely remember that the armistice was at 11.00 in the morning, although I may be thinking of World War One.

Mon Veau seemed much more interested in the creek than the safe house so I did the inauguration on my own.

The sun shone brightly, not a cloud in the sky but there was a light breeze. I made a speech. I said aloud to the accompaniment of the creek behind me, and a wayward crow high above, what the purpose of the memorial was.

I recited the names of the people who were associated with it.

Then I sang the Buddhist hymn, like I did for Jean-Claude and Eveline.

I sat there for a while and felt very peaceful.

There was a sense of completion and I hoped that the souls whose presence I had evoked were happy with this memorial to their earthly deeds.

And that was it.

I felt no need to visit Saint Fé.

She liked it.

I know that because in meditation she came. It was as if she and I were in one body, she had merged with me. The sensation built slowly. I had bowed before the objects on the altar in the chapel, a whole array of symbols. I had settled back onto my cushion and closed my eyes and it was calm and warm inside. Then as if coming towards me out of a mist, she became evident, appearing, a bit like adjusting focus on a camera, getting clearer and clearer. She wasn't exactly as I have come to recognise her from the photos, but it was her, no doubt. She was much more ethereal, formless but unmistakable.

And then she became a part of me, inside me, filling me almost physically but certainly psychically.

And she was pleased.

That was the feeling of it rather than an explicit message.

She has not spoken and I wonder if she ever will.

She conveys what needs to be conveyed and I am more than content with that.

When the meditation released me, I sat there, deeply satisfied, incredibly happy. There was no sense of being alone at all.

There is renewed energy and I launch myself into whatever the day has to offer. Most of my decisions are weather-based.

On a good day I am outside, in the garden, trying to fix things like shed doors or walking with Mon Veau. I have conversations with Ma Vache, Boris and his harem, George, even the field mouse under the woodpile (actually as I suspected, there is more than one but they all look the same.)

I go down to the memorial often and bring fresh flowers for the altar.

Now and then I encounter other visitors to the safe house.

The hedgehogs have been there and a small snake. There are some deer droppings and there might be some kind of water creature hiding in the creek, but I have only seen small footprints.

I have been wondering what hedgehogs eat. I have a pair of *hèrrisons* , who trundle about the garden. They have three new babies, tiny little toddlers, who scuttle here and there as if they are incredibly busy. When I first saw them they were pink, but now they are turning hedgehog brown. I like to imagine them going off to hedgehog kindergarten and doing artwork.

Up till now I hadn't seen them eat anything, so I decided to sit and watch them.

They are valuable!

They eat bugs. I watched one of the parents chase and capture a beetle of some kind. So that's good. The hedgehogs are insectivorous, so they can help to keep the veggies unbugged. I don't know which is the male and which is the female. They look the same and I am certainly not going to try to catch one and turn it over. They seem to share the parenting duties evenly. They might even be a pair of ladies for all I know while the gentlemen hedghogs have gone off to play golf.

I have been exploring Jean-Claude's sheds.

Do I dare try to start his tractor?

I am no mechanic so the likelihood of it being useful is small. What would I do with it anyway? I can't see myself working out how to attach a plough and churn up a field. There are various agricultural machines in his shed too but I don't see myself using any of them. There is a rotary digger that runs on two-stroke, of which there is a half tank, but even that I am wary of. The same goes for the chain saw.

There's a whole shed full of hay, which I was lucky not to lose when I burned the house. If I am still here in winter, I can feed Ma Vache and her son with it. There are bags of chicken feed too.

There are ropes and cables, poles and fencing wire, all the kinds of stuff that I'm sure farmers everywhere always amass. That could be useful.

Standing in the midst of it all I feel a great surge of joyful gratitude, and I laugh out loud and I send the soul of Jean-Claude, wherever it might have gone, my happy thanks.

I will visit these bountiful sheds often.

On rainy days I read, I root around in the dark recesses of the château, I drink an occasional wine, I make fancy meals, as fancy as my garden and the chickens will allow. Every now and then I feel compelled to eat a chicken but I go through so much guilt chopping off a chicken's head that I don't do it too often.

I do all this on rainy days to keep myself in good spirits.

Rainy days have the danger of darkness and I don't just mean clouds.

There is some direct correlation between the greyness of the sky and the condition of my mind.

If I am not careful my inner weather deteriorates.

When I see the sky getting dark, I hunt for distraction.

I look at the sky a lot.

Every morning it's the first thing I look at as soon as I go outside.

The skies are untroubled by human flight so very often the sky is absolutely clear. I set myself the inner discipline of making sure my mind is as clear as the sky.

The sunrises can be gorgeous, so I always take those as good signs.

I can think of my mind as the sky.

And hopefully, just as I know I am not the sky, while I can observe it, so I should be able to do that with my mind.

My mind can be rosy in the morning, or bright and clear all day, or it can be dark and thunderous, as long as I don't let it control me, then I can observe it just the same way.

I could imagine my thoughts as clouds. They just float across the sky of my mind, changing shape as they go. Some are dark. Some are fluffy. Some look like something, others carry portents. But they are just clouds. So if I regard my thoughts the same way I do clouds, they are just thoughts and they don't affect the sky at all.

Some days this works. Other days not so much.

Some days are better than others.

The silent freeway shimmers in the midday heat but nothing else moves on it.

How long have I been here?

Maybe two months or more by now and there is nothing to suggest that anyone is out there.

I think of the tales of isolation, like Castaway or Treasure Island or The Swiss Family Robinson, stories I came across as a kid. I am in the same boat, only it is the scrubby countryside of the Lot that surrounds me, not the ocean.

Will I find a Man Friday? I would prefer a Woman Friday actually but anyone would do. There is a part of me that deeply craves human company.

Other than the beasts I have no-one to converse with, and although they are erudite in their own wonderful way, I need someone who uses words.

Then again this gathering appreciation of solitude is something to treasure. At last I have begun to find a way to feel more or less comfortable in my own company.

And then there is the subtle presence of those who join me from some other planes of consciousness.

Are there such things as planes of consciousness?

I have read about them, but it all strikes me as a bit theoretical. It would be nice to have someone to discuss this with.

Maybe I will become so good at solitude that I will move beyond the need for human contact.

The few books on Indian mystics that I have discovered in the château suggest that most mystics achieve their greatness by learning that solitude is the goal of life.

The Desert Fathers were like that, living back in the early Christian times. I found a thin little book about it, where they lived in the Egyptian desert and had a very direct experience of the existence of God.

If being isolated offers a relationship with God, that could be interesting.

If that's true, I have all the ingredients for it.

For the last few days there has been a light that comes on in the late afternoon, about three hills away.

The first time I saw it, I thought it was just my hopeful imagination. But the next night at about the same time the light came on. The third time convinced me. The light always came on in the late afternoon, I checked the time on my solar watch, and then the light was turned off again at sunset.

I began to wonder who was doing this.

Was it some kind of automatic signalling device?

Or was there a person there?

I couldn't let it go.

I worked out where it was by lining up the two lower hills between the château and this light source. I put on the best boots in the château and took a good strong walking stick.

I locked Mon Veau in the field, which he was not happy about, and I walked away from the château like an explorer.

I could hear his indignation for quite a while.

I passed Jean-Claude's sheds and then went down the winding track to the road below.

Then I struck off in the direction of the light. I followed the road beside the freeway before a side road run underneath it.

I climbed the first of the two hills and looked back at Le Domaine de Buveny.

My mint tea turret stands out starkly against the sky. Then I made sure I could see the hill where the light came from. I could see some kind of building and began to feel very excited.

I crossed a couple of deeply grassed fields, climbed a couple of fences, and then found a track going up the hill.

And there it was.

I stood there staring at it. It was very modern, mostly huge glass windows at the front with a high gabled roof. They had used old stones for the structural walls but it was obviously brand new.

I approached warily, wondering if there might be dogs, but I heard nothing.

I tried a few doors but everything was locked.

This was before I remembered about the virus and touching things.

Having reminded myself about that, I peered into the big windows which did not have curtains. I could see a large lounge area, luxuriously furnished with fancy light fittings and a massive flatscreen television, but showed no sign of having been recently inhabited. Looking in other wndows I saw a fully equipped gym and round the back a very big and fancy kitchen. Across from the back of the house was a massive garage and through the windows I saw several what looked like vintage cars. Between the house and the garage, there was a big in-ground pool with a hot tub, all covered over by a retractable glass roof. The pool had been drained. Beyond it was an enclosed garden, with trellises and walkways, but had become quite overgrown.

I began to think no-one had been here for months and that I had come on a fool's errand.

Who or what turned the light on at the end of the day, but only recently?

Did someone come here in the late afternoon to do that?

If they did, why?

Was there someone trying to signal?

If that was true why only do it before sunset and not into the night when it would be more visible?

I decided, having come that far, I would wait until the late afternoon to see how the light came on.

I climbed into the overgrown veggie garden and found quite a few strawberries and other fruits, lots of self-sown veggies and a million snails and bugs having a feast. I joined the feast and lunched on the garden's offerings. Then I took a walk around the property to see if there were any signs of recent activity.

It didn't look like it. The grass had not been mown for months and was high enough that if anyone walked through it, they would leave evidence.

There was none. I kept to the stony track as much as possible not wanting to leave my own evidence.

There really was nothing there. Whoever owned this place maybe only came in the summer.

If no-one appeared by the end of the day, did I dare to break in, in case there were things I could use?

It was tempting.

I took a walk behind the garage to see what else might be there and I came across a shed with a door that stood ajar. I carefully pushed it open and walked into a head- maze of spiderwebs. I backed out, clawed it all off my face and used my stick to destroy months of careful webbing.

It was primarily a wood shed and junk store. There was one object that filled me with joy.

A bicycle.

Quite a fancy Peugeot off-road kind of bike with thick, but flat tyres. Luckily it had a pump attached to the frame. If no-one turned up, this I would keep. There was nothing else in that shed that tempted me.

The afternoon wore on and as I wandered about, I found nothing else that suggested recent human presence and nothing that was useful to me.

At about the time I thought the light would come on, I went round to the front of the house. It had a very clear view of

Domaine de Buveny. I wondered if whoever owned this place was acquainted with Chloé. They were certainly of the same monied class. I had looked for a mail box but there wasn't one. Unless I broke in and found something to reveal who owned it, I would never know whose it was.

Keeping an eye on my solar watch, I waited for the light to come on.

The time passed. Nothing happened.

The sun began to go down, right behind Domaine de Buveny, eventually highlighting it in silhouette.

Then I found myself bathed in light. I turned around and saw what it was.

I had to laugh.

The setting sun, as it sank behind my château, reflecting back to me, was bouncing off the huge glass windows.

I stood there, amused by my own mild stupidity and looked at this outlandish piece of rich man's folly and decided, other than the bicycle, I wanted no part of it.

I got the tyres pumped up and they seemed to hold, so I rode it down the track in the gathering dusk. What took me maybe an hour and a half to get up to the house took me fifteen minutes to get back.

The last hill was too much for me and I had to walk, even though the bike had gears. I realised that I was not very fit, but now I had wheels.

Mon Veau was incredibly excited to see me back and I gave him a long and loving head rub to make up for my betrayal.

I parked the bike in one of the sheds.

Realistically I couldn't think of where I would want to go on this bike, but it gave me a sense of the ability to go, if I wanted it.

Well that took care of a whole day.

The ironic thing is that the next day it rained and there was, of course, no light on a far hill.

I have run out of toilet paper.

I have been very careful to use very little to make it last.

Long ago I stopped using the toilets so that whatever water was in the tank on the roof behind the turret, could serve for the more important things. Without electicity or the generator, I can't fill the tank, so all it gets is rainwater runoff.

I never went camping as a kid so I have been a user of civilised toilets all my life.

Here I have had to retrain myself.

With the help of yoga I am now a good squatter.

I used to march out into the garden with a trowel and one square of tissue to a different spot each day.

When I was in India I saw plenty of people going off to squat, even by the road, with their little can of water.

I treasured my precious one square each day.

When I was in India, I also learned that you don't touch anyone with your left hand, that's for post toilet cleaning.

So now, without my little square, I am teaching myself a new technique.

It is not easy and I am glad I am the only human here, so there are no witnesses.

I still have the trowel.

Over the months, the garden has received lots of human manure, each with one square of precious toilet paper.

Now it's unaccompanied manure.

I don't know why my parents called me Simon.

What prompts this question is that, because it is raining cats and dogs, I am reading.

I found a book, in French, about the Albigensians. They were a religious group, considered heretics by mainstream

Christianity. They were called Cathars which, if I am getting it right, meant The pure ones . Back in the 12ᵗʰ century they were radical Christians who didn't like all the pomp and glitz of the Catholics. They also hated the system whereby the priests got to be the intercessors with God. The Cathars believed you can have a direct and personal relationship with God without a priest running interference.

The Catholic church hated them and the Pope of the time, whose name ironically was Innocent the Third, decided to have a Crusade against them and he asked Simon de Montfort to do it.

It looks like my namesake was a bloody Crusader and wreaked havoc wherever he went. He wiped them out pretty well and became overlord of the whole southern part of what was then Gaul.

I don't think my parents knew about him.

I waded my way through as much of this history as I could, but what really struck me was a description of what the Cathars believed in. Instead of believing in just one God, they embraced the idea of two gods or deistic principles, one good and the other evil. This was outrageous to the almighty monotheistic Catholic Church. The Cathars believed that the good God was the God of the New Testament, creator of the spiritual realm. Whereas the evil God was the God of the Old Testament, creator of the physical world. The Cathars thought he was Satan. Here's the interesting bit, assuming I am getting it right, the Cathars believed that the human spirit has no gender but is the spirit of angels seduced and then trapped in the material realm of the evil god.

Here comes reincarnation again.

They believed that humans have to be born again and again until they achieved salvation by what they called 'consolamentum', finally working out who they really are. Self-realisation, like the

Eastern religions. When they got that, they would return to hang out with the good god forever.

No more reincarnation.

They were interesting people these Cathars, because they believed that you could become Perfect , both men and women. A Perfect was someone who had achieved one-ness with the good God. They believed that Jesus was the good God's agent and that anyone who was perfect would escape from the cycle of birth and death. The Perfects were venerated, treated as saintly. They were vegetarians, celibate and, as far as I can tell, really good at debates. There was a chapter about a woman Perfect who so out-debated the local Bishop that he ordered her whole town to be destroyed. The army of Simon de Montfort arrived, laid seige to the town and then when the town finally surrendered, having run out of food and water, the army General asked the Bishop whether they should spare the Catholics who also lived in that town. The Bishop said : Kill them all, God will know his own.

So they did.

The Catholic church has a murderous track record.

The last part of the book is depressing. My nominal forebear, Simon de Montfort, made himself incredibly wealthy and powerful by obliterating the entire culture and people of the Cathars. He and his army were brutal beyond belief. Many of the Cathars were burned alive.

The Pope was happy.

There are no Cathars alive today.

Then again there is no one else alive either, except me.

Maybe.

All this set me thinking, yet again.

Why am I her?

Why am I still alive?

Why only me?

This is what happens on rainy days, when thinking takes the place of doing.

In my mind, I can gather up all the seemingly disparate fragments and see if they gel into something coherent.

All those men, through the ages, called Simon. Obviously there were plenty of them who remained anonymous and unrecorded by history. Ordinary Simons, simple Simons. Then there are the more famous amongst us, the crusaders, the minor aristocrats, English Lords, even Saint Peter, who started life as Simon. All these Simonic dots to be joined down through history to now. Here sits perhaps the last of all the Simons, sheltered in a half-restored château as a half-restored person.

What does it all signify?

Is there anything significant about the name?

Is it just the accidental labelling by doting parents at the birth, or is there more to it? I could have been a Barry or a Herby.

I wonder if anyone ever wrote a book about all the Simons in history.

I doubt it.

On the other hand, ignoring the repetition of the name Simon down through the ages, there is still the tricky question of whether we are born more than once.

Not to be funny, but reincarnation keeps coming up.

It seems like a lot of people subscribe to the notion that it exists. So if it is real and the cycle goes round and round, then who was who?

Who came back as what?

I came back as me.

Who was I?

Who am I now?

Am I who I am because of who I was?

And Clo? Who was she? How come she and I seemed to be so familiar to each other as soon as we met?

Why isn't she here?

And then there is Adèle Dieulefait.

Who is she? I know who she was but who is she to me now? That's assuming she was something to me before. The evidence for that is getting rather overwhelming.

Why is she here now?

Did she wait for me?

Did she call me here?

Is she the reason for all this?

Alright! Too many questions and no way of knowing the answers to any of it.

Can't Google anything these days.

Can't ask the head of the monastery.

Can't use any of Chloé's information source: Tarot, Shaman, i Ching.

There's just me and I don't know anything.

So much mind wrestling, I need to take a break from it.

Luckily it never stays wet for too long. No monsoons here. I can get out of the château and get my hands dirty and my mind clear.

I can hang out with my four-legged and feathered friends.

There is quite a relief in doing all that.

I can work up a sweat digging and clearing. I have to get physically much fitter and I have to occupy myself.

I am planning new garden beds. The tomatoes are coming on. I have the beginnings of lettuce and other leafy things.

It looks like I have zucchini and *potimarron* and some of their cousins.

Plenitude.

What more could you want?

It must be Ascension Day about now, forty days after Easter.

France is the world champion of holidays. Even though there is supposed to be a separation of church and state, the state happily acknowledges all the major Christian Days and everyone gets a day off.

So around now, according to at least some Christians, Jesus went to heaven.

He ascended.

The Cathars thought of Jesus as basically ethereal, not really in a body at all, so they wouldn't be having a day off. If they had survived that is.

I don't know why I am thinking about this. Jesus was never one of my super heroes, although the stories back in Sunday School were tolerably entertaining. Some were a bit hard to believe, like walking on water and all that.

Anyway for some reason it came to me today in meditation. Jesus went to heaven about now.

Later in the day, I went down to the safe house memorial and put some fresh roses on the altar and I thought about it some more.

It kept coming back to me.

Jesus went to heaven.

What does that mean?

It would be instructive to ask Arturo, because I'm sure he had his opinions about that.

So now I have dug out the château's bible, hunting for the bits about Ascension. According to the Gospel of John, Jesus told them all about it. I found this bit: No one has ascended into heaven but he who descended from heaven, the son of man .

Does he mean just him, or everyone?

The Cathars would have said Jesus went back where he came from because, as he was an angel, that was his home base.

If I entertain the idea of heaven at all, I prefer the idea that everyone goes.

I can't buy the concept that only one branch of Christianity has the keys to heaven and no-one else.

The Muslims claim it's theirs, and the Jews think they are the chosen people.

I suspect heaven has lots of doors or gates and every denomination goes in by their own special gate to fool themselves that they are the only chosen ones. Then when they get inside, I like to think that they are so ecstatic they forget all about their own exclusiveness and just have a heavenly time.

I don't think there is such a thing as hell.

Maybe because I am all alone in the world, at least the world as I know it, I think about all the ways people believe life ends and what happens after that.

At some point, I will join the rest of humanity in dropping my body. Putting aside the tricky question of who would conduct my funeral, where, once I have no body, will I go?

The notions of what heaven is supposed to be like that I learned about in Sunday School seem no more real to me than Disneyland. I haven't been to either of them.

Well not that I can remember.

Disney I am sure about.

This is yet another of those unanswerable questions.

I may have to die before I find out.

I won't be going to heaven just yet, the way things are going, but I have been thinking about going to Saint Fé instead.

It's got a church.

Why do I find myself wanting to go to a church? I really don't know.

This comes from a meditation in which I think I might have seen Jesus. It was vague and there was nothing explicit about it. The figure was willowy, cloudlike, but I had the sense that it was Jesus.

I came out of that meditation feeling an impulse to go to a Jesus place .

That's the best way I can describe it. The nearest is Saint Fé and now I have a bicycle. And, while I am there, I can see whether the memorial to Adèle is still there.

My hesitation is of course corpses and the virus.

It is weird that I am afraid to catch the virus. Do I want to live longer?

What for?

What does it serve for me to eke out my days up here, tending lettuces? If I get the virus, I might die or I might not.

At least when it first started, I heard that most people did not die from it. I might even get it and not know I had it. Or I could get a mild dose and become immune.

I could agonise on this for days on end and what would that serve?

Either I go or I don't.

I decided to go.

The day was warm, the tyres were pumped up and so was I. There was quite some adrenaline throbbing through my system as I started out.

Scared, no doubt about it.

Once again Mon Veau got locked up and complained.

I shot off down the track to the road at the bottom and turned in the direction of Saint Fé.

I passed several houses on the way, but I saw no signs of human life.

A dog ran out of one of the places and barked at me, but I was going downhill at the time, so I was fast. That dog was all skin and bones, so I knew there was no-one taking care of it.

Saint Fé has seven or eight houses, the Mayor's office, a few sheds and barns and the church. The church stands back from the road a little bit. There is a small open area in front of it with big platane trees, a bus stop and a notice board. The posters for the local elections back in February were still informing the electorate of who they could vote for.

There was no-one there.

I had dreaded finding dead bodies in the street but there was nothing.

No cars.

No dogs.

Most likely everyone had evacuated to somewhere. That was my hope because I did not want to be conducting multiple funerals.

I propped the bike against one of the trees and went looking for the memorial.

I circumnavigated the church, looking for a stone structure or a plinth. There was nothing there. I began to think that maybe the article in the Sud Ouest was speculative and nothing had ever happened.

Then, as I was about to try the door of the church, I looked up.

There it was, on the wall at head height. I had been looking down, as I walked around the church and I had missed it. It was a simple plaque, no bigger than the cover of a shoe box. It was engraved brass but quite badly weathered. So it was not easy to make out the words.

Adèle Deiulefait died as a martyr for France on this spot and it gave the date of her execution.

I stood for a long time looking up at it.

Such a little thing, a little brass plate, to signify such a momentous and hideous event. I felt a wave of sadness, both for her, what happened to her, and that this memorial was so pathetic. I found a stick to knock off a wasp nest that used the bottom corner of the plaque as a platform. The wasp was not happy about that and I had to back off while she circled angrily.

At last, I turned away and tried the door of the church. It was heavy but it moved. I was hoping not to find a dead priest inside, although in most cases country churches in France now only have priests for special occasions. There is one priest per district if they're lucky.

The only dead things in the church were flowers on the altar and a pigeon on the floor.

It is a very simple and unassuming church, probably built at a time when every village had to have one. It has no stained glass windows, just simple diagonal panes of opaque glass that only let in dim light. There are several statues of saints, all of them in need of a good coat of paint. The altar is basic and the crucifix above it simply the tortured figure of the Christ hanging on a wooden cross.

Wooden chairs are the pews.

The floor was thick with dust that swirled when I opened the door.

The whole thing was deeply sad.

I stood there in front of the altar and wondered why on earth I had wanted to come.

I felt there was nothing for me here.

I had thought I might meditate in here, in this Jesus place , but once there, I felt no desire for that at all.

I scooped up the dead pigeon and buried it outside.

One small funeral.

I just wanted to go home.

That was the thought. Go home.

I got back on the bike and did just that, at least this time managing to ride the bike all the way up the track to the château without getting off.

I have no idea why I went there.

Jesus certainly didn't put in an appearance.

The outing revealed nothing new.

At least I could feel relieved that Saint Fé was not littered with corpses.

Maybe I would go back and see if there was anything useful in the houses, but not now.

I have decided to cut my hair.

There are mirrors in the château, but it is rare that I look at myself.

When I do, I see a wild man. My hair goes up and out all over the place and my beard is thick.

I found a small mirror in one of the en suites and scissors in the kitchen.

I chopped off as much of it as I could. Now I have stubble on my chin and on my scalp. It is not exactly haute coiffure , but it feels better.

I gathered up the clippings and took them outside. I put them on the teak outdoor dining table for the birds.

The Merle, the sparrows and the swallows can make nests with my discarded tonsure.

The Merle is a kind of blackbird. The male is black and the female is brown. They hop around as a couple, always close. They are used to me, both of them and they hunt about, even amongst the chickens doing their bit to de-bug the garden. Their nest is made of sticks and grass and is round. I found it in a hedge behind the sheds.

The sparrows live here all year round. They find their way in under the tiles on the roof or in corners of the sheds. Their nests are made of sticks and grass and they somehow get all that to hang together. Right now they are wrestling with each other in mid-air which I think is a part of their mating rituals. They are incredibly aerobatic and quick.

The swallows have just arrived. One day there were none and then suddenly a whole flock turned up. I think they winter in Spain. They have nests already built in nooks and crannies of the château from years past. It is extraordinary how, with those tiny little beaks, they bring mud to fashion their beehive-shaped houses with little round holes at the front, and then line them with soft stuff, like my hair, to welcome the next generation when they hatch. They make tiny little whistling sounds as they flash in and out.

So my hair will go to good homes.

Now I have begun to roam a little further, I am becoming painfully aware that there is no-one out there, at least not in my neighbourhood.

So how come I am healthy, untroubled and, not to put too fine a point on it, still alive?

Jean-Claude and Eveline died and I assumed it was the virus. But was it? Did they decide to end their lives? There they were sitting in their kitchen. They didn't look like they were sick. They were just dead.

It never occurred to me to try to see what killed them.

Now I have been to Saint Fé and seen that there is no-one there, it makes me wonder. Where did they go?

There were no cars. If they were all dead in their houses, like Jean-Claude, their cars would be outside. The most plausible explanation is that they might have all been evacuated, but why? Where to? Are there places far away from Saint Fé, where there are refugee camps or something? If there were, would I want to go there? I have seen refugee camps on TV. They are not attractive places to hang out.

There is no way to find out the truth.

If I went back to Saint Fé, what would that do? What if I verified that all the houses were unoccupied?

Would it mean that there are people alive and well further away somewhere?

But why no aircraft?

Why no trucks on the freeway?

The converse of all this is to say to myself: OK, maybe you have to accept that you are the only one left alive.

You're it.

Then what?

It would stop me wondering about what's over the hill or whether there are other people somewhere. If I could convince myself that I am indeed utterly and completely alone, now and forever, what would that do?

In my mind, the choice seems to be between going back to Saint Fé or committing myself to the total acceptance of being here, like this, by myself.

I am going to try the latter, because I really don't want to go back to Saint Fé.

There was nothing there.

I have decided that I will do serious self-talk.

This is it. There is no-one out there. You are the last man standing. Get used to it. Get to like it. Get to the point where it is so natural you don't have any conflicting thoughts.

That feels right to me.

This morning I started my meditation with that. I did some of the self-talk, then I chanted the Buddhist hymn aloud, like it was my own funeral, then I closed my eyes and began silently repeating the Buddhist mantra.

It was fabulous.

As the meditation began I found myself going deeper and deeper.

There were waves and waves of happiness.

The mantra dropped away into a warm, still silence.

There was a subtle throb that emanated waves of light from inside me that shimmered out in gentle ripples. I felt full of light, I was the source of light but I had no body sense at all.

I could imagine myself as one of the Cathar's Perfects , seeing myself as an angel illuminated and being liberated from the lead weight of human existence.

I was quite happy to go to heaven if this was my time.

And in the middle of it all, there were what I instinctively recognised as other angels, but I knew them.

My parents were there. They were smiling and peaceful.

Clo was there. She looked radiant, as happy as I had ever seen her.

Diedre Temple-Harmsworth floated by,

Tante was there, vaguely in the distance, quite ethereal and then Adèle, closer than the others and clearer, sitting very still.

Then I could see where she was sitting. She was in the safe house, not as it was before the Germans blew it up, but now, as I have reconstructed it. She was sitting in the open air, on the stone that is now the altar. She had the same presence as the statue of the Buddha in the Chiang Rai Temple, radiant and magnificent and worthy of reverence.

In my meditation, even though I didn't feel I had a body, I bowed before her.

When I eventually ascended, ever so slowly, I was filled with emotion, tears flowing but they felt so good, so joyful.

So that worked.

I didn't Google. I didn't do an i Ching, I didn't import a shaman, but I certainly got some confirmation.

This is it.

I am here for the duration.

And I have guardian angels.

As I absorbed what had come to me in meditation, on one level it was incredibly comforting and affirming.

On another level there was something very different and very hard to accept.

It was a kind of grief. I sensed that all the beings who had graced my meditation no longer had bodies. Some of them I knew about, like Adèle and Tante, but not my parents, or Diedre, and certainly not Clo.

Are they dead?

How could I be sure?

The feeling was very powerful, carrying a certainty that was impossible to ignore.

Did I need to mourn them?

I felt deeply that perhaps I did.

The hardest was Clo.

Up till then I had not really lost hope that somehow we would get back together, but if she was gone, then I really was alone.

That was hard to deal with.

I took several meditations to get there.

I dedicated one to my parents and felt a lot of love for them.

We were never much good at expressing overt love and I don't recall ever saying I love you to either of them. Not even when I was leaving.

Now, in this meditation, I could.

I thanked them for everything they had given me and I asked them to forgive me for not being a more loving son when I was with them.

I reached a sense of conclusion with them.

They did not appear in the meditation but I felt my energy, full of love for them, flow towards them and I felt it was received.

I came out from that meditation at peace with them and with myself.

Diedre was easy. She was not a young woman when I knew her, so it was natural that she might have passed on. She'd had a great life, full of creative drive, generosity and *joie de vivre*. She was a great person.

My meditation dedicated to her was infused with my gratitude.

I came out feeling completion with her, too.

Clo was something else.

I left her to the last, because she was the hardest to face.

I felt fear in me as I sat for that final meditation of mourning.

I chanted the Buddhist prayer for her and had trouble finishing it because I was crying.

Then, as I tried to calm my anguished breathing, I went inside and my breath deepened and there they were together, Clo and Adèle.

It was as if Adèle had come to help.

They were both ethereal but also very clear. They seemed to hover, sometimes quite separate, but at others seeming to merge into the one body.

I tried to focus. I wanted so much to say how much I had loved Clo, how much I missed her presence, how much... but there were no words in the space where they both floated. I had to be willing just to be there with them.

When I finally rose out from that meditation, it was almost agony to rediscover my physical body.

I lay full length, face down, in front of the altar and breathed and breathed, trying to re-find myself.

Adèle had played no active part in this meditation. It was if she had been there simply as a witness, perhaps as a guardian angel.

As I lay on the floor in the chapel, I looked up at her photo and I thanked her for that.

It bothers me that I have no photo of Clo.

I will have to hold her in my memory.

And now I move on, alone and yet not alone.

I had some more grieving to do, but I also had to accept that there was a powerful force that seemed to be supporting me.

I can go on.

The whole reason the world has gone the way it has is because of a virus, a miniscule living thing that does its best to replicate itself, like all living things.

Everybody thinks of it as evil. At least that was how it was being portrayed when I left Toulouse. The invisible enemy, the plague, the killer in our midst, and all that.

But how would it be if I were to think of it, not as evil, but as just another living entity trying to survive, perpetuate the species.

It's just the nature of things.

Maybe the human race evolved out of something as little as that. Bit by bit, persevering against the odds, the one-celled being became a two-celled being and then a three-celled and bingo, after a million generations and evolutionary steps, by way of neanderthals, cavemen and troglodytes, it turned into Beethoven and Einstein. How about if this virus wiped out the current evolved species, meaning us, so that it could begin to evolve into our replacement.

The natural cycle of life on the planet.

Maybe we should graciously step aside and welcome in the next generation.

Maybe it has happened many times.

The world gets to the point of a need to start again, so it gets cleaned up and a new virus starts up and away we go again.

It doesn't change anything for me to think like that, but it prompts me to see that it is possible to see anything from different points of view. So from the point of view of the virus, everything is going very well. If it has managed to eliminate all humanity, except me, then it has done well.

So how come it doesn't seem to be able to get me?

I must be a thorn in its side!

I can imagine the virus in their headquarters or central command raging: That damned Aussie up on that hill in the Lot, he's the only hurdle left before world dominance. Why can't we get rid of him?

Aha! Maybe I am a superhero, without being aware of it, the only human left who can single-handedly see off the virus and restore humanity.

Well, if I am the only one left then reproducing humanity might be something of a challenge. I might need help from a divine power to turn one of my ribs into a woman. Quite frankly I have always had trouble with that story. It's too incestuous for me. I mean who did Adam's son Cain mate with, the son who didn't kill the other one?

I think it must have been edited out from the original version.

Phew. I am starting to get lost in delusions. Once the mind starts to run, it gets out of hand.

Funny idea, taking my mind in hand. Image of a brain sitting in the palm of my hand and I am talking to it: Mind, behave!

Am I getting deluded about delusion?

Actually, when I get a bit more objective about it, from my point of view, the virus is non-existent.

I haven't seen it.

I have only heard about it, or the threat of it coming.

The whole thing could be a hoax, or fake news, or some wild political strategy by some new dark force. Maybe it's all being run by Russian bots for all I know.

Jean-Claude and Eveline died of something but I don't know if it was the virus or not.

The population of Saint Fé is gone, but I don't know why.

So what if there is no virus?

Does it matter?

Somehow, whatever it is, has brought me here.

What would change about my current situation if there were no virus?

My situation is what it is, irrespective of the cause.

Something happened to close the freeway and stop the planes from flying and marooned me here.

Does it matter what did this?

I have to accept that the answer to that is: No. .

What matters is what I do for myself with myself from here on.

How do I prosper now, where I am, as I am?

I think this is the most important thing.

I have to learn to accept, totally, that this is what is happening.

Then I have to go a step further.

I have to see this situation as beneficial. I have to tell myself what an opportunity it is.

This could be me, sitting like the Buddha under the bodhi tree and becoming enlightened.

Why not?

What would that be like?

I actually don't really know what enlightenment would feel like.

I could sit under the Linden tree and try it.

If I find out, I will be sure to write it down.

Enlightenment.

It could just be the opposite of en-heavy-ment.

Everything is light, light as a feather. En-light-en-ed!

I could do that, if I put my mind to it. I could make sure that I accept that nothing is heavy, it's all light, then I would be filled with enlightenment.

I suspect it's not that easy, or there would be a lot more enlightened beings in the world.

That actually might be the case but I haven't met any of them. Not that I know of anyway. Maybe they are around, but are heavily disguised so their enlightenment doesn't scare the natives.

Kind of like the Cathar Perfects who scared the cassocks off the Catholics, especially Pope Innocent. If they hadn't been so evident, they would have survived.

In the meantime, I can think of this château with gratitude, as my last resting place.

I will live here and I will die here.

Just like Adèle.

It is all very well to ruminate on my situation, but I have to do things.

So I have to focus on my daily routine.

I still rely on Boris to get me started. He is totally reliable. Then each of the activities that follow need to be kept.

Meditation is precious, even on those mornings where I seem to have basically fallen asleep and I come out of it with saliva on my chin. Other mornings there are rushes of the sweetest energy and I come out of meditation feeling quite ecstatic.

I have decided I should do some more physical things, so I am trying to remember the yoga poses I learned from Ramanuja in Varanasi. Clo shared with me what she learned when we were in Saint Jean de Luz.

I can do the down-facing dog, but the corpse pose is my favourite.

Maybe I am practising for the inevitable.

Then there are things to do in the garden and things to fix, like shed roofing or the door on the hen house. Prince Charles would not approve if the door doesn't shut properly on the replica of his poultry palace.

I walk every day and that now includes always a few moments in the memorial. I sit there for a while, in a kind of open-eyed meditation.

Adèle is present very often but not always. I think that is a product of how my mind is doing in the moment. When my mind is quiet, there she is.

There are nature's visitors from time to time, which I am coming to treasure. By sitting still, all sorts of creatures venture out. I wonder if they are drawn to the energy of the memorial, the safe house. Little lizards bask in the sun on the warm stones. The hedgehogs snuffle about. Pies, those noisy birds, come and cackle in the trees above my head. There are other little furry things that I am not even sure I can name but they are very welcome. I catch sight of a tail or a bit of fur but it's hard to tell to whom it belongs.

Then in the afternoon, up the stairs I come with the mint tea and I gaze out over the still valleys and limestone hilltops and write whatever comes into my head.

The evenings are getting long now as the summer comes on and the sunsets are often spectacular. This is God's version of TV.

No two sunsets are ever the same.

Sometimes I read by candle light. I alternate betwen English and French.

And then sleep.

My dreams are often filled with the re-workings of my day's mindset. I am beginning to recognise that. If I can keep my thoughts quiet, or at least benign, then I sleep better.

I could be a sleep therapist.

Better than a sex therapist.

Well my only problem is that I will never have any clients for either, unless of course something changes.

Ah, watch out!

There's the mind again, subtly going negative.

Redirect!

Here is a very good redirect: I find myself thinking about gratitude. I have a lot to be grateful for. It really helps to remind myself about that.

I have plenty to eat.

I am healthy as an ox, certainly as healthy as Mon Veau!

I have a roof over my head, quite a fancy one in fact. And I find myself being grateful for living a new kind of life that has no money involved, no work for pay, no financial planning. I had a wallet when I got here, I used my credit card when I went shopping in Gourdon. Since then I've put that wallet somewhere and haven't given it another thought.

It is a relic of a bygone era.

Mon Veau is a teenager! At least he is behaving like one, although unfortunately a bit oedipal. He was mounting his mother this morning. She wasn't having it, but still it's a sign that natural life goes on. He is now as tall as my shoulders and beginning to fill out. He is totally loveable, utterly tame and still loves a good horn scratch. I don't know anything about cattle but I am hoping his breed has benignity in males.

The sex drive is universal. Boris does his husbandly duty on a regular basis. The ladies squawk indignantly when he does but they reproduce. The chicken and egg cycle keeps going.

But in other than humans, though, the sex drive has only one function. The rest of non-human life is intent only on reproduction. They all go on industriously fertilising their females, regenerating their species, as if the world will go on indefinitely. They want to be sure their species is represented.

My species? Not being able to clone myself, I am thinking we may be leaving this earth to other species to dominate.

Without us, who will come out on top?

Talking of sex drives, Mon Veau's mother took off.

She has been gone for a whole day.

I don't know whether she was fed up with her son's amorous advances or whether she just decided to go for a walk. When I went out to get my morning cup of creamy beverage, my source had absconded.

Mon Veau is still here and from time to time, he yells: Mum!

I wonder how she managed to go without him following.

I am sick. Or I was.

I haven't touched this exercise book for a couple of days. Too busy trying to eliminate what did not sit well inside me.

I'm sure it's not the absence of my one cup of milk per day but I was as sick as a dog.

I think it was mushrooms.

I found a whole group of what looked like ordinary mushrooms and made myself a great omelette. I had done it often enough to be confident.

An hour later I was throwing up like a mad man. And regretting that omelette like hell.

Since then, after a whole day without anything but a few sips of water, I am still cramping much of the time and trying to throw up whatever vestiges might still be there.

At least I can say I am grateful that I don't think they will kill me and I am grateful that I have been so healthy up to now.

If I do get really sick, then, other than miracle cures, that'll be the end of me.

It's starting to wear off but it was scary while it lasted.

It makes me stare my own mortality in the face.

How easily I took the good French health system for granted. It is, or it was, more or less, free. And the doctors, the few times I ever saw one, were great. They all speak English too, all the ones I met anyway.

Now I have to be happy with self-help health care.

No more chemicals in my system, which I suppose is a good thing.

All natural remedies from now on.

God help me if I need a root canal!

She's back.

Three days since she went walkabout, Ma Vache appeared late in the afternoon. Mon Veau was ecstatic and got himself a vast bellyful of milk, butting his mother mercilessly.

I guess I will never know what she got up to, but my suspicion is that she went for a naughty weekend and found herself a stud bull somewhere. I guess in nine months or however long it takes for the gestation, I will find out.

I am begining to think about winter which is weird because, by my calculations, I think we are getting close to June. However, like a good squirrel, and I have seen a few, little brown fellows with bushy tails, I have to start storing for the next cold season.

This is on the assumption that I will survive that long.

There is plenty of wood in the wood pile but all that was cut to size with a chain saw. There is a chain saw in the shed but I have never used one. I do know you have to resharpen the chain and I haven't a clue how you would do that. Or maybe you have to put on a new one. There is a spare chain in its packet, but there's no way I would ever work out how to put it on. I can't Google it.

So I will have to saw and chop my winter wood supply. There is a big hand saw and there is an axe. It'll make me fit.

Then there is the storing of enough to eat. I have planted all sorts of things and I will store them in the cellar which will work just about as well as a fridge.

What was stored from last year has certainly served me well so far.

Then there are seeds. I will have to collect and label the seeds for next year.

It's like I am going back in time to how it must have been when they first built this château. They would have done all this as their traditional way of life.

Except Simon de Montfort, or whoever built and owned this château would have had a small army of peasants to actually do the work. I wouldn't mind having a crew of peasants.

I will just have to accept that I am my own peasant.

So part of my daily routine now will have to be winter prep.

George has gone.

I rather enjoyed his low key company. He was just our local friendly goat. He didn't actively contribute to the wellbeing of our little commune but he was our resident goat. He did help to keep the grass down. I wonder if he was on his last legs and went off to find a quiet place to leave his body. He did look a bit wobbly lately.

I will miss him.

I have been thinking about all those things we used to do as regular citizens. I don't do any of them now.

Paid taxes (not that we did that too much, we never earned enough!)

Bought cell phone packages

Posted on Facebook

Checked emails

Used headphones

Went to restaurants

Had a bank account and credit cards

Owed debts

Earned money (not much)

Carried coins and grubby notes as money

Worried about money (not too often, mostly the lack thereof)

Bought clothes

Got haircuts

Took painkillers

Gave and received presents

Listened to music

Watched TV

Went to the cinema

Carried ID

Voted (well I never actually did, but I should have)

Had political opinions (now I am an autocracy!)

Owned property (actually we only ever owned Tante's house)

Went on demos (the French are world champions at that, I tended to watch rather than join in) and the companion activity, that is to go on strike, which I never did.

Flew (take a plane somewhere, it's the only kind I know)

Travelled (having a bike doesn't count)

Drove cars and had drivers' licenses, observed the rules of the road, more or less

Had neighbors (human ones)

Did sports

Did theatre (wow that one was an interesting throwback)

And on it goes.

Looking at the list, so many of those words have no meaning now. The actions of each of those things were required by the society I used to live in. Now it's non-existent, none of them are relevant any more. Whatever culture evolved to think that all those activities were important, has ceased to function.

I realise that here, high on a rocky hill in the middle of nowhere, I am free of all that.

I am a free man.

In lots of different religions and spiritul paths they talk about liberation.

I may not be liberated in the highest sense, but I am certainly liberated from all that stuff.

It is a weight off.

I have no baggage.

It is actually rather exciting to hold that kind of awareness.

I am free.

I am totally free.

I have such a feeling of euphoria that I have found myself singing old songs, simply because I am feeling so at ease.

I have nothing to worry about.

I am free.
I am happy.
It's fabulous.

That rascal!

George completely fooled me. He didn't go off to die under a friendly tree, he left to round up his family. He was hanging out with us as a bit of time off from his familial duties. He must have decided to take responsibility, as a good goat should.

He was only gone a couple of days and has just turned up with a nanny and two kids. I wonder where he found them. And I wonder how he found them. Certainly not on Tinder!

I am inclined to think he knew where they were all along and had now decided it was time to bring them out of hiding.

The nanny is shy, but little by little she is getting used to me. I wonder if I can milk her like I do with Ma Vache. When I asked her what her name was she said (in a goaty accent) Beeeee, so I'll call her Betty.

I will have to think of the kids' names. I think they are twins because they are about the same size, a male and a female, I think. They jump about and neither of them has let me pat them yet.

I suppose he can be Billy the kid and she can be Kid Glove.

So now I can hang out with Billy and Glove and their parents, George and Betty.

We are becoming quite a pleasant little community.

Adèle has decided to show up, not just in meditation.

I had been chopping firewood for about an hour and I was bathed in sweat. I stood up straight for a moment to rest my sore back and there she was. My heart missed a beat, or maybe several. She was, just like in the first photo I found, slightly obscured in the shade of the Linden tree which could well have been the tree she was standing under in the photo. She was watching me. She was dressed exactly as in that photo and she had her hair down. She smiled ever so gently. I brushed my hand across my eyes because the sweat was pouring off my forehead and when I looked back, she was gone.

Does it mean something?

Why does she show up now?

Is something about to happen?

When I sit for meditation, I am looking to see if there is something.

I do this till I realise that I am trying to make it happen.

I know that won't work.

I have to let go and she will come when she wants.

I will just go on with my daily routine and leave her alone.

There could be goat's milk on the menu soon.

Today Betty let me fondle her nipples which was generous of her. She's still feeding the kids and I did get some milk, although not much. The technique has to be different because her nipples are not very big.

I will bring a cup next time I try. The kids watched me and I am not sure they liked what they saw. I was raiding their food source.

I love these two, Billy and Glove.

They are silly goats very often. Sometimes for absolutely no reason I can see, they jump in the air. It's like a physical form of Tourette syndrome. They tend to send each other off. One does it, then the other one does. I would love to see them on a trampoline.

They seem quite friendly towards Mon Veau. I have seen Billy and Mon Veau have a bit of a headbutt fight but it was pretty gentle. Two teenage boys butting heads.

It's been a couple of days since Adèle appeared and I admit to be looking for her, hoping she might turn up when I visit the safe house or even if I chop more firewood. It is so hard to let go of my desire to see her.

She came that one time because I wasn't expecting it.

I have been thinking about water.

Up to now I have taken water for granted. The tanks have been filled from the rain and they gravity feed into the house. It hasn't rained for a while and I am wondering what happens if the tanks run dry. There is a well but the pump is electric. Do I have to try to start the generator to run the pump? Will I have to become aquarius the water bearer? It's a bit of an uphill hike if I have to carry water all the way up from the creek. I will cut back on laundry, not that I ever did much. I tend to wear clothes till they stink or I spill something nasty on them. I have been most derelict with bed sheets. The problem is that I grew up in the era of washing machines. Having to wash by hand is not my favourite activity, so I do as little as possible.

Now I can justify that as water conservation.

Who am I kidding!

Something weird happened in meditation.

The ring that sits snug on my finger seemed to get hot. It felt like it was burning me. If I am to understand that this ring comes from Adèle, what am I supposed to do with it?

If it is burning me, is that to urge me to do something?

Should I take it off? It actually sits so tight it would take some effort to remove it.

It disturbed my meditation so much that I came out much earlier than usual.

Then the ring cooled again.

What is this?

Adèle, what's going on?

For the rest of the day I had an expectation that something would come of it and nothing did.

Would she appear again? Would I get some insight into something?

By afternoon when nothing had taken place, I walked down to the safe house with Mon Veau trotting happily alongside me.

He still likes to nudge me now and then but I think he is beginnng to recognise that he's a big boy now and he could hurt me.

While I knelt in front of the altar in the memorial, he had a drink in the creek and nosed about in the grass for what he considers to be sweet and juicy.

Nothing came to me other than feeling calm and relaxed.

The ring didn't burn and Adèle did not appear.

Did I imagine the whole thing?

High above me I saw a pair of big raptors, eagles probably or maybe some kind of vulture or buzzard. They were too high to tell, but what I loved about them was that they circled often opposite each other in a thermal updraft. Going up and up without any wing effort. Were they talking to each other or simply serenely circling? Then when they were just tiny specks in the sky, they both took off, with still wings using their altitude to take them wherever they wanted to go.

How I envied and admired them. It would be so good to be able to fly like that, to get so high, to sense the updraft, where no effort is needed and to use the newfound height to go wherever I wanted.

I fantasised about how that image could be translated into my own human existence. How woud I do it?

I would flow with whatever was carrying me along. I would rise without effort when my life uplifted me.

From my lofty height, I could simply glide wherever I wanted.

It's a nice concept but bears little resemblance to my current situation.

If I had a hang glider, and I knew how to use it, I could jump off the hill right in front of the château and glide over the valley.

Then what?

I would probably run out of air space and land on the freeway, and I would then have to fold up my hang glider and stagger back up the hill.

Well that killed that image.

I have lost time.

I have no time.

I am now living in a timeless time.

I accidentally bashed the face of my solar watch against a rock when I was crossing the creek and slipped. My dear time-keeping companion now says its 11.36 and refuses to move.

What a strange sensation it was to realise that perhaps one of the last links I had to the way things were before, has gone.

And yet that too is a kind of freedom.

The notion of time, as determined by a device, is a human invention.

Man invented seconds, minutes, hours, days, months, years, centuries, so he could pretend he had control over time.

It was an illusion.

Apart form anything else, man was pretty inaccurate in trying to tame time.

Now here, stuck on this hill, time will become something else.

The sun will be my determinant and the turning of seasons too.

Other than that, I will know it is time to wake up when Boris tells me. I will know it is lunchtime when I feel hungry. It will be time to go to bed when my eyelids droop.

I have put my now useless timepiece on the altar with other things that prompt me to contemplate my existence.

I can thank it for its help up to this point. I had always considered that it was very useful.

I can thank the brilliant watchmakers who built it to be so precise.

I can thank my own good sense that, now it's a useless ornament, I don't think it is a tragedy to be without minutes and hours.

The untanned band on my left wrist can now join the rest of my body's colour scheme.

Chickens!

One of Boris's harem has produced a very welcome surprise. I didn't see it happen, but one of the ladies had created a nest inside the hen house in a corner and I totally missed it. She let me know today by staying in when all the others came flying out to start the day. She clucked away in her corner so I went to see what was going on - and there they were. She has three of them, tiny little yellow fluffy beings who mostly shelter under her feathers.

This is another of those interesting natural lessons in letting Mother Nature do what she does best.

I had been trying to help by leaving eggs behind and marking them but they never turned into anything. I can now throw them out and leave the ladies to do what they know how to do.

And God bless Boris.

It's funny that the appearance of the chickens made me think about the purpose of life. Chicken and egg maybe?

I was thinking about myself as a chicken. Chickens start out as fluffy little bundles, then become hens or roosters, do what poultry does and usually get killed by humans before they die natural deaths.

What's the point of being born as a chicken?

What's the point of being born as Simon Teague?

Having arrived at the not so ripe old age of forty, what has been the point up to now? Somewhere, I don't remember where, I read about how your soul chooses the mission for your life. This is predicated on your having had a whole series of lives, one after the other, in which you built up a record of good and bad karma. So your soul sets you up with certain circumstances and you get to see if you can achieve what your soul intended.

OK, if I am to believe this, then what did my soul intend?

I have no idea.

I could look at it another way: what have I achieved in this life? What did I do that was good and worthy, and what did I do that was not?

How do I judge which was which?

I did things as a kid that were not so great. I wasn't so hot at telling the truth. I stole some money from my Mother's coin box and bought myself fish and chips, more than once, and felt terrible about it afterwards. I don't think I ever deliberately hurt anyone, that I can think of, at least physically. In other ways, emotionally or psychologically, I am sure I hurt people and was blissfully unaware of the damage I caused.

I wonder if that counts, if you do something unconsciously. Maybe motive is the key to good and bad deeds.

So what is the balance?

Oddly I can't think of much of what I did that was good. I have to think about what that means. What is a good deed?

I wasn't too active on the charity front. I never gave coins to the homeless. I never did volunteer work for some worthy cause. I suppose I was helpful, but I don't feel a strong sense of having done anything that was remarkably good.

Have I wasted my life up to this point?

I don't know what that means.

OK, so now I am sitting all by myself, having done so for months, very comfortable on a warm afternoon, with my mint tea, in my turret, in a château, in the middle of France.

Is this what my soul wanted?

What's the point?

It's not much different from being born as a chicken.

Lady chickens at least grow up to be hens and lay eggs

I haven't laid anything worth recording.

But I don't want to sit here and be morose about it. What took place for the last forty years was what it was. I kept looking for something and every now and then I thought I had found a hint of what I was looking for.

The monastery was good for that, but it was only a hint.

Finding Clo was good for that. She taught me how to be a less selfish person. So that was good.

Taking care of Tante was good, although I got as much out of it as she did.

Now what?

What can I do now, for the rest of my life, that would be in line with what my soul intended?

Which means I would have to find out what my soul intended in the first place.

I could meditate on that question.

And anyway, who knows how much life I have left to live.

It worked in a strange way. After writing all that philosophical questioning, I did put some serious effort into meditating on the question.

What came to me is the simplest question of all.

I have to know the answer to the question: Who am I?

I know that's a horrible cliché, but I think it's the one.

So I sat with it.

I breathed in deep, the way I learned in the monastery.

I breathed out as fully as I could, as recommended.

Then I began to use the question : Who am I? in place of the mantra.

This went on for quite a while and I disciplined myself to keep at it.

Then suddenly there was a flash of light, blue-ish in colour, and I felt like I was dissolving.

I couldn't keep the question going any more, because I was floating in some kind of fluid space with no ability to think at all.

I don't know how long I was in that space, but when eventually it faded away, I was left with a feeling that the answer to the question was given, but not in an articulate way.

It was a state of being.

Something like : I am what I am. The Am-ness is not describable as a thing. It is how I am.

And that helps.

I have used this new meditation technique a few times and it works pretty well.

I have to learn to just be as I am and say to myself: I am, whatever that state is and that's fine.

That's as good a result as I could have expected.

I only thought about it afterwards, but Adèle was not part of that. She has some rôle to play in who or what I am or what I was, but not in way.

I guess Adèle is karma material, unfinished business perhaps, but this is not attached to karma at all.

This is deeper.

I just am, when I get down to it.

I could be a philosopher.

The garden is begining to be incredibly fruitful. There are tomatoes coming on, the zucchinis are getting big, there are beans and peas on the vines, red fruit coming, all sorts.

I could open a health-food shop.

The hens have been pretty good at keeping the the bugs down, although every now and then I find myself chewing on an insect which I hadn't noticed. Nothing worse than finding half a caterpillar in your tomato.

I found an old fashioned scythe in the shed. It was a bit rusty and horribly blunt, but I also found a sharpening stone so now it works pretty well. I am teaching myself how to use it.

To start with, after about ten minutes, I was exhausted and my back hurt, but little by little I am learning that if I let the weight of the scythe do the work and swing without too much effort, using gravity, I won't do myself any permanent damage.

So the grass gets cut and lies there ready to become cattle food.

I am thinking about winter and how I might have to keep my menagerie inside and feed them. There are some bags of animal feed in Jean-Claude's sheds but I might need more than that. And anyway the grass is growing amazingly fast in the field and there is no way Ma Vache and Mon Veau, plus George and his tribe, are going to keep that down.

I am making hay while the sun shines.

After I cut it, I will leave it there for a day or two then I will rake and turn it over and then I am going to make what I think are called stooks, so the grass is piled up to dry. I am inventing my own farming technique and I am rather proud of myself.

Aagh! It's raining and my hay is getting wet.

It rained all night and by the time I thought about it, there was no way to rescue any of the cut grass. So much for drying the hay. I think I will have to make silage. I have smelt it in some of the local farms and it is not nice but I know cows will eat it. I guess farmers have to live with this kind of uncertainty all the time.

I will have to learn farmers' resilience.

I have to take what nature throws at me. It's not the end of the world.

Although that might be closer than I think.

I have been making myself less prone to feeling upset about small things.

I suspect this is how farmers have to be.

So my hay turns into silage. It could be good. I believe that silage goes on cooking and making useful chemicals while smelling like manure. Of course I will have to work out how to store silage. I have seen it in pits covered with tarpaulins so maybe that's what I have to to do, but digging a pit is a big job. This château does not have any manuals on silage management. On the other hand there is a whole shed of hay that won't get used at Jean-Claude's place, so it's not all that disastrous.

I think I was getting too proud of myself as a scyther, so Mother Nature took me down a peg or two.

A day later the sun is shining and the steam is rising off the wet cut grass in the early morning. It looks very tropical, and I am resigned to making of it what I can. Although I know it won't last, right now the scent of the cut grass is intoxicating. Billy and Glove have been jumping around in the cut grass, so they like it.

Maybe I will leave it and see if the sun dries it out enough to still be considered hay.

Over to you, sun.

Betty is giving me quite a lot of milk now, a good cup full. She stands there and lets me milk her just as Ma Vache does.

I wonder how you make cheese.

Unfortunately I have no idea. I am sure you don't just let the milk go off. I haven't found any books on cheese making on the château shelves. I think there has to be something about churning but I don't actually know what that is and I haven't seen anything that looks like a churn, although maybe Jean-Claude's shed might be forthcoming. Even then, if I found a churn and I put milk in it, then what?

I am sure cheese doesn't just make itself.

I have been thinking about the dog that ran out and barked at me when I rode the bike to Saint Fé. I wonder if it is still there. It was all skin and bone when I saw it, it might even be dead by now, although dogs should be able to look after themselves. I have seen a pack of dogs chasing deer, up here on the hill, so I wonder why that dog didn't just go off and join his race in the wild. Maybe it is protecting something.

I have decided to go and have a look.

I haven't ventured down the hill for weeks.

I pumped up the bike tyres and took an empty backpack in case I found something useful.

Mon Veau watched me go, but now he seems to know that he and the bike don't go together.

When I reached the house where the dog was, there is no sign of it. I propped the bike near the house and took a walk around.

There was junk everywhere.

It was a property that had the look of a residence of hoarders, an old couple or even an old man by himself who never threw anything away. There were car bits and bodies, tractor parts, rusting farm machinery, boxes and cartons, all sorts of what I would have thought of as rubbish.

There was no sign of the dog. And nothing else moved. I peered in through several windows but it was very dark inside.

I tried a door, mindful that I was not wearing gloves, but I felt that the virus couldn't still be on a door knob after all this time. The door gave easily. I took a careful step inside.

At first I thought the house was deserted. There was no-one in the kitchen, then I ventured further in.

They were in bed.

It was indeed an old couple and they had died together. They were far apart so I assumed they had died in their sleep.. The dog was dead too, at the foot of the bed. That's why it stayed. There must have been a dog door somewhere so it could come and go, but faithful to the end it died at its master's feet.

I had another funeral to conduct.

I wondered if there was any indication of who they were and I did find some letters addressed to Monsieur et Madame Dupuy. They were the sort of letters everyone gets, the electricity notice, and the bank statement. They were not a wealthy couple. Then I found their note written in a very rounded script on blue paper. It was taped to the mirror.

In deciphering it, I got the drift even if I couldn't read some words. They were telling their two sons that they had decided not to evacuate like everyone else. This was their home and they preferred to stay and take their chances. They hoped that when the virus had passed they would all meet again. They sent their kisses to their grandchildren.

I stood still for a long time just looking down at them. They were probably in their eighties, weather-worn poor farmers. I think they made the right decision. Where would they go? What would they do? Here at least they died together and their loyal hound kept guard. It was quite moving.

They were obviously Catholics, by the ornaments and wall hangings. Every room had a crucifix and flyspecked pictures of saints.

I walked around the rest of the house through the different rooms, all of them full of stuff. I checked the food pantry but they had used almost everything. I found a few tins and some good knives which I put in my backpack.There was no wine but a vast stack of empty bottles. At least their final days were well fuelled.

I found more matches and candles in the kitchen. They had a gas cooker but the bottle was empty.

In their sheds there was more junk and I began to feel like I really didn't need any of it. All I needed was the fuel for the fire.

Their garden was overgrown with wild roses, so I picked an armload and arranged them on their bed. They had one large red unused candle with a picture of Saint Therese of Lisieux. I lit it and placed it on the dressing table under the picture of the Virgin Mary.

I found a can of petrol in a shed. Enough for a good funeral pyre.

I piled flammable material around the bed, heaps of backcopies of the Sud Ouest and firewood to make sure it burned well. I poured the petrol copiously everywhere, running a trail outside from the kitchen so I didn't get singed like the last one.

I was getting better at conducting cremations.

I stood by the bed for the last time and I sang the Buddhist hymn. It wasn't the same as it was with Jean-Claude and Eveline, because they were people I vaguely knew. These poor folk, were just a couple of dead bodies.

Nonetheless, I did what I thought was respectful.

I moved the bike and the back pack well away, then went back and lit the petrol. It whoofed immediately and the trail of flame ran into the house and it exploded with a huge noise.

The heat was intense and I backed away.

Then I waited as the black smoke spiralled high up and then off in the gentle breeze. I was certain no-one would come, but I still felt responsible to stay until the fire had died down.

While it burned, I walked around the property a bit. It was all rather sad. It was not a well run agricultural enterprise. They had a tangled veggie garden and I helped myself to a few things but I had my own, more than I could eat. He had planted a crop of sunflowers and they were doing well, great round yellow heads bowing gently in the wind created by the fire.

The roof came down with a crash and cinders flew everywhere. The trees around the house began to burn and then one of the sheds. Now I had to pull back out into the road as everything began to burn.

And that was it.

Eventually the fire ran out of things to consume and it all started to die down. The house was a bed of smoking ash and all the sheds had gone. Even some of the car bodies had burned.

The sunflowers were the last untouched evidence that someone had once lived there.

The backpack was quite full as I got back on the bike and headed back to the château.

As I rode I had the feeling that I had done something good.

At least their souls had been released.

I wondered if there would be more excursions like that, but I began to think that I had done enough. What would be the point in touring around and setting fire to houses with dead bodies in them?

What about Saint Fé?

I saw no reason to go back.

I would leave it in peace.

The more I thought about it, the more I began to feel that this hill, this château, these fields, the creek and the safe house memorial, all these were my world now.

Beyond that world, there was nothing of value.

I had everything for a good and simple life.

I washed all the traces of the excursion and the funeral out of my system.

I stood naked in the garden and soaped myself thoroughly and washed my hair and beard, then rinsed all the soap off into the grass.

I even washed out the empty back pack.

I used quite a bit of precious water but it seemed appropriate.

Then, having purified myself, I went in to the chapel.

I lit my own candles and I looked at the Buddha for a long time.

I was asking that if I had done anything accidentally disrepectful, could I please be forgiven.

I hadn't meant to do that, it just came out of me that way.

I sat with my back against the wall and closed my eyes.

I went deep, fast.

It was like I was on one of those water slides you see at aqua parks. I went down and down and plunged into a dark and welcoming place. It was incredibly peaceful there.

There were no thoughts at all but a sense of presence. A benign, friendly presence. I could not tell what it was, or who it was, but it created an atmosphere of utter contentment and safety.

How long I sat there, I have no idea, not that time matters any more, but I came slowly up and out of that state feeling full and complete.

It wasn't Adèle, or the Buddha or the dead couple or anyone else.

It simply seemed that I had been bathed in benevolence.

I bowed to the Buddha with a deep feeling of gratitude.

I have made my last cup of coffee. I left the generic coffee till last but even that has gone.

It's all mint tea from now on.

I realise how attached to my morning coffee I was. At a certain time in the morning my body sent out craving signals: Coffee please!

Not any more.

The cut grass is a bit drier but not like it was, all fluffy and airy. I have spent all day raking it and my body is aching. Even damp grass is heavy. I raked it to turn it all over and even if I don't have a massive acreage to harvest, still it's back-breaking. It makes me very appreciative of what farmers used to do before machinery came in. How much we have taken for granted in this modern age, all these inventions to make life easier. And yet, very directly, without machines, my life is easier. Just more physical.

If the weather holds then in a couple of days I will start to make a silage dump or hay stacks depending on how the hay behaves. There's no way I am going to dig a huge hole with one spade, just for silage.

While I raked away, my menagerie thought it was great fun. The kids jumped and ran through the cut grass while Mon Veau, who is not so playful these days, tried eating some of it. The goat couple and Ma Vache came and watched. Even a few hens turned up to see what sort of bugs would be hidden.

Never having been much of a physical person, I am finding that my body is hardening up. It likes a bit of hard physical toil. I have a bit more muscle mass and a pretty good tan.

Pity I have no-one to flaunt it to.

The berries are coming in and I have a fight on my hands. There are blueberries, cranberries, groseilles and mûrs, the blackberries. Just as they are all starting to ripen, the birds have swooped. Flocks of them. The word must have gone out on the bird radio : easy pickings at Domaine de Buveny. They are very keen on the raspberries. I have found some netting in the shed, and Jean-Claude's shed had some too. I will try draping it over the vines to see what I can protect.

I might even try a scarecrow or two.

Mother nature battles her self.

Some afternoons, mint tea in hand, I sit here and wonder.

It happens pretty much every day if I am honest with myself.

If I am going to learn how to be at peace with being utterly and permanently alone, what is my purpose in life from now on?

I should have a purpose.

Every creature has a purpose, they are all the same, no matter where they are in the food chain. The purpose of life is to recreate itself.

I don't have that, I have no one to recreate with, so what is it?

What is the way I should be, when there is no-one to take any notice of what I do? There are no laws now, no prohibitions, nothing is legal or illegal, nothing is considered morally reprehensible or morally admirable.

I could do anything.

So what is my culture?

I am forced to admit that the influence of my parents and the social circles I grew up in, the Methodists, Australian society, my age group, my peers and all their commonly accepted ways of being, have created in me a set of values.

I could change them if I wanted to, but they are in there, deeply embedded.

When I ask myself the question: Who am I? where do I end up?

I can run through a list of labels as a response, but each of them is a limited description of me, just an aspect of my age, gender, colour, race, language, talents, shortcomings, life history, temperament and all that.

The problem with all these labels is that although they might be true, no one of them is the whole answer. When they are eliminated as being only partial answers, what is left?

The bottom line is something that transcends all the labels I can think of.

The best of my meditations get me close to glimpsing that.

There is an occasional and sadly fleeting moment when I experience myself as being something conscious but not labelled.

I sense myself as just being, not being something.

Is that the point?

If I could get into that state on a permanent basis, how would that be?

It would be pretty good.

Then why would I want to go on living? Why would I want to have this body? After all it is a fragile mechanism that needs to be fed, watered, rested, exercised, relieved and all the rest. It is a very demanding creature.

It's tiring having a human body.

On the other hand I wouldn't want to be a goat.

In the middle of the night, in a full moon, I woke up because the ring on my finger was burning again.

Suddenly I was very awake. I went up the stairs to the turret and looked out across the hills. These hills are made of limestone and they have a whitish tinge to them. Now in the moonlight they seemed to glow. The sky was clear and the moon was at its highest, shedding its silvery powerful light everywhere. And the ring was burning my finger. It was hot to touch and I could not get it off.

As I stood there in the moonlight, she came. It felt like she was just behind me. Of course when I turned I saw nothing but when I turned back and looked out over the valley her presence behind me was stronger.

"This is our country," she said, and I felt her arms around my waist, holding me from behind.

"My Jacques," she said, and I felt her head against my upper back.

"How many times have we stood here, you and me, one life after another?"

Her voice was inside my body. I could feel the vibrations of it in my chest and my heart was racing.

Then I felt her hand reach around me to my left hand and take the ring in her hand.

"Now you must finish what we started."

Was she speaking in French or in English? I couldn't tell.

But I knew what she was saying.

What did we not finish? I didn't ask that verbally but as a thought.

Our country."

What does that mean? What do you want me to do?

"Bring it back to life."

What does that mean?

I felt a rising sense of panic, something momentous was surging through me, but I didn't know what it was. I was getting terrified.

"Do you mean the Germans?"

"That war is gone. "

"There's only me."

"You are enough, my Jacques. Bring our country back to life."

The pressure inside me built until I couldn't stand it any more and I passed out.

When I came to, the moon was much lower in the sky and I was shivering.

The ring on my hand was cold.

I was cold.

She was not there.

I staggered back down the stairs and wrapped myself in a blanket and lit the fire in the kitchen.

I made tea and sat with it warming myself and trying to understand what all that was about.

La terre. I know that this term is precious to the French. It refers to the relationship with the earth, your land, your country. Very much like the Australian Aborigines. Tante told me how most of her friends and aquaintances would make sure that everyone knew where they were from. Every part of France has a name for the people. Here in the Lot, the people are called Lotois, or Lotoise for women. The capital of the Lot is Cahors and those people are called Caducien or Caduscienne.

What the locals are called round here I have no idea.

Is that what Adèle meant?

The most alarming part of it was her telling me that I was Jacques. Who was Jacques

Gougnard? I have the photo of him, so I know what he looked like.

Why wasn't he there when the Germans attacked the safe house?

Was he a resistance fighter, a Maquis, like her?

What is the point in me asking these questions?

How will I ever know the answer?

So then the other side of it, what does she want me to do?

Maybe she just means look after the property. I am doing that, as best I can.

But it wasn't that, it couldn't have been that. It was too strong a command. She wasn't just saying mow the grass and tend the garden. I was more and more feeling that it was La Terre.

What am I supposed to do about it?

I eventually went back to bed and tossed and turned.

All this swirled in my brain too tumultuously to let me sleep.

In the end I got up, made more tea and went into the chapel.

I lit candles and sang the Buddhist hymn. Then I arranged all the photos of Adèle, including the one with Jacques in front of me.

Then I did some inner talking.

I need to know what you mean? I don't know what you want.

Then I closed my eyes and repeated the mantra, trying to be as released from expectation as I could.

Absolutely nothing happened.

I eventually got up, stiff and sore and deeply disappointed.

All morning I felt sad, dragging myself from one distraction to the next.

Around the middle of the day, she was standing under the Linden tree in the shade.

I had thrown myself into tasks, as physical as possible. I raked the nearly dry hay into piles and worked up a good sweat. It was hot and I only wore cut off jeans. I was building one pile at the end of the field where the Linden tree stands. It's a huge tree, with a wide solid trunk and must be hundreds of years old.

She was leaning back against the trunk watching me.

At first I caught a sense of her presence and then, out of the corner of my eye, I could see her.

Just as she was in the first photo.

This time she let me look at her. She was standing still but as I looked and kept looking, her face slowly broke into a smile. Then she spread her arms out wide, as if showing me her *Terre*.

Then as I watched, she kept looking at me with this half smile and unbuttoned her white blouse. She was bare-chested underneath. Her breats were small and her skin was very white. Then she stepped out of her long skirt and the white bloomers underneath. Totally naked she looked at me with that smile.

I hadn't noticed before but she was barefoot.

In any other circumstance I would have taken that as an invitation, but not now.

I could not move.

What was she trying to show me?

It was symbolic of something, it was not just her naked body.

And then as I watched, she dissolved into the tree.

She kept looking at me as she faded, literally disembodied, melting into the texture of the trunk of Linden.

I waited, willing her to reappear but she was gone.

I wanted to run to her, beg her not to go, but I seemed stuck in place with a rake in my hand.

After quite some time, Mon Veau gently nudged me. It was almost as if he had been sent to wake me up.

I went over to the tree and ran my hands over its smooth bark.

I imagined it was her, her naked body in the smooth coolness of the trunk.

Then I sank down underneath the tree and closed my eyes.

I stayed there a long time and Mon Veau left me in peace.

The nakedness of her haunted me as much as I had been haunted by her presence before.

I couldn't get the image of her white body out of my mind. It was not a sexual thing. I was not aroused when the image of her came to me. It was something much more mysterious.

It meant something very powerful that I could not get.

From then on she would appear like that in my dreams and she would appear like that in my meditation.

Most often the vision would be of her in the shade of the Linden tree and fade in and out from the trunk. There was great beauty to her body, its texture and shape, but my admiration was like I felt when I saw the Venus de Milo in the Louvre. I loved gazing at her and the look she gave me as she stood there.

What tormented me though was not knowing what it meant.

I loved those inner moments while being tortured by them at the same time.

Whenever I looked at the Linden tree I wondered if she would reappear physically there too.

She didn't.

What came to me next was a subtle but clear message. It was a sense that her people, or our people as it came to me, needed to be taken care of. It took me a while to understand what this meant.

Over several meditations and other instances of a kind of daydream state that I would get into sometimes, the message became clearer. I might be raking hay or chopping wood and I would just stop for a moment and close my eyes and there would be something there.

I kept feeling it was to do with ancestors or members of the family. Then I sensed that there had to be a cemetery or something like that, somewhere close and I needed to go there.

Then I remembered that Jean-Claude had spoken of some headstones, long neglected at the bottom of the hill where our track joined the local road.

This came back a couple of times till I could not ignore it any more.

So I went looking.

At first there was just scrubby bushes on both sides of the road. The two letter boxes and the old bus shelter were on one side and a small ditch on the other. Beyond the ditch there were brambles and clumps of acacia bushes. It was all quite thick. I pushed into it as much as I could despite the thorns, and ended up getting bloody scratches all over my arms and legs.

I found nothing.

However, as I stood there I had a very strong sense that I was in the right place.

I decided that I would have to come back with the right tools. I was experienced now, having cleaned up the safe house.

I was about to head back up the track when I thought to check the mail boxes. In all the time I had been there, it had never occurred to me.

There were two of them, one for Domaine de Buveny and the other for Jean-Claude and Eveline. The boxes open with a key but they are flimsy things. With a deft finger I could see if there was anything in them by going through the slot.

There was something in both boxes and I couldn't prise either of them out.

More tools were required.

I went back up the track.

When I came back I forced the mail boxes open and wrecked them both. Not that it mattered, there would be no more mail coming.

In each was the same letter. In French it was informing them that the whole area was contaminated and all residents were to be evacuated. It was dated March 14th, the day after I got here.

I read it over several times to make sure I understood. It explained one thing and left a whole lot of questions. That's why Saint Fé was empty. It explained why the Dupuys had decided not to go.

Maybe the whole of Gourdon was getting ready to go somewhere, but I didn't sense it when I went there. Everything seemed normal.

What these letters did not explain was what does it mean when it says this area is contaminated. I thought the virus was global and everywhere had the same exposure, more or less. Why was here described as being contaminated?

Also why did no-one come to see if Domaine de Buveny had been evacuated?

What about Jean-Claude and Evaline? Did they do they same as the Dupuys? Better to die at home than to fade away in a refugee camp somewhere?

I put the letters in my back pocket and started to attack the brambles beyond the ditch.

I cut and slashed my way in about a few meters then I hit the first headstone. At first I just thought it was a rock, but when I scraped away the moss and the mud I could see some writing on it. I worked at cleaning it up until I could make out the letters of the name.

It was a Dieulefait.

At least I think so. Some of it was missing or chipped off so I was guessing, but there were enough letters to make it fairly certain. The date was something in the eighteenth century. I could make out the 1 and the 7 but not the last two numbers.

I stood back from it and took stock.

So the messages were clear.

I had listened and here was the evidence.

I knew I should do what I did to the safe house, clean it all up and pay my respects.

I did no more that day.

I went back up the hill and took a dip in the dam before I went up to the turret with my tea.

On the one hand I now have a new task and I am happy about that. On the other hand the two letters had me worried.

I couldn't find a satisfactory way to think about the fact that I was perfectly healthy in a contaminated area. In other places, I knew they were asking people to stay home, shelter in place, but why were they evacuating here instead?

It made no sense to me.

The reason there were no trucks on the freeway might be because the freeway passes through a contaminated area, but that doesn't explain the total absence of aircraft.

I exhausted my brain trying to get a sense of it.

She came as the sun was setting and I had closed my eyes. The warmth, the goldenness of the last rays of the sun had bathed my face and I lay back against the warm stones of the wall of the turret.

I could only see her face. Her hair was long and draped partially over her face like a veil.

"You found yourself," she said

There was a softness in her eyes that made me melt.

And then, ever so gently, she evaporated.

I came back slowly and sat there with a wide smile on my face.

OK, I thought. If I was that Dieulefait, then I have been here a few times. I just dug up my own grave.

And then I remembered what she had said earlier and I knew that this is indeed my country, our country. Now it made sense. I am recycling.

I suppose Jacques came somewhere in between then and now.

If this is where my previous incarnations took place, then why on earth was I born on the other side of the world?

If this is my country, our country, why didn't I just come back, to be born here again?

For the next few days, I toiled away in my family cemetery. There were a dozen stones, but none there were Dieulefaits. Of course some could have been part of the family by marriage. Unfortunately a lot of the headstones were indecipherable, so they could have been anybody.

I did my best to clean up both the headstones and some of the slabs attached to them. I hacked away at the brambles until the area was clear. I dug out the roots of the acacias so they wouldn't grow back.

I began to clean the area behind and a little higher up the slope from the head stones when I heard running water. I hacked in further and found a spring, running a small rivulet of clear sweet water out and down towards the road. I dug around it until I got it to divert and I ran the little stream down between the headstones to the ditch by the track.

I was becoming a landscape architect.

I found rocks here and there that I brought to line the new stream. After about five days, I had made what I thought was a rather fancy little irrigated family plot for me and my ancestors, of whom I was one.

All the time, while I did all this physical labour, I felt incredibly happy.

I could feel her close to me and every now and then I thought I almost caught sight of her.

The day when I knew I had finished it, was the day she came, fully visible and unclad. She knelt by the new stream and dipped her hands into the water, then she lifted the water over her head and let it run down her long hair and over her face. Her whiteness seemed to glow in the late afternoon light. The water shone as it ran across her breasts.

I felt such love for her.

I could not move.

I watched without breathing as she bathed herself several times, deeply absorbed, until at last she looked up.

Mon Jacques, she said, and looked at me with as much love as I was feeling for her.

And then very slowly, she dissolved into the water.

So now part of my day is taking care of the safe house and taking care of the cemetery.

I hope there isn't any more familial archeology to do.

Two holy sites is plenty.

Now we are into the baking days of what must be July. It's too hot in the middle of the day to do anything and we all find shady spots to rest. The kids are growing fast and love to run around, but when it gets hot even they lie down in the shade.

I've got more tomatoes than I know what to do with, even when the birds get quite a few. I've got cucumbers, and zucchinis by the box full, some red cabbages and some aubergines.

I could open a greengrocery if anyone else lived in this world.

The grass is browning but the animals all seem happy with what they get.

The dam is only half full now but I think it will last.

I have the best suntan of my life.

Now that I was more or less convinced that I had deep roots in this place, I went hunting in the boxes and shelves in the dusty unrenovated parts of the château. There was a lot of stuff. I wanted to find anything about the history, anything about the Dieulefait dynasty. The more I dug the more interesting stuff I came across. I began to make a pile of things that I wanted to study maybe later, maybe in the cold of winter when going outside would not be attractive. Somebody in the past liked history books and I was getting a good collection.

Nothing about the Dieulefaits though.

Then I found it.

It was a leatherbound book with dog-eared pages which looked like it had not been opened for years. Quite a few of the pages were stuck together and would take real patience to separate them.

The title of the book was Une Histoire du Domaine de Buveny , by Gervais Dieulefait, and was written in 1910.

I put it in the chapel with all my other precious objects of worship.

Now part of my day would be one chapter read and understood.

I was going to need Monsieur Larousse to be ready at hand.

Gervais, my supposed ancestor, was not exactly the most exciting author. He liked details rather than narrative. It was heavy going, with lots of dictionary checks. No wonder it was at the bottom of a box of long neglected tomes. It also explains why Chloé never found it.

It's a pity because she really wanted to know the background to what she had bought. Chloé was not the sort of person who had the patience to spend time rooting aound in dusty boxes. She moved way too fast for that. Most of her research was on the internet and the Toulouse Library. She had not found anything to do with this château. Obviously she had not gone deep enough.

I can only imagine her excitement if she had come across this.

In his workman-like coverage of the history, Gervais has included several artistic drawings of what the château would have looked like when it was first built, several reproductions of noteworthy ancestors including an army general in Napoleon's army and one grainy photo of what the château looked like in 1900. It was a long distance shot and there was not enough clarity to discern who several of the figures standing near the entrance might be. It didn't look all that different from now.

After a very flowery and somewhat poetic opening about the glorious history of Le Domaine de Buveny, Gervais gets down to the details.

The château was commissioned by Alphonse de Poitiers in 1298 when he was the Count of Toulouse. He was the brother of the French King Louis IX and good friends with Simon de Montfort. He ordered the château to be built, and several others, to take command of the road to Paris. There had been dwellings on this hill before that, but Gervais dismisses them as humble structures of no historical importance.

When he ordered the construction of the château, Alphonse rewarded the Dieulefait family for the part that one of them, Charles Debonâme Dieulefait, played in the Crusade that Alphonse financed and co-led to Palestine. Charles was a chevalier that Gervais describes as courageous and headstrong. He barely survived the Crusade coming back with some debilitating disease, which Gervais euphemistically refers to as a socially contagious affliction so I assume it was a gift from the Ladies of the Levant.

So there we are.

We go way back.

The name Le Domaine de Buveny , according to Gervais, comes from one of the heros of the Crusade.

He was a young English chevalier and a distant cousin of the Dieulefaits, Geoffrey Laroche Buveny of Steny. He led a victorious charge in Acre, during which he received a mortal wound. He supposedly kept on fighting and only dropped dead at the moment the city of Acre surrendered.

The name was chosen by Alphonse himself.

Gervais claims that there are artworks depicting the feats of Geoffrey Buveny in a Toulouse museum. They adorned the parlour of the château until it moved out of Dieulefait hands, and they went to safe keeping in Toulouse.

I wonder if I will ever get to see them.

The Dieulefaits were notables at the Court of Toulouse in the thirteenth century and several of the women married into aristocratic families in that Court, and through their connections the Dieulefaits became very wealthy. Effectively they were the overlords of this whole district. Gervais doesn't mention how they treated their peasants.

This went on for a while, with subsequent generations ruling the area and extracting taxes. Gervais needed an editor to tell him that pages of tax records do not make fascinating reading.

I skipped a few pages here and there, and wondered if it was worth continuing.

I did a lot of gardening before I ventured back.

I was glad I did because suddenly it got more interesting.

Religion got in the way.

In 1572 a major war erupted between the Catholic establishment and Protestants called Huguenots. Evidently this area had lots of Protestants who had been mistreated by the lordly Catholic rulers, including the Dieulefaits, for years.

Gervais at least admitted that much.

According to Gervais those pesky English got involved and supported the anti-Catholics and it is clear whose side he is on. He is no anglophile in his depiction of what went on.

I have read elsewhere, as I studied the history of my adopted country, that England has been annoying France very consistently for more than a thousand years. This was surely a good example.

The château was captured by the Protestants and Gervais hints at English mercenaries.

The lord of the château at the time, Henri Arche Dieulefait, was executed and his head paraded on a pike and the family was thrown out. Gervais avoids too much gore in his rendition but I got the picture.

After that he tells the pitiful story of bands of homeless Dieulefaits finding shelter in very humble dwellings with distant cousins who were not hospitable.

The Protestants, having taken a string of Catholic châteaus and towns, then restructured the whole area, redistributing property. This château was held by the de Beaurepaire family.

I had to laugh when I got to this part. The de Beaurepaire family!

Alain de Beaurepaire had to be a descendant. This was getting more and more weird, although pretty exciting at the same time. If Alain was part of this lineage, then he (or at least his forebears) actually owned the château centuries before his American wife bought it back. It makes sense, because the old château that Chloé had wanted to buy was not too far away.

Chloé would be amazed. I really wish she could be here to discover all this.

I can just imagine her shrieks of amazement.

Maybe it will happen.

The de Beaurepaires held the château for more than a hundred years. Gervais is surprisingly generous in his praise of the de Beaurepaires, admitting they were good farmers and looked after their peasants well.

They built a Protestant Temple on the property.

I will have to go hunt for it, although it was a long time ago and often stones from buildings that get destroyed are then used in others, so there might be nothing of the Temple left.

I spent a couple of days looking in parts of the property that I hadn't spent so much time in, but I didn't find anything that suggested a Protestant Temple.

When I got back to reading, along came the Sun King.

He had a name rather like ours. He was called Louis Dieudonné, God given.

I learned all about him when Clo and I lived in Versailles. He was not only appallingly flamboyant, putting on vast dramatic spectacles, he was also very vain and responsive to flattery.

Gervais is obviously rather proud of his ancestors' relationship with the Sun King.

Several of the Dieulefaits were in his retinue. The Sun King did not like the Protestants at all and he instituted something called the Dragonnades , where loyal companies of Dragoons were stationed in the châteaux and other main establishments of the Huguenots to intimidate them. Somehow the Dieulefaits got to persuade the Sun King that their loss of property during the religious wars was illegal, or unjust, or, to put it bluntly, shameful to the Dieulefaits. He was quite sympathetic and he sent in the Dragoons.

Now that I am entertaining the possibility of having been born now and then in France, I wonder if I was around at that time? The Sun King, Louis XIV, loved drama and had many new plays commissioned including by Racine and Molière. I bet I was in there somewhere!

I am enjoying imagining how that would have been.

Back when I was in drama school, I had to do a play reading of Racine's Iphigenia for classwork. It was very long, horribly wordy, and lacked any significant action.

I remember getting halfway through it and saying to the student director: What the hell am I saying? Maybe in the time of the Sun King it was all about good costumes and well-spoken dialogue.

Anyway, in relation to this château, when the Dragoons moved into the area there was some kind of very local action in which a company of Dragoons, not content to just annoy the locals, went so far as to throw the de Beaurepaires out of the château, destroy the temple, and reinstate the Dieulefaits.

Gervais suggests that the head of the Dragoons was invited to marry the daughter of the Dieulefait family which stood to regain the château.

From then on, to make sure the local peasants did not rise up, the Dragoons evidently terrorised the community and murdered a few of the most senior local Protestant leaders as a warning.

So now we got it back.

We do seem to have rather a lot of blood on our hands, although I suppose back then it was the manicure of choice.

It would have been regarded as a practical necessity. Keep the peasants too frightened to rise up.

The locals were clearly not happy, but Gervais passes over this rather quickly with some gentle euphemisms.

So, other than those messy and insignificant details, life went back to normal for the Dieulefaits.

Again Gervais gets a bit lost in long chapters that tend to dwell on who bought and sold what and who married whom.

I tended to skip read those bits.

His sense of narrative rhythm leaves a lot to be desired.

The most colourful scenes of this history describe how, although the Dieulefaits got the château back, some of the senior members of the family stayed in Versailles with the king. The second sons of the several Dieulefait families ran the château and the farms, while the first born sons paid homage and sought favour.

The most noteworthy member of the family in Versailles, according to Gervais, was Catherine Dieulefait, who was considered a great beauty, a favourite of the king. She was senior amongst the ladies in waiting and was said to be a confidante of the King himself. It was the King who had organised her betrothal to the heir to the dukedom of Cointreau, a handsome young man who was a champion at jousting. It was considered an excellent match and they were destined to be a couple of note in the Court.

However just before the wedding, he was killed in a tournament.

This was so shocking to her that she withdrew from the Court and returned to Le Domaine de Buveny, where she very quickly died of tuberculosis.

In the book there is a small portrait of her in Versailles. She has regal bearing and is looking straight at the artist with a subtle smile. She is dressed in a long white gown with a jeweled necklace and a tiara.

She wasted no time in showing me her outfit in more detail.

She swept into my meditation.

She wore the full-length thick rich white gown, with fancy embroidery on it. The small tiara in her piled up hair was embedded with stones. Around her throat, glittering jewelry set off her white skin.

She stood above me, looking down.

Her eyes pierced me.

There was no smile.

"We are Dieulefait." she said "We take back the territory that was ours. No-one shall live here but Dieulefait."

I found myself bowing before her.

She radiated a light and a power that I could not hold.

"You are Dieulefait," she said, her voice commanding and resonant.

"En effet, on es Dieu. In fact you are God."

I passed out into some dark region of unconsciousness but the sense of what she had said flooded me.

I was terrified in one part of me, elated in another part of me.

The rest of me swam in the darkness of unknowing.

When eventually I came out of it, I was lying full length on the floor in front of the altar with all its little symbolic objects of worship.

I gazed up at the photos of her.

Can we please have a conversation about this? I begged.

On some level I understand this, but it is all a bit too mystical for me.

I had enough trouble accepting that reincarnation was even possible, but this was something altogether more strange.

What came to me as I tried to make sense of it was that, in a way, it's like a piece of theatre, certainly a period drama.

It might go like this:

The dynasty of the Dieulefait family occupied long ago this château and commanded Le Domaine de Buveny for centuries.

Then they lost it. The souls of the Dieulefaits kept coming back to try to regain what they had lost. Sometimes they did, but they never managed to keep it. Adèle was the Doyenne of the family in at least one of her early incarnations and in her last one, she and maybe some others (although Jacques was not a Dieulefait, as far as I can tell) fought the Germans trying to get it free. Now the soul of one the Dieulefaits has come back, in the form of a terribly ignorant Australian, with no idea about any of the history. The soul of Adèle makes herself known and guides the last of the Dieulefaits to regain the territory of his ancestors. To make sure it happens, a plague descends on the region and this benighted Australian is the only living being left.

So he alone reclaims the territory.

End of story.

Is that it?

Well, if it is, then I can wander about, playing God.

I can be God.

Dieulefait.

God the Fact.

I could wear a white cloth like the medieval portraits of God and have a shepherd's crook. George and his tribe can be my flock and we can all play God.

Pity there is no audience to enjoy the play.

Chloé would love it.

The weird thing about the whole idea is that in the most obvious way, it doesn't change anything.

Whether I tell myself I am God or not, nothing will be different.

Unless of course, I am actually God. In that case I could simply recreate a world to my liking.

Now that would be fun. I would make sure Clo reappeared.

I could easily imagine she and I creating a new world.

What fun.

It is very tempting to get into fantasy about that, but that's all it is.

Fantasy.

If I really was God, then Clo would be right here.

The fantasy doesn't serve any good purpose.

To get myself back to reality, I go back to my daily routine as I have done all along.

However I do notice that there is a subtle change.

I keep the idea of being God alive in my mind.

It is always there.

I look at everything around me from the perspective of accepting that this is my country and I have been here, generation after generation, having gained possession and then losing it again and again.

I am Dieulefait.

The other perspective is a strange detachment from reality.

It is as if I am on a film set and we are pretending, acting out this scenario.

I watch myself going about the daily tasks, but at any moment the director could yell: Cut! And I would revert back to being me.

Whoever that is.

One day when I was back in Versailles, they were shooting a film about Louis the XIII who was the father of the Sun King. His main advisor was Cardinal Richelieu. That day they were filming the Cardinal arriving at the palace in his fancy coach with an escort of six mounted cavaliers . All the actors, dressed in very fine period costumes, even the horses, were standing about waiting to be called.

The funniest thing for me was the anachronistic vision of the Cardinal in all his finery speaking to someone on his cell phone.

It's all an illusion really.

The hay is all done and it is quite dry. I have filled one of the sheds to the roof with it and I am rather proud of myself.

The fruit trees are coming magnificently. I am harvesting big reddish apricots and purple plums. What I will do with them all, I have no idea. I realise there is plenty for all the birds and for me. The goats really like the ones that fall. I would make jam except you need sugar for that.

The veggie garden just goes on giving too. The pumpkins and *potimarrons* are starting, and it looks like I will have a massive store for winter.

Everything is so bountiful.

Somehow the danger that must be lurking out there is not a reality for me when I have all this.

I am finding myself more and more content with my lot.

There are flowers and fruit, there are the animals to keep me company and the chickens go right on doing their poultry duties.

If I am God then I have made a rather splendid world for myself to live in.

Although I was feeling more than a bit euphoric at playing God, I took a bit of a break from Gervais after Adèle appeared.

I had a certain fear that she might become very active in whatever might happen next, if I kept reading, as if reading might bring her to me in ways that might scare me to death.

Perhaps it's the idea that if I don't know about something it can't hurt me.

If I read about it, then I know it.

Ignorance is bliss?

However, finally I succumbed.

I couldn't resist wanting to know what happened next.

There was still three centuries to go.

I sat back in the chapel, apologised to Gervais for my absence, and plunged back in.

In 1715 the Sun King got gangrene and hobbled off into the sunset.

The court of the new king brought many changes, but the Dieulefaits stayed on.

Those at Court needed to be financed and a lot of pressure was placed on the lesser members of the family to produce. After the death of the Sun King, the senior Dieulefaits tried to keep their previous place at Court, but they had lost favour and were struggling with the demands to look the part of courtiers. It was not cheap and, with not enough money, they had no influence. It's a truism of history. Money equals influence. There was a lot of pressure on the country cousins to cough up.

The lesser Dieulefaits struggled on here in the Lot trying to meet their demands. The harvests were poor and the government was applying taxes. The Dieulefaits put pressure on their workers to produce more. They were obviously not great at industrial relations. After the death of the Sun King the quasi military support they had been given was taken away.

The Dragoons were gone.

The Dieulefaits were left to their own devices and had to try to control the locals without any security back up. There were several minor insurrections as the peasants began to fight back. Gervais is surprisingly candid about that. He obviously was not impressed with his ancestors during that period.

Then along came the French Revolution.

The locals, led by the next generation of de Beaurepaires, who were shamefacedly posing as champions of the poor, grabbed the opportunity with both hands. They seized the château and did nasty things to the incumbents.

Gervais uses euphemisms at this point.

He's a bit squeamish I think.

I am glad about that because I wouldn't want those images floating about in my meditation. The head of one Dieulefait on a pike is enough.

The château was ransacked and the tricolour flag flew over the turret. The locals declared themselves to be Republicans.

We still have a flag pole up there, although I doubt it's the same one.

Gervais tends to slip through the period of the French Revolution rather fast, as if he finds the whole thing rather distasteful.

The bloody years from 1789 to 1799 were covered in not much more than a paragraph, full of dates and details, but no shocking images.

I think lots of French people, except far-left leaning ones, find the Revolution rather embarrassing.

What happened to the Dieulefaits in Paris, he leaves as a vague They did not do well and describes the state of the château as being chaotic and unmanaged. The peasants took what they wanted and left it as a ruin. The doors found new homes and the window shutters became firewood.

All that remained was the solid structure.

Evidently the de Beaurepaires were not keen to take it back. Gervais doesn't seem to know why. I suppose if they were posing as champions of the poor, they couldn't just move in, it wouldn't look good.

They might risk getting their own heads on pikes.

I stopped there for a day or two, although I am getting rather fond of old Gervais.

I feel like I am getting to know him.

He's a gentle soul, wanting to catch the history of his family for future generations.

I imagine he is writing this in his last years. He is quite articulate but conservative. Although what he is writing about is more than a little scary for me, I am happy to be in his company.

I suppose given the company I have, he is as good as I can get.

He's more forthcoming than Adèle at the moment and a lot less enigmatic.

I went back to my daily chores, but all the time I was thinking about what had happened on these grounds.

Where I walked, blood had been shed, lives cut short, revenge taken.

Not having had any life experience like that, it is hard to imagine.

The cemetery took on a whole new meaning.

I wondered if any of the corpses was missing a head.

And somewhere on the property there are the ruins of a temple.

Of course a Protestant temple is nothing like a Thai Buddhist temple. I have seen these French temples in various places in France and they are extraordinarily plain, both inside and out, perhaps as a counter to the flamboyance of the Catholics. The Protestants had that in common with the Cathars.

Even as I harvest the garden's bounty, draw milk from the cow and the goat, and amass fruits and berries from the trees and vines, I sense how what I am doing has been done, in one form or another, by my ancestors, of whom, from time to time I was one.

It jangles the brain, that's for sure.

When I went back to Gervais, he was into Napoleon.

During the chaos of the revolution, the château remained an abandoned wreck. Gervais passes over this as the saddest time of the château's existence.

He doesn't approve of neglect.

At first, Napoleon's early efforts to reconfigure France, after the Coup d'Etat that brought him to power, left this part of the country to fend largely for itself.

After 1799, the focus was on military matters and reorganising the bureaucracy. In the midst of all this, our area was just a backwater that no-one seemed to care much about.

However at some point, in 1804, when Napolean became the Emperor, a local government official was appointed to look at what happened to the châteaus and large estates of the aristocracy. The Dieulefaits petitioned him for restoration of their rights to Le Domaine de Buveny.

This went on for quite some time.

Luckily one of the descendants of the family who had stayed in Paris had risen through the ranks of the military and had served with distinction in the Egyptian Expedition, becoming a colonel. His name was Henri Dupont Dieulefait and he had the ear of the Irish General who had worked alongside Napoleon.

That Irish General was Edward Fitzgerald Teague.

What!

Teague?

I stared at this sentence for the longest time. How can that be?

Here was another of my ancestors, I assumed, getting involved. This was all becoming more and more scary as it went along. I don't know if we had such an Irish General in our family tree, but as far as I know all the Teagues came originally from the Galway region of Ireland, although my father claims we came from Cornish forebears.

As I stared down at this tatty page of history, I knew he had to be connected.

Too many connections were being made for it not to be all part of something bigger.

After I recovered from my shock I steeled myself to read on.

It turned out that the Dieulefait family were more or less penniless. They were trying to keep up appearances as best they could but after the French Revolution, being an aristocratic family, especially with no money, was not an easy life.

Many of them were scattered around the country with distant relatives, all of them living in wretched conditions. Old aristocrats were dying in rotten chateaus.

Henri Dupont Dieulefait was the only member of the family with any influence. With the help of General Teague, he persuaded one of Napoleon's senior advisors that the ownership of Le Domaine de Buveny should revert to the original family. This petition was successful enough that the local administrative official was persuaded that the Emperor wished for it to happen, and so it did.

Henri Dupont Dieulefait organised a trip with the General to see the property and was suitably horrified at the state it was in. The funds needed to restore it to its previous glory were, however, well beyond the means of any of the family.

This is when General Teague came to the rescue. He suggested that his third son who had not inherited much land in Ireland, could be persuaded to come to the Lot and oversee the recreation of the property.

Gervais suggests that perhaps the third son had committed some kind of indiscretion and needed to be quietly expatriated. He is discreet when it comes to details.

Anyway, General Teague seemed to love the project and he provided the funding and the supervision of the rebirth of the château and its grounds.

He seems to be a bit like an earlier version of Chloé!

Evidently in those days there was quite a bit of Dieulefait property that was claimed, various fields and woods scattered all throughout the valley.

While the restoration began, Henri Dupont Dieulefait took full advanatge of the patronage of the General and therefore the Emperor himself.

He saw his reputation and his fortunes rise and rise.

He did not stay in the Lot, as the work proceeded, because he was engaged in military campaigns. However, he did manage to get a company of soldiers to be billeted on the property which meant that once again the château had security, both financial and military.

It turns out that the young Teague, Thomas was a good property manager.

He was also handsome and single.

The Dieulefaits were delighted when he asked for the hand of Fleur Dieulefait, oldest daughter of Henri Dupont Dieulefait, in marriage.

This was dutifully granted, the marriage taking place in Saint Fé, and they went on to produce a small tribe of Teague Dieulefaits.

Unfortunately, Henri Dupont Dieulefait was hit by a cannonball in Russia and died an agonising death on the battlefield.

By that time he had become a General in his own right.

Gervais claims there is a statue of him somewhere in Paris.

Over the next fifty years, the château-based family prospered, while the rest of the Dieulefaits, scattered all over France, faded into obscurity.

Gervais is rather disdainful about many of them, who were still trying to play at being aristocrats. He spends a long time going through very boring minor details about his immediate antecedents, who they were, where they lived, who married who.

It seems like a lot of second sons became priests in minor parishes.

This was the part of the book where he had wads of documented evidence and he copied it copiously. It was long and tedious and I began skipping pages.

The one thing I did learn was that there is a family crypt in the Saint Fé cemetery.

I will probably have to get on my bike again soon.

I wondered who Adèle was in all this. However, if she did appear during all these years, she didn't let me know about any of that. Although I was fascinated to see what happened to the château through the turbulent French centuries, I was still held in the state that she created in me, when she appeared as Catherine in the Court of the Sun King.

The power of her, the stature that she emanated, has kept me in awe of her.

It all creates a desire in me to do deeper and deeper search.

I have lived for forty years and a bit, thinking that I was this Australian man with certain physical characterisitics, mental capacities, emotional equipment and a reasonable amount of talent.

But that's all been thrown into a new perspective.

I am a Teague, and probably have been before, now and then.

I am a Dieulefait, and have been, now and then.

I am also God.

And if that's true, then it's not just now and then.

Is it all just about labels?

The I that became all these labels, who is that?

Historically, we journey on.

The final chapter of Gervais's book talks about the château as he knew it. The great Depression of the late 1880's led to the loss of almost all the outlying properties so that only the château and its grounds, some one hundred hectares of mostly non- arable hilltop land was left. Gervais was the oldest son of one of the other lines of Dieulefaits. He was not a direct Teague descendant but he and his family had lived close by, in Saint Fé, for generations. His father had worked for the Teagues running their vineyard, which sadly no longer exists.

Gervais himself had gone into the wine trade and had run a wine cellar in Gourdon. At the time of writing, the château was still owned and operated by the Teagues.

So now I knew quite a lot about the history of the place up to 1910.

What I didn't know was what happened from then on. I do know that Chloé bought it from an English family who used it as a summer house and had managers taking care of it. I wonder if that English family had Teague ancestry?

The managers seemed to have left when the family did.

The head of the family was a banker and had a lot of cash to blow on vanity objects.

It all came crashing down when he was discovered to have quietly run a private investment scheme of his own inside the bank without the bank knowing anything about it. As I recall, as told by Chloé, he got caught when some of his investments went bad, incurring huge losses for his bank.

He blew his head off with a hunting rifle in Surrey.

Another headless corpse.

Naturally the family had to sell up in a hurry and Chloé, with her never-ending good luck, picked up the château for a fraction of it what it was probably worth, well furnished with sturdy items of quality English workmanship.

I know all this from Chloé herself.

I sleep in a fine chestnut double bed with a canopy frame.

So who owned it before the English family?

When I look at the first photo I found of Adèle, the people all look French.

Are they the owners?

Maybe they were the farm managers.

Where did Adèle fit into this?

She is a Dieulefait, not a Teague, at least as far as I can tell, but she probably has Teague forebears.

I got back on the bike.

It was time for exploration, social archeology.

But it was more than that.

I had a vague idea where the cemetery of Saint Fé was.

I needed to pay my respects to the Teagues as well as the Dieulefaits.

I took some tools in the backpack in case there was some repairing to be done.

We are definitely in mid-July sometime and it's blazing hot, so I started early.

The morning was still cool as I ratttled off down the track. The animals watched me go. Mon Veau had no opinion and watched me from the shade.

Nothing moved on the road to Saint Fé. When I passed the cremation ashes of the Dupuy house, I saw that the sunflower crop had withered and browned.

Nothing drew me back there.

The buildings of Saint Fé were exactly as I had left them last time.

I propped the bike under the plaque devoted to Adèle and poked around the houses. I wondered which of them had been the house where Gervais had lived, but there was no way of telling. There were letter boxes with names on them, but there were no Dieulefaits or Teagues.

The only other building of note, other than the church, is a solid stone building opposite the church with the sign Mairie in carved stone over the the portal. Even a tiny little place like this has a Mayor and his office. On one side was a brass plaque with the names of the Mayors of Saint Fé. And there was Gervais. He had been Mayor for the last fifteen years of his life. I suppose in a town this small there aren't too many people who want the job. He was the only Dieulefait and none of the Teagues or de Beuarepaires had ever taken office.

As I peered into windows and tried the doors of the Mairie , I saw nothing that told me what had happened. I thought about breaking in, but I couldn't think of anything that I wanted to add to my collection of stuff. I tried a few other houses with the idea that I might find some coffee or toilet paper, but the doors were all locked.

I had no real inclination to break in.

I headed for the tombstones.

The cemetery is, as I had suspected, hidden behind the church. Between them is a small park about a hundred metres from the road. It has a gravel driveway lined with shrubs that had been carefully topiaried but had now gotten quite bushy.

The cemetery has double sculpted iron portal gates with the Fleur de Lys on them.

The gates were not locked.

The whole thing is probably no more than a hundred square metres, surrounded by a a high stone wall.

Nature was enthusiastically reclaiming its own. The pathways between the graves were thick with weeds, and creepers were laying claim to many of the stone angels and crosses adorning the headstones. A big beech tree had come down in the wind at some point and taken out part of the surrounding wall.

I went hunting for my forebears.

It didn't take long. The Teague Dieulefaits had by far the biggest burial building, whatever it might be called. I suppose it's a family vault. The French word is, if I remember correctly, caveau which I suppose could also mean a tomb. Maybe it's a family mausoleum, a little one.

This one dominated one corner of the walled-in enclosure, sheltering under wide branches of a massive oak that stood just beyond the wall.

The structure was shaped like a small house, built of stone with a pitched slate roof, a stone cross on the top and stone statues of angels at each corner, each the size of a small child, with benign smiles and open wings.

As I gazed at it, I sensed there was just a hint of a similarity to a miniature Thai Buddhist temple, but I am sure that was not intended.

Above the door, which was solid oak, was a blonde head stone with the two names engraved across it. Dieulefait Teague.

Everything in that corner was overgrown with ivy and grandpa's beard creepers and the weeds were waist high. I had brought a machete so I hacked it all back. It wasn't exactly neat but an improvement.

When I tried the door it did not move. I wondered if it was locked but I couldn't see any key hole.

In the end, I used a rock and with a few good whacks, I got the door to move without doing too much sacrilegious damage.

The first corpse was lying on the ground.

How a little hedgehog got in was a bit of a mystery but it never got out again. Maybe it thought it was a Teague with bristles.

I gave it a decent burial outside.

It was pretty dark inside but I could see plaques everywhere.

I think maybe the bodies in their coffins go down into some kind of underground chamber but it was too dark to really tell. Luckily I had matches and went off and found enough long grass to make a bit of an old-fashioned torch.

It wouldn't last long so I had to be quick.

There she was.

With her date of birth and death Adèle Isabelle Dieulefait was buried here.

This is what I had come for.

At least I knew where she was buried.

While the flame lasted, I saw the plaques of many Teagues and Dieulefaits from different generations, some indicating to whom they were married.

When the torch threatened to burn my fingers, I retreated.

I sat outside for a while taking all this in.

It took me back to that age old question : Who am I?

More and more I was willing to accept that I had been various incarnations all connected to the bodies interred here. It was quite possible that more than one of the bodies in this vault had been inhabited by me, whatever that me is.

It is strange, I have to say, to be sitting in a graveyard and thinking that I had lived in some of the dead bodies in front of me.

The weirdest thing is that I have no sense of that, other than beginning to accept that it might be so.

I have no memory of being these people.

I pushed the door closed and then hacked away at a few more weeds, so that it had a neater area around it.

I was going to have to come back to finish it and I would bring candles so I could study the plaques inside.

I went for a walk around the cemetery and there diagonally opposite and not quite so fancy was the family vault of the de Beaurepaires. As in life and history, the two families faced off across the buried bodies of their compatriots.

How Chloé would have loved all this. She would have mocked her husband unmercifully but also she would glory in knowing the history.

I could imagine her drilling the history into her sons, the latest generation of de Beaurepaires.

I gave the area around the de Beaurepaire vault a bit of a clean up, in honour of Alain and the boys.

I had a very strange sensation as I rode the bike down the hill out of Saint Fé.

I was a physical person sitting on a bicycle saddle with my feet on the pedals.

But I was another person looking at this person pedalling along. This other person was just watching the legs going up and down, but had no opinion.

It, he, just watched.

I felt like I was both of these at once.

It almost got to the point where I couldn't work out how to make my feet push on the pedals when we got to the incline up the track, back to the château. I was too much into the one who watched and I had to will myself to be more in the physical body to keep the bike going.

Back here, I needed some time to digest all that. I was sweaty and hot so I dropped into the dam for a while and lay there cooling off.

I was lying in the water on my back, drifting, floating.

There was the physical pleasure of the hot sun on my skin with the cool water underneath, when I sensed her.

As naked as I was, she walked towards me from the Linden Tree, her hair long and loose, her feet bare.

As she came she looked right at me with that hint of a smile.

She came into the water and came right up to me.

Now I was aroused.

I felt she was really there.

I desired her intensely.

But unlike other times in my life when I was in that state, there was no physical consummation.

Instead, she simply walked into me.

She entered my body, hers melting into mine.

I was filled with an enormous rush of energy, more of an orgasm than I had ever experienced, but at the same time not like anything I had known as physical sex.

This wasn't that.

She had unleashed something in me that was much more powerful.

I could barely keep myself was passing out and running the risk of drowning in the dam.

I threw myself up onto the grass and lay there.

She was still there, but yet not still there.

I passed out.

I was brought back to wakefulness when a shadow passed in front of the sun and the change of light brought me back to alertness.

I was staring into a goat's face.

It was Glove.

She has become very friendly and sometimes comes up and rubs against my legs to get a head scratch like her Dad. Now she was standing over me looking into my face. I gave her a very fond head scratch and she gently butted me in the chest.

It was the perfect way to recover.

Since that encounter in the dam, I cannot get that sensation out of my system.

How can I describe what happened?

She became me, she melted into me.

Just as I am wrestling with the idea of having inhabited different bodies, now I have to add the sensation that she became part of this body. Not physically. I don't mean that. She was not a physical being. It was some other kind of body and she entered me, into some kind of other body that I have. I think it's a bit like the body I have when I am dreaming. That body does all sorts of things, like it could fly when I was a kid. My physical body lies asleep on the bed, but this other body goes off on adventures, has wet dreams, or gets terrified by monsters.

It's all part of the same old question: Who am I?

Or to put it another way, if I go in and out of different bodies, who is it that is the same Me that does the going in and coming out?

I really wish Adèle and I could have a conversation about all this.

Wherever she exists now, I am certain she knows a lot more than I do.

I really need the distraction of other things.

If I keep thinking too much about it, I will go nuts.

So I work.

I make myself work hard.

My body likes it. I am all muscle now, deeply tanned and as healthy as Mon Veau.

I am chopping wood like crazy which is insane in the middle of summer but I have to do something very physical.

Should I still exist in this body in winter I will not regret my efforts.

I take care of the little cemetery on the property and the safe house. I visit them both every day.

I fix things, as best I can, having very little skill with what the French call bricolage , handyman skills.

Anything to keep me busy and out of my mind.

I have been puzzling over the two cemeteries.

If there is the big family vault in Saint Fé, why are there a few graves, unvaulted at the bottom of the hill? Perhaps they were what happened to those pour souls who got massacred during the Revolution.

There is so much that has happened here that I cannot understand.

Do I need to?

Or do I just do my best to take care of whatever I can?

I went back to the other cemetery, in Saint Fé, this time with candles so I could read the plaques.

I took more tools to hack away the undergrowth round it.

If I am buried there, I should take care of it.

Nothing had changed in Saint Fé that I could tell, although the weeds were growing at a great rate.

I worked on the exterior of the Teague Dieulefait tomb for a while till I thought it looked pretty neat.

The door gave more easily this time and I went in and lit several candles so I could see very clearly. There were many plaques and I knew who some of them were. The fanciest plaque was for General Henri Dupont Dieulefait. It seemed the size and style of each plaque indicated how significant the person was in life.

It's a bit ludicrous really, they all shrivel up into skin and bones, no matter what they did.

One of the least signifcant plaques was my old friend Gervais.

He got that book done as the last gesture of his life.

He died in 1912.

I gave his plaque an extra polish to thank him for his historical contribution.

I paid special attention to Adèle's little plaque and passed a cloth over all of the Dieulefait Teagues. After all, some of them might have been me.

I looked for Jacques Gougnaud but he wasn't there. I had a feeling he wasn't a Dieulefait.

No doubt there are other corpses from my incarnations dotted all over the place, maybe even in other parts of this cemetery.

I cleaned up the inside, got the moss off the stone floor, and removed cobwebs and mouse poo from the corners of the ceiling.

As I closed the door on the now pristine family vault, I realised that I didn't learn anything new.

But that was OK.

I was paying my respects and taking care of my own.

I walked around to see if I could find any Gougnaud graves but I didn't see anything. Maybe I, as Jacques, came from somewhere else entirely. After all I, as me, came from the other side of the world.

I stood at the gate of the cemetery and felt like I should wave to all my acquaintances buried there.

It made me smile.

As I rode back I felt very happy about it.

I think I am getting used to the new world order.

The château family just got bigger.

Betty was looking like she was about to produce for a while and her milk had dried up. Old George had evidently done his husbandly duties.

Having been through the birth of Mon Veau I was now certain that I did not have to do anything to assist at the birth. They know how to do it, these mothers.

As it turned out, she gave birth at night in the shed that I had rearranged for the goats to stay in at night. There was always the danger that a fox could take one of the kids.

Anyway in the morning when I went to let them out, there in the hay was a tiny little brown goat. It was the cutest little thing I had ever seen.

I stroked Betty and congratulated her on her newborn.

Betty let me pick it up. I should say I picked her up. She wasn't much bigger than my fist and so delicate. As I looked at her, she made a tiny little bleat, just saying Hi . I decided to call her Adèle.

As the other goats all went out of the shed, I gave each one a good head scratch, especially George as I congratulated him on the newest member of his tribe.

Betty stayed in the shed. I guess she was convalescing and also waiting till Adèle was more steady on her tiny little legs.

I went off and made myself some breakfast, and just as I was cleaning up, I saw Betty emerge with a tottering Adèle behind her.

I spent most of the morning hanging out with them and watching how Adèle got stronger and stronger. Obviously the milk was now flowing and she helped herself often, with the same headbutt motion that Mon Veau used on his mother.

He doesn't get that anymore. If he tries it now, she turns on him. I suspect she is not far off having her next one.

As I had suspected, she went off to find herself a friendly bull. I don't think it is all that soon but she does seem a bit more round in the belly.

Adèle loves me.

She totters over to me and I can fondle her as much as I like. Betty totally approves. The other two kids, Billy and Glove like to join in. They seem mostly uninterested in their new sister but they play along with me.

They are excluded from the milk supply however. If they try, they are butted away.

That's reserved for Adèle.

As the baking hot weather goes on, the dam begins to dry up.

I will have no water soon. The little creek down by the safe house is a trickle and likely to disappear very soon. I wonder where the tiny fish go when that happens.

The same with the spring in the cemetery, not a drop.

The little stream bed is rock hard.

I have to be very abstemious in my usage of water now.

The mint tea and a few sips of water during the day, little dips in the now quite muddy dam is all I allow myself. I come out not much cleaner than when I went in.

The animals all drink from the dam and Ma Vache and Mon Veau drink a lot!

The milk still flows, so that's good.

If I was a praying person, I would say that my prayers were answered.

It's raining buckets.

I can't say I literally prayed for rain, but I was hoping.

I woke up to the sound of incredible thunder and brilliant lightning flashes, then I could smell the rain coming. The land is so parched that I could almost feel it calling out : Over here! Over here!

Then when it came, it was torrential.

I ran upstairs and let myself be drenched standing in the turret. It was so delicious. I got some soap and had a rain shower in a rain shower.

I have never been so grateful for rain in my life.

In the morning, the rain was tailing off but there were great rivulets of water running into the dam off the gutters of the château. Whoever designed the dam used the topography of the land to create channels that catch the water that would have missed the dam on either side. Now they were pouring water into the dam like taps.

When I went down to the safe house memorial there was water running everywhere. The creek was filling from little springs feeding into it along the banks.

It was the same when I went down the track to the cemetery. The spring that Adèle had bathed in was running again, making little gurgling noises as it ran.

I marvelled at how one day everything seemed so parched and life threatening, and the next I was bathing in sweet benevolence.

It just goes to show that I should take every day as it comes and accept that whatever is to come next will come and there's not too much I can do about it.

The day after it rained, there was a small miracle in terms of greenness.

New shoots of grass appeared in the brown fields, limp plants stood erect and proud of themselves, and happy weeds seemed to grow almost as I watched them.

The combination of heat and wetness spurred everything.

For the first time in my life I am really aware of nature and the extraordinary way it works. Everything in it has a relationship to everything else. The only example I can think of that does not conform to that is the human creature.

Me.

Everything else seems to know what to do, who or what to eat, how to reproduce and how to protect yourself.

I am not very confident about any of that.

Then again if I am God, as I have been led to believe, then I constructed all this.

I did a great job of symbiosis with almost everything except myself.

Why did I do that?

Why did I design humans to be so out of sync with everything around them?

Well maybe, going back to obscure Indian texts, I did it to fool myself into forgetting who did all this.

It seems to have worked perfectly.

I was fooled.

Frankly, thinking of myself as God, the creator of all this, is not helping.

I don't feel like God, whatever that means.

What does God feel like?

Does God feel?

What kind of feeling would I have to feel like I was God?

It's all very well for Adèle, from the other side, or wherever she hangs out, to tell me, because I am a Dieulefait in Teague disguise, that I am God.

Even if I believe her, it's just a leap of faith.

In reality, my reality, it doesn't change anything. I am still stuck in the sense of being a limited human being, identified by my male-ness, my Australian-ness and my alone-ness.

I am Simon Teague sitting on a hill.

Maybe one day I will suddenly wake up to my Godliness and say to myself: Oh I see it now. Yes indeed, I am God .

It hasn't happened yet.

I suppose it must be August by now.

The days are hot again, but now we have a more or less full dam.

I am enjoying it.

I work hard, get up a good sweat, then spend hours in the water. Now and then the goats will venture in. They seem to like the water. The two older ones are full size now, but they still play like kids. Little Adèle is adorable and loves to follow me around. Mon Veau has given that up. He's a big boy now and keeps more to himself, although he still likes a good head rub now and then.

I think he is going to be a gentle bull and I have no fear of him.

This time last year, in August, we went to Lourdes.

The fifteenth of August is the day the Virgin Mary went off to heaven. According to legend she was collected by a squad of angels and ascended, so they call the day Assumption and it's a big French day off. Un jour fériée.

Lourdes is one of the places in France that is revered as a holy site. It's a bit like a miniature Disneyland for devout Christians, Catholics anyway.

Chloé wanted her boys to see it and maybe get a sense of some kind of belief in God. She had no religion herself much, other than her worship of money, but she considered herself a spiritual person.

She was certainly eclectic in that regard.

She had an endless list of spiritual visitors, like the shaman or the fortune teller, and she would consult all sorts of spiritual references. In general, it all served her rather well, at least in purely material terms, but she never really settled on one of them as her main spiritual path.

She always thought of me as Buddhist and said I was lucky to have found my path.

Secretly I had no notion of having found any path to follow, but I let her enjoy that fantasy.

She took us all off to Lourdes on a pilgrimage.

We piled into the family Mercedes SUV, Chloé, the two boys, Clo and me. Alain had no interest in that at all. As far as he was concerned matters of the spirit were to be found in Armagnac bottles.

Chloé had booked a splendidly provisioned, big stone house high on a hill overlooking the town of Lourdes and with towering snowy peaks above it on all sides.

The town itself is jammed into a narrow deep valley following the winding river Gave de Pau that tumbles out of the Pyrenees high above with its rushing iceblue water.

In the middle of the town is a small medieval château that has been attacked on and off like so many in France down through the ages. It's about the same size as this château, sitting on a rocky promontory with steep steps leading up to it. However, it's not the château that draws the pilgrims.

In 1858 a shepherdess call Bernadette Soubirous, who was an illiterate fourteen-year old, had visions of a woman wearing blue and white in a cave, what the French call a grotte, on the banks of the river. She believed that she was having visions of the Virgin Mary. This went on for a few months during which the woman in the vision instructed her to dig a hole in the grotte and water would appear, which she did. It took quite a while before the religious authorities of the day believed her, but eventually they accepted that there was something to this. Once Emperor Napoleon the Third had one of his sons miraculously cured, supposedly, by the holy water, Lourdes was assured of a future as a spiritual resort.

Today that spring is considered the holiest site in France, and the water is considered to have miraculous healing properties.

There is a vast ornate basilica sitting on the rock above the cave, and nearby there is a vast underground church which looks like an underground parking lot and is surely the ugliest church in the world

Back then, while we explored the town and the sites, I read all about it, saw the short movie that they show in the town, stood in line to get a close up of the grotte, took a bath with a crowd of naked Christian men of all shapes and sizes (not to mention hygiene habits!) and dutifuly drank the holy water. I didn't get any significant experience out of any of it, but I was fascinated by how devotional everyone seemed to be. There were nuns and priests in black kneeling in the baking sun, sweating and praying with incredible fervour. There were hordes of pilgrims from all over the world. Why so many Indians come to Lourdes is something of a mystery. I always thought India had almost a monopoly on saints and miracles, so why were they coming here? The raucous Italians I can understand why they are here, although their apparent lack of decorum is something to witness. They are the loudest and rudest pilgrims you could ever imagine.

The town itself is a maze of narrow streets winding up a steep hillside where every second shop sells replicas of the Virgin Mary as statuettes, candles, coffee mugs and plastic drinking bottles, where her head is the top of the bottle. All the other shops are for coffee or pizza.

You can't buy regular groceries. For that you have to go down the valley to a supermarket.

What is weird for me now, as I recall where I was a year ago, is that here, in the Lot on a hill in a thirteenth century château in the year 2020, I am having something of the same experience.

Not the statuettes or the pizza, but at the core of it all, back when a lonely simple girl met the Mother of God in a cave, I am seeing things like her. Visions. Water runs spontaneously out of the ground and I am being told I am God.

I have a newfound admiration for that girl, Bernadette, who stuck to her story, against the odds and eventually became a saint. It must have taken some strong self-belief to withstand the heavyweight doubters in the established church who cruelly attacked her.

In French the word lourdes means heavy. I am not sure I understand the connection.

Maybe it is the heavy burden of trying to convince the authorities that you are telling the truth. She got there in the end.

Once she was officially credited with saving the life of Napoleon the Third's child then she got to be a saint and is worshipped to this day.

The French do make a habit of treating their future saints cruelly until they change their minds.

Look at Joan of Arc.

First they burnt her then they loved her.

Now she is the patron saint of the country.

Down through the ages, in the annals of Christianity, there have been encounters like Saint Bernadette.

Probably more than we know about.

I suspect some of the smarter witnesses of such events decided to keep it to themselves.

I won't have that problem.

There is no-one to doubt what I am seeing, except me.

Is this a holy site now?

I don't really know what constitutes a holy site.

The nearest I came to feeling I was in one was the Monastery in Chiang Rai. It felt holy.

Maybe now, if I went back to Lourdes, I would have an entirely different experience.

It doesn't look likely to happen.

Anyway, if today, or around now is the fifteenth of August, then salutations to the lady in Blue and White who ascended to heaven with her angel escorts.

Maybe Adèle sees her from time to time.

Maybe they catch up over heavenly coffee and compare notes on how their protèges are going.

I think Adèle has an easier task than the Virgin Mary who is on a par with Jesus in the popularity stakes.

Adèle just has one, at least that I know of.

Simon of the tribe Teague.

I got inspired, by thinking about Lourdes, to go back to the church in Saint Fé.

I vaguely remembered seeing a small statue in the church of what I think might be the Virgin Mary.

There were a few rather battered saint statues and I think one of them was a woman in blue and white.

Something had drawn me to the church last time but I had never worked out what it was.

Maybe it had something to do with the Virgin Mary.

There was only one way to find out.

I started early because it was going to be another hot August day.

I took a backpack of tools and cleaning stuff. The family vault might need a bit of maintenance and maybe the church itself could do with a little bit of sprucing.

As always, as I pedalled along, nothing moved on the road, except a scuttling squirrel shocked to find someone else on her private road.

She paused for a second in disbelief before shooting up an oak.

I went to the cemetery first. The heat had inhibited the enthusiastic growth of the weeds and there was not too much cleaning up to do.

I polished all the plaques and said bonjour to each of my ancestors as I did.

It was deeply peaceful in the vault and I felt strangely honourable taking care of it.

Doing my duty to the family.

I ignored the de Beaurepaires this time.

Then I went into the church.

Nothing had changed.

There was a statue of the Lady in Blue and White.

She had her own little altar off to one side, made of stone. She was about a foot high and had a very benign expression on her face. A small brass plate underneath let me know who she was : Notre Dame de Compassion .

I gave her a good clean, including getting rid of her veil of cobwebs. Outside I found a tap that still worked and I gently washed her. She had some cracks and chips but in general she was in reasonable shape.

When I had finished, I told her that I had been thinking about her and that I thought I knew more clearly who she was, than I did this time last year.

Now that I was the only person left in the world, I had no worries about talking to a statue.

I wished her a happy Assumption.

I brought over a chair and sat in front of her for a while and I felt myself dropping into meditation without any resistance.

I felt that I was being gently wafted around in the air inside the church.

I was floating and the walls of the church were made of fabric and they billowed in the breeze.

It was very calm and still, even as I floated about.

And then at some point, even though I had my eyes closed, I could see her statue begin to move. She grew larger and life infused her form. Her blue and white robes gently moved in the breeze and she turned her eyes to look at me.

There was just the hint of a smile and the slightest nod of her head.

Then everything went very still inside and I sank deep inside myself to where there was no sense of being at all.

How long I stayed like that I don't know, but when eventually I came back, I had moved out of the chair and was kneeling with my head on the floor in front of her statue.

I had no sense of having moved at all but I felt incredibly good.

Finally I staggered to my feet and put my hands together as we used to do in the Monastery in Thailand.

I thanked her for a great meditation.

She certainly was our lady of compassion.

Now she was a statue again, inert but uncobwebbed.

While I was there I did a quick clean of the other statues.

Saint John of the Cross had a big chip off his face, leaving him with almost no nose and half a jaw. He looked like he had leprosy but I cleaned him up as best I could.

I had to wonder why no-one did anything about it. He's probably been like that for years. I can imagine there must have been little old ladies, locals, who came into the church now and then, did a little genuflect and prayed for salvation, before scrubbing the saints.

You would think they couldn't stand to have their saint defaced.

Maybe they just got used to him like that.

Saint Thomas was in better shape and only had cracked feet. His face was intact, but he needed a good podiatrist.

I did my best.

Before I left, I stood in the middle of the church and told them that I was happy to see them and asked them to take care of Saint Fé.

I promised I'd be back.

Riding the bike back, once again, I was feeling very light-headed.

Journeys to Saint Fé were turning out to be rather pleasant.

I suspect I will be coming back as a regular pilgrim.

My little world had just got a fraction bigger.

Now sitting up here in the cool of the evening, I am indulging in the pleasure of my newly expanded community.

I have been gifted with some new saintly friends.

I am beginning to treasure an inner world that I can inhabit with more and more ease.

It must have always been there, but I never took the time to acknowledge it.

Maybe I just didn't notice.

Perhaps when I was very little I had that world. I know kids do have it. They can play with imaginary friends, or have conversations with their dolls and all that. I suppose the modern world kicks in at some point and says: Stop that fantasy stuff, get real.

Maybe the modern world was wrong all along, but we weren't strong enough to hold on.

Perhaps I am getting it back.

I wondered why Adèle did not appear when I was in the church, but I guess she comes when she comes.

I certainly have no control over that.

Then again our meetings lately have not exactly been the sort of thing you associate with churches.

I will let her choose when and where she appears, and what she wears.

I have decided to harvest lots of bulbs for next year. Does that mean I expect to be here next year?

Who knows.

Around some of the ruins of other houses and buildings there were tulips, daffodils, hyacinths, irises and narcissus. I have dug their bulbs up and I will plant them in the area around the safe house and the cemetery.

If I am still here, then I will enjoy their spring presentation.

If I am not, then they can all come up in their own good time just to be whatever they are.

While I am busy planting I think about that. Does it matter whether I am here or not? Not really.

I am happy to be planting bulbs just for the pleasure of planting bulbs.

Nightmare!

Hot humid night and restless sleep, suddenly Adèle is there but scary as hell.

She is riding a huge wolf, whose eyes match hers, red glowing coals. She is wearing animal skins and carrying some kind of spear.

She is yelling at me in French:

Dépêche-toi! Hurry up!

Travail!Work!

Lutte! Fight!

I wake up bathed in sweat and terrified.

What the hell was all that about?

Work on what?

Fight? Who with?

I can make no sense out of it but it has shaken me horribly.

It feels like some kind of omen, something is coming and I have to be ready.

I spent the rest of the day nervously looking over my shoulder.

The answer came as the sun was setting.

I was upstairs enjoying the pale pink changes in the low clouds when I heard screaming, horrible screaming.

I looked down.

There were three big dogs attacking Billy.

I flew down the stairs and grabbed the gun from the cupboard.

I had no idea if it had bullets in it, but I ran outside yelling.

They were hunting dogs. I don't know what the breed is called but I have seen them in the dog-trailers of the registered hunters. I suppose now they just roam free and eat what they can catch.

As I ran towards them, I pointed the gun and pulled the trigger.

Nothing happened. Obviously it was empty. I cursed myself for not thinking to have it ready. I had seen dogs before and I knew it could happen.

When they heard me and saw me coming, they backed away. I pointed the gun anyway and they obviously knew what it was. They bunched together and bared their teeth, growling.

I walked towards them slowly, still pointing the gun.

I was yelling at them in as strong a voice as I could manage : *Allez-vous en*! Go away!

I got to Billy, who was bleating piteously and bleeding from a big wound in his neck.

Deep inside myself I was a bit terrified. If those dogs decided to try my bluff I would be mince meat. They were big strong creatures with teeth.

There was a tense moment when we all held our ground.

And then my saviour came.

Out of nowhere, George came charging towards the dogs with his head down.

As they sensed him coming, they leaped back and turned to face him.

He ran headlong into them with his big horns catching one of them in the belly and lifting it off the ground. Then somehow he managed to throw it off and turned on the other two. They took off and the one he had hit dragged itself away after them. I think he had really done some damage to it.

I stood frozen as all this happened and it was only when the dogs retreated that I found myself able to breathe. I realised that my hands were shaking. I doubt that my aim would have been much good, even if the gun had been loaded.

The dogs stopped by a clump of trees and watched us from a safe distance.The injured dog was licking its wounds. I took a few steps towards them and raised the gun and they turned and were gone, the injured one obviously badly wounded.

I crouched down next to poor little Billy, and George came over and sniffed at him. Billy was lying still and making little mewling noises. I put my hand up to his neck and blood flowed across my fingers.

Billy was in bad shape.

I picked him up and carried him towards the château.

As I walked, the other goats all came. George had stayed close but now the three females all came too. I suspect they must have run away when the dogs attacked.

When I took him into the kitchen, they all came in. They have come inside now and then which I didn't mind. They never pooed indoors which I was happy about. Now they were the patient's family, so I let them come.

I put him on the kitchen table and tried to patch up his wound. Glove jumped onto a chair to watch. I am not great with blood at the best of times, so this was a bit stomach churning, but I managed.

Once I had laid him on the table he stopped making any sound and just looked at me with his soft goaty eyes. I used a tea towel, as I tried to put a bandage round the wound. He looked like he was wearing a cravat..

I filled a box with hay and lay him there. He seemed to be a bit calmer and he lay still. The others hung about for a while, coming over to the box and making little soothing noises.

It was a very moving sound.

Finally I herded them out and locked them into their shed. I made sure that Ma Vache and Mon Veau were safe too. The hens and Boris had already retired so they were safe.

I found the bullets for the gun and worked out how to put them in. Then I went outside to make sure it worked. I put an empty can on a fence post, although it was pretty dark by then. I pulled the trigger. The gun bashed into my shoulder so that I nearly dropped it and the can stayed right where it was.

At least it made a good noise.

Now the gun stays loaded on top of the not-working fridge in case of emergencies.

I suppose I should teach myself how to use it, so that next time it is needed it is a useful weapon.

I said goodnight to little Billy and hoped that he would be better in the morning. He was pathetically weak, but he seemed to be aware of me when I stroked him. He gave the tiniest of little bleats as if he was saying thank you, as best he could.

He didn't make it.

Sometime in the night, Billy quietly left his little goat body behind.

I wonder if goats have after-lives.

Do they come back as other goats?

He could become a goat ghost and hang out with Adèle.

I had to decide what to do with his body.

Realistically, I ought to eat him. I do need the protein and I am sure his little body would be quite edible.

The problem would be my emotional reservations and my lack of butchering skills.

I thought long and hard about it, but I couldn't do it.

I buried him under the Linden tree.

We had a little funeral, me and the goats.

They watched me carry his body out and they came along.

I dug a grave and then wrapped him in a sheet and laid him in the hole.

I chanted my Buddhist hymn and then gently covered him up.

I planted a circle of bulbs round his grave so that next year he would have quite a nice floral display.

I found a wide piece of wood, maybe cedar, and carved his name into it, then nailed it to the Linden tree.

So now that tree has various significances.

Was that dog attack connected to the nightmare, or was it just coincidence?

How come dogs didn't attack us all this time, until I had the visitation from Adèle the warrior queen?

All this mystical stuff is so hard to get a handle on.

Trying to analyse it seems fruitless.

I suppose I will just have to see if there is something else I have to fight.

If there isn't, well, that was that.

But still there are endless questions.

Why was Adèle dressed like some prehistoric heroine warrior?

Was she appearing as a really old incarnation? If it was, then maybe we go back even further than I thought.

Why was she mounted on a gigantic wolf?

What do their red eyes mean?

Or is it all just symbolism?

Of course the other question is : Are dreams real?

They seem to be, at least while we are in them.

Then again, when you think about it, our everyday life seems real till we drop off to sleep and then it doesn't exist.

So what's real, the world we dream in or the world we live in?

I tried a few meditation invitations, trying to invoke Adèle's presence, but she was not having it.

I don't think she likes being summoned.

Clo was a bit like that, she needed to be in control.

Anyway, Billy was dead and buried and life went on.

Every time I passed the tree, I thought of him.

I tried a few more practice shots with the gun but my ability to hit the can did not improve. Instead my shoulder got sorer and sorer. There is probably a correct way you are supposed to hold a gun when you pull the trigger but I don't know what that is.

I swear I will only use it if it is really, really necessary.

It feels good to know that it's there, loaded and in a place where I can grab it in a hurry.

We must be close to the end of August by now and it is harvest time.

I am picking fruit and veggies like crazy and trying to decide what to do with them all. I have no fridge or freezer, so I have to think of ways to preserve them. For jam you need sugar and I don't have much. Anyway, I have dozens of bottles of jam thanks to Eveline.

What will I do with all these tomatoes? The best I can think of is to keep them in airtight jars in the cellar and hope they don't ferment and explode. It seems to be such a waste to have received such bounty and have no-one to give it to. I could feed a small refugee camp for weeks with what is coming.

And the goats don't seem all that interested in tomatoes.

As a break from endless harvesting food that is probably going to waste, I built myself a swing.

The lowest branch of the Linden tree was calling me. It is solid and thick. I got some chain lengths from Jean-Claude's shed and with bolts and screws, teetering on his highest ladder, I attached them to the branch then dropped them down and looped them round an old tyre of which he had dozens.

Now when the fancy takes me I can swing back and forth like a kid.

The thing about this little project is it was such fun to do.

No-one critiqued my skills and I made myself a swing.

When I was digging out the materials for the swing, I came across a small cart that was lying behind one of Jean-Claude's sheds. I can't imagine what he used it for, maybe just a kind of hand cart. It is about a metre square and has wooden sides. What drew me to it was that it had tyres. When I used the bike pump, they filled and held. It has two short shafts at the front, kind of like a big homemade wheelbarrow.

When I found out that the tyres were good, I fantasised about having a bullock cart, with Mon Veau between the shafts.

The shafts were too short for Mon Veau so I added a longer shaft to each one. My craftmanship was horribly amateur, but I used lots and lots of wire and ties and some round bolts with nuts.

It was a cartwright's nightmare, but I hoped it would all hold together.

Then to keep my beast of burden between the shafts and enable him to pull, I found leather harnesses in Jean-Claude's shed, maybe from back when he had horses. I worked out a way to have a kind of breastplate of leather for his chest and a strap to go over his back to keep the shafts in the right position.

Now the most interesting part of the project was to see whether Mon Veau would pull it.

He loves carrots so I got a bag full of sweet young ones as bribes. He stands easily with me, specially when he gets his head rubs, so it's no problem to hold him. I put a halter round his neck and tied him to a post. He didn't like it much but every time he complained he got another carrot. Then I manoeuvered the cart up behind him and ran the two shafts up on either side. He watched all this warily. Then I attached the shafts using the harness pieces to go across his chest and over his back. Now he was inside the shafts and held there by the harness. He shook them and he was not happy about it, but more carrots kept him tolerating what I was up to.

Then I untied him and led him round the field, pulling the cart and offering a carrot every now and them. It wasn't heavy and he pulled it with ease but he didn't like the noisy thing that rattled behind him and he kept turning his head to look at it. As we walked, I continued talking to him and offering another carrot now and then, holding his halter with one hand. We did a couple of turns and then I stopped him, undid the harness and let him out. He walked away and then turned to look at me.

I had no more carrots. He did a little jump in the air and ran round the field to show his independence.

Then he came back just in case I had another carrot.

I gave him one last loving head rub and thanked him for being such a good boy and left him to himself.

The next day we did it again, more carrots on hand and we went further. He seemed to accept what I wanted and as long as he got a carrot every now and then, he was good. I always had to walk beside his head to get him to move, but other than that we were getting there.

Within a week, doing a practice every morning, he had got the hang of it and was doing long walks with no need of carrots all the time.

I don't really know why I was doing it, but it was a wonderful exercise in working out how to do something for which I had no training.

If I ever needed to have something carried a long way, then he would be my truck.

I am beginning to wonder, if I am going to be here more or less forever, why don't I see what the houses in Saint Fé have in them?

Why don't I break into the modern house on the far hill or the old farm house where Ma Vache came from?

Up to now I have felt that it would be inappropriate somehow, wrong, sinful.

But if I am the only human left, then it's all mine anyway.

I am looking for adventure, I have to admit.

Day in and day out doing all the same things, all of which I like, is all very well.

I have to come up with new projects to keep myself happy.

So I went.

The one house that I haven't yet visited is the farm where Ma Vache came from. It's not that far, a bit more than a kilometre. I decided that I would take Mon Veau and the cart.

I might find good stuff to bring back.

Once I had him in the cart, which carried a good bag of carrots, I walked him off down the hill. The only problem with that was that I had no brakes. Even though the cart is not heavy, I pulled it up from Jean Claude's house myself, still it tended to push Mon Veau down the hill and the unexpected weight of it prompted him to run. I had to run too, to keep up. I tried to stay calm as I talked to him but he wasn't having it. Luckily with me pulling on the halter in desperation he slowed and by the time we reached the bottom of the hill, the cart was still upright, I was out of breath, but we were all intact.

We paused for carrot refreshment and then headed across the road to the other side. The track to the old farm wound up a hill and like so many of the properties in this area the house was built to have a view over its own fields.

Just before I reached the house I came across the mail box.

They were Dieulefaits.

So here I was, not trespassing but visiting my own folks. At least it gave me a little relief from my secret guilt.

I was happy to know who they were.

Maybe they were descendants of Gervais. Maybe this is where Adèle lived. I was certain she would have set foot here often enough, even if this wasn't her immediate family.

It was quite similar to Jean-Claude's house, made of stone with rounded terracotta tiles on the roof. The front verandah was dominated by a very old and far-reaching wisteria, almost completely obscuring the front of the house. When it had been looked after, the garden must have been quite pretty, but now it was a jungle of weeds and overgrown creepers and vines.

I tied Mon Veau to a fence post with the cart still attached. I told him this is where his mother had come from and gave him a few carrots. I hoped he would stay put, then I went exploring.

I walked all round the house, before thinking about trying to get in.

Like every other farm, there were multiple sheds full of all the things you would expect. Plenty of useful things, like tools and equipment, but mostly duplicates of what Jean-Claude left me. There was one old tractor but no other vehicles.

There were no animals or poultry. They had really evacuated everything. I wondered how they had missed Ma Vache.

I checked back with Mon Veau and he had decided to sit down. The shafts of the cart let him do that, which was good, because otherwise he would have tipped it over.

Then I faced the house, knowing that if it was like the others I was going to find dead farmers.

Before I tried the front door, I paused and said to the spirit of Adèle: I hope you don't mind me poking about.

I waited to see if there was any kind of signal, but the wind blew gently and the scent of honeysuckle wafted in the air.

I decided she had no objection.

The front door, which was solid oak, didn't move and did not invite any attempt to force it.

I went round to the back and there were several doors of lesser thickness, none of them unlocked. This made me think that perhaps this house was unoccupied by the corpses of its inhabitants, unless, I suppose, they locked the door first. Both Jean-Claude and the Dupuys had not locked their doors.

I was about to attack one of the doors when I felt I was being watched. I looked around and at first saw nothing, but then looking up into an elm tree I saw what it was. A huge and well-fed orange cat was regarding me with big amber unblinking eyes, as if to say, who are you and why are you encroaching on my territory? I went over to it and reached up to see if it was interested in human contact, but it continued to stare and made no move, so I left it.

One of the doors had small square glass panels and so it was easy to break one with a stone and carefully reach in to the bolt. I did cut myself a bit and left bloody evidence of my break-in for forensic detectives in the far future to work out who the culprit was.

I started wandering around in the house when I heard Mon Veau yelling. I went back out to see what he was up to.

He had tried to stand up again, pulled the hitch away from the fence post and had tipped the cart over and was stuck with it dragging it round the overgrown garden on its side. He was really annoyed.

I caught him and uncoupled the cart, gave him a carrot and I think he forgave me. I stood with him for a while rubbing his head. He's just a big baby really.

Then I let him unhitched him and let him wander. I just hoped when I had finished exploring that he would not have gone off too far. I took the carrots back into the house so he wouldn't find them and destroy my bribe cache.

I went back to exploring. The house was quite dark as they had closed their wooden shutters. I opened the windows and then the shutters to let the light in. It was pretty clear that they had evacuated. Apart from how neat everything was, they had left the evacuation letter on the kitchen table.

Monsieur et Madame François Dieulefait.

They had packed things up, emptied their fridge and taken a lot of stuff from their food storage.

The best thing I found though was a family photo in an ornate polished wood frame, with lots of them in it, including Adèle. It was quite a large sepia photo taken, I am pretty sure out the front of this house, when the wisteria was much less wild and the garden much neater. It must have been taken around the same time as the photo I first found, because Adèle looked much the same.

She was standing in the back row with some other girls who looked about her age. I looked carefully but I did not see Jacques in the photo. I suppose it was just family.

I dug around in the house looking for other photos of her but, although there were lots of photos, there was no other with her in it, unless she was one of the young children in some photos and I couldn't recognise her, but I don't think so.

I did find another copy of Gervais's book on a bookshelf along with a few history books that I decided to keep.

I wandered into different bedrooms but there was nothing I wanted to take other than that. There were a few tins of tuna that would make a nice change.

I carried the big photo and the books outside and found a box to put them in. I would be back to take more stuff from the sheds when I felt like it, but by now I was done.

I had made my little adventure and I felt really ready to go home.

I apologised to the cat, who had not moved, for my intrusion and went looking for my beast of burden.

Mon Veau had been good and not wandered far. The garden was full of things that he liked so he was happy. I let him graze for a while as I sat on a wooden garden bench that was rapidly being taken over by a clematis vine, and looked at the house. I could imagine the life of the family over the years, maybe there was just an old couple left as the young generation went off to careers in the city.

I didn't feel sad, so much as I needed to sit there and acknowledge that I had been there and seen another part of my self.

Then I turned the cart back up, caught up the halter trailing from Mon Veau's neck and reconnected my transport. He wasn't so keen and the carrots were losing their allure, but I got him hooked up after a few tantrum moves. I put the box of little treasures in the cart and we headed off. This time I made sure the weight of the cart did not send Mon Veau charging down the hill, by holding him tightly. We made it safely to the bottom of the Dieulefait's track.

Before we started up the other side, I tried an experiment. I hopped into the cart and yelled, gently, at Mon Veau. He turned his head and looked at me and didn't move. But then he decided that if I needed a ride then he could manage, and he towed me up the track back to the château.

I gave him a very loving head rub when I uncoupled him and told him he was a very good boy.

He headed for the dam for a long drink.

I hung the big family photo on the wall in the meditation room, and that afternoon dedicated my meditation to that family, wherever they might be.

I felt happy about the whole thing.

I didn't have to burn down another house and cremate more dead people, I had another photo of Adèle and I had enjoyed a little outing.

Life is good.

Is it September?

It could be.

The weather is still blazing hot, which is normal and I am just guessing.

Really for me now, who cares what month it is. I go with what God provides, or whatever I provide and if I am to believe Adèle, we are one and the same.

We can call the month whatever we like.

And anyway months are lunar cycles. If I chose to follow the moon then I would say it's new moon plus however many days.

I like looking at the moon but I don't do any calculations about where we are in the lunar cycle.

I'm sure if Chloé's astrologer were here, he would tell me why everything is happening according to what's in the sky, but I don't have a clue.

We went back, Mon Veau and I, to the Dieulefait house one more time and came home with a load of useful stuff from the sheds. The cat was not to be seen, maybe hearing us rattling up the track it hid away.

I filled the cart with materials and tools, so it was quite heavy. I walked alongside. He is getting used to the cart now and doesn't need much bribing at all. He even braced against the weight as we headed down the track and he pulled mightily on the way up our track.

I have discovered that I am turning into an animal trainer.

Did I train him, or did he just work out what I wanted?

Often when I sit for meditation, the notion firmly planted in my brain about being God comes up.

Most of the time, it is just too impossible to contemplate directly, so I tend to just let it be there, but sometimes I get into it and try to find that Godness in myself.

If, like some of the Indian saints that I have read about claim, God exists in all things at all times, including us, then God is, in fact, present in me.

The point that some of them make, at least in the few books that I have explored, is that God isn't hidden inside us, but is fully manifest.

If you know how to look, there is God.

Look in the mirror and you will see God.

I have tried that, but the mind can't stand the notion, raising endless intellectual skepticisms. And even more difficult is the inner critic who quickly shuts off any possible revelations.

What is easier for me is to see that everything here is God made.

I like that notion. I can accept, even with all my flaws, that God made me and he made me out of himself.

So from that perspective I can say it.

If God made me out of himself then that is what I am made of.

I am Dieu (God) le (the) fait (fact).

I found a very simple example of God's creative skills.

Look at all the different kinds of grass that God dreamed up.

I thought about this as I lay in the field on my back in the late afternoon sun with the goats and Mon Veau nibbling juicy varieties all round me. Some grasses grow seeds and drop them right there and they propagate. Other grasses run long roots underground and pop up in new places. Some grasses make little light fluffy balloons with seeds in them that the wind carries to new spots. Some grasses the goats and the cows really like, and they eat them and excrete the seeds in ready-made fertiliser wherever they walk.

God was very grass smart.

You could say the same for how he made humans of course, no two the same. He puts musical genius in some of us and homicidal pathology in others. He plants some humans in what are often called God forsaken places which, of course, they are not because he made them. He puts others in gilded mansions where people appear to indulge in godless lives of exploitation and sense pleasures.

God must have a wacky sense of humour to have come up with so many oddball variations.

I remind myself that God made the Germans who blew up the safe house and tortured Adèle.

God made the men who wrote the farewell letters hidden in the tin.

He made the Maquis and he made the Milice.

To be so detached from his creation must be one of the qualities of God, if in fact God has qualities.

I can recall how when some disaster happens somewhere in the world the journalists interviewing survivors report them saying : How could God do this to us?

I can't recall anyone saying, Well, God did this and that's just the way it is , except maybe in Arabic when they say : Inche Allah God willing.

I never heard any Methodists come out with anything like that. I think in general the Methodists just let God get on with it and they try to behave well, whatever happens. At least I can say that about the Methodists that I grew up around.

All this thinking about God does make me yearn for Adèle to teach me what she knows.

Who is she, other than the different disguises she has shown me?

Is she something greater than that, just taking on the forms of different women to keep me intrigued?

Does she think I am not ready to see her true form?

Is she some kind of angel?

Is she God?

Days of fruitless meditation ensue when I try very hard to get her to pay a visit.

She is not to be commanded.

By now I should know that meditation is what it is and I have not much control over that.

Especially her.

Now for the first time there is cooler wind, coming from the north.

We are definitely into September. The days are getting shorter.

It is full on harvest time and the pumpkins, potimarrons, potirons, melons and all those other members of that family are producing prodigiously. The goats really like the melons, both the watermelons and the yellow ones. I am happy to share them because they won't keep. Every now and then I will throw a big watermelon out into the field where it shatters and the goats are delighted.

The plums are ready to pick and the apples and the pears are really close. In a few weeks I will have two different kinds of figs, the purple ones and the green ones. Lots of fruit salad coming up.

What a pity I have no-one to cook for, no-one to share with.

I don't know what to do about the grapes. I have no idea how wine is made and a lot of the grapes are quite sour. I think wine grapes are meant to be sour. Sadly the edible ones all seem to come from Italy. Anyway, with all this very sweet fruit in abundance I can do without Italian table grapes.

Not only are the château fruit trees producing but so are the trees around Jean-Claude's house. He has pomegranates and kakis, those big orange coloured fruit that are very sweet. He has kiwi vines too and they are very ready to be eaten. It's a pity the vines smell so bad.

So there is fruit and fruit and more fruit.

What bounty!!

Accident.

Can't write.

I think it might be three weeks or more since I wrote those last two incredibly painful lines.

I am writing very very slowly because every word hurts.

I had decided to go back to Saint Fé.

It's too far to take the cart so I took the bike. My idea was that, now that so much time had passed, I was certain there was no danger in breaking into the houses, no virus and no danger of being caught at it.

I was just interested to see who lived there and what was there.

Kind of like going to a museum, except there are potential take-aways.

I never made it.

I got about half way and was coasting down a slight hill, when a deer, quite a big one, came flying out from behind a hedge and hit me full on. I crashed to the ground and put out my right hand to stop myself and it went snap.

The pain was instant and incredible. I knew I had done myself a serious injury. I don't know about the deer because it just scrambled to its feet and took off.

I sat there for a while, wondering what to do. I had smacked my face on the gravel at the edge of the road and had blood running down my face. It felt like someone had sandpapered that whole side of my head.

The hand however was the real worry. It was unusable. The slightest movement made me scream.

I couldn't ride the bike any more, you need two hands for that.

I was hit with a great wave of despair.

Then I think I passed out, because I woke up lying by the side of the road holding my hand against my chest. It was a hot day but I was shivering, going into shock.

I was very scared.

I imagined I could just lie here and be found as a rotting corpse, although I don't know who is left to do the finding.

Then from somewhere inside myself I found the will to stand up.

I had a face caked in dried blood and a completely useless right hand. However I did have two good legs still, so using only my left hand, I began to wheel the bike back to the château. I willed myself to put one foot in front of the other and keep going. It seemed like a marathon.

What I had cycled in a few quick minutes now took a pain-soaked eternity.

My left-handed technique got me as far as the bottom of the hill, where our track winds up to the château. But uphill was impossible. I just couldn't do it one-handed. On every attempt, the bike kept veering off to one side and I would be forced to drop it.

I was rapidly running out of energy.

Finally I left it there, lying near the cemetery. Maybe it would become another corpse, just an unburied rusting frame.

I began taking tottering steps to head home. Making it back up the hill was one of the hardest things I ever did. I was only half conscious, the pain was severe and I was shaking.

I have the indelible memory of looking at my feet with my eyes half closed, just begging them to take one more step, one more step.

When I finally made it, staggering towards the château, my breath was coming in gasps and I was in danger of passing out.

I was sure I had broken something and being right-handed, that was serious.

I found painkillers in the medicine cabinet. Every now and then I had cut myself or needed some other kind of first aid, so I knew what we had. Chloé is like all the Americans I have ever met, absolutely in need of having all sorts of medications on hand, they are fixated on health, petrified of germs and squirmy at the sight of blood.

I washed my wrist gently, and tried to reduce the scabby mess that the right side of my face had become. Although the pain was intense, I wrapped a couple of tea towels round my wrist with a wooden spoon inside to keep it still and then I crashed onto my bed and disappeared.

When I came to, it was morning and the pain was awful. I gently undid the tea towels and saw that the wrist had swollen up a lot. I couldn't move it without shooting pains that threatened to make me pass out again. I took more painkillers and made tea left handed which was a tough assignment. To make tea, I have to light the fire, get it hot enough to boil the water, then pour the water into the tea pot with the mint leaves. After all that effort, the tea tasted so good when I finally got there.

I had not put the animals away the night before but they had all survived and were none the worse for wear. I tried to milk Ma Vache and Betty but my left hand just didn't have the dexterity. I ended up with a teaspoon full of each. They were very sweet and patient about it. Their milk is heavenly to drink, especially still warm.

The lesions on my face were mostly superficial and all I could do was keep it clean and wait for nature to take its course.

I was not going to win any beauty contests until it healed. Even then I would be the beast in a Beauty and the Beast contest.

What followed were days of self pity and suffering, clumsy actions and fear. I avoided the mirror and lived on the painkillers.

I had to be disciplined to make sure I rationed them so I didn't run out. The prospect of pain without alleviation was not to be contemplated. I had to decide how much pain I could stand and how long I could stand it. I worked at waiting longer and longer before I succumbed to the numbing comfort of painlessness.

In terms of food, I avoided cooking and food preparation, except the tea, so I lived on fruit, although it meant that I had constant diarrhoea.

The body needs variety.

Life was miserable.

And diarrhoea when a right-handed person can't use his right hand is also unpleasantly clumsy.

I couldn't do all the things that helped to fill my day.

I took to reading to distract myself.

I found another history book about Quercy, what this region was called in medieval times. The most interesting part was about the Lords of Gourdon, the town where, until I lost my electric wheels, I went to the supermarket. Evidently they were supporters of the Cathars, which this book calls heretics. So even before this château was built, there were constant battles concerning faith. Some local lords went with the Catholics and got rewarded in the end by my old friend Simon de Montfort, but a lot of them were sympathetic to the heretics and refused to arrest them. When I read about Raimonde de Mazerac, one of the most famous female Cathar Perfects , I felt a strange sense of recognition. This got even stranger when I came across the name of the family that supported the Cathars, her kinsman was Guillaume Donadieu. So that was too close for comfort.

Or was I reading too much into all this?

I had a horrible suspicion that here was another window into the past that had some connection to the present.

Maybe it was the effect of the painkillers, but I found myself almost terrified that Adèle was about to appear as this Cathar

Perfect and tell me I was Guillaume. How many people have I been?

I put the book away and read some English Whodunnit books written by well meaning English ladies, to divert my mind.

I did need diversion.

I was in danger of falling into a deep well of self-pity that lurked in the corners of my mind.

This was a time to marshal my inner strength and detachment.

I was grateful that I had spent days, even in the heat of mid-summer, cutting wood, so that now I have a good supply for making the fire.

I couldn't garden.

I couldn't fix anything.

I spent hours on the swing tyre, rocking myself back and forth. The swing is very soothing, almost meditative. There is something mystical about the parabola of the swing. You go up to the apex, there is a fraction of a second of complete stillness before you change direction into the descent, where you gather speed, flash through the nadir and decelerate on the upswing before another split second at the apex of inertia. I found myself becoming more and more conscious of each of these stages. The absolute stillness at the top of the swing could be expanded if I concentrated on it. I could do the same when I focussed on the exact moment at the bottom of the swing.

I am sure physicists could explain the whole thing mathematically, but for me it was a mystical experience where I could stop time with my concentration, just for a microsecond.

As good as my experience of the swing had become, the first meditations, after the accident, in the chapel were hard work. If I had taken the painkiller early enough before I sat to meditate, then the pain was hidden but even then, while I sat and repeated the mantra and tried to go deep inside, it was hard not to be aware of the physical body's messages.

The oddest moment in meditation was an image of the deer coming at me, my intense fear as I watched it, more or less airborne but in slow motion and then seeing the deer's face become the face of Adèle. It was fleeting but it happened more than once, so there was no mistaking it.

I could not read the expression on her face but there was no mistaking who it was.

What it meant, I have no idea, but it didn't make me feel any better.

After a few days, the scabs began to fall away from my face and I felt the swelling of my wrist beginning to go down just a bit.

Very gingerly, I felt I could move my wrist just a little. That came as a moment of quiet joy.

At least I hadn't broken anything and with a bit of luck I could get my hand to work again.

So here I am, I am writing again.

It is not easy and what I just wrote has taken several days, doing a little at a time.

My wrist is by no means healed but I can use it with care.

I keep it bound and when I unbandage it I do gentle wrist exercises getting it slowly and painfully back into shape.

It is going to heal, I am sure.

Hopefully I have only torn tendons or muscles or something, and I am pretty certain that I didn't break any bones.

Thank God.

I thank God, whoever I decide that is, that I didn't do something more serious, like break a leg. It would have been the end of me.

I would be lying on the ground by the side of the road, like so many historical figures dying of gangrene, or even worse just dying of hunger and thirst. Horrifying to even contemplate.

I would end up being a crow's morning breakfast, like a runover cat on a freeway.

As the pain began to subside, my meditation began to be more easeful and I began to feel that it was therapeutic.

I could go inside, go deep and leave the pain and the suffering back there on the surface. It was the one time each day when I was free from it and I looked forward to it every day.

Although there were no visitations, no fireworks, no insights as such, it was a welcome escape from the physical burden of incorporation, having a human body.

I would slowly ascend at the end of the session feeling light and re-energised.

The pain in the wrist would come back, but having had a rest from it, which I cherished, I could face the rest of my challenging day.

At this point, I have begun to cut back on the pain killers, trying to take only one a day.

Maybe when I am brave enough, I will go back to the Saint Fé houses and see if they have any medicines.

The French are not like the Americans in that way, so I am not that hopeful.

At last I have rescued the bike.

It lay there for weeks.

I apologised to it for my neglect, when I saw it there, weeds starting to use the spokes of the back wheel as a climbing frame.

I pushed it back up the hill mostly left-handed.

Actually I am getting much better at doing things left-handed. Tooth brushing is tough and basic toilet necessities are painful, but I am getting there.

I can get a full cup of left-handed goat's milk now.

Luckily the garden is going quiet and doesn't need much work. I gather more fruit and veggies one handed and store them away.

I have started going for walks again with Mon Veau and sometimes little Adèle comes too. She is very affectionate and when we walk she trots beside me and bleats every now and then, like she is doing a little commentary on what she sees as we walk. She and Mon Veau stop for refreshments, here and there. They seem to like the same things. It is funny to see them together. He is so big now that she fits easily under his belly when he stands. Sometimes, when he sits down, she hops up on his back and stands there and he doesn't seem to mind at all.

We have to be in the middle of October at least. The days are short now and the air is cold. The trees are changing colour, ready for winter.

I have found some good clothes stored away in neglected closets and I am building up to be ready for winter.

I won't be winning any fashion contests that's for sure.

Another calf!

I could see that Ma Vache was growing rapidly lopsided, like she did before Mon Veau took birth.

Now we have a beautiful little heifer. I had to hunt for the right word in French with the help of Monsieur Larousse. The word is génisse , so I will call her Jenny.

She is very delicate, tiny and wobbly on her pins but she has gorgeous big eyes. She is quite different in colour from Mon Veau and I think she might have different paternity.

Obviously Ma Vache found herself a new stud.

Jenny is not blonde like her mother or brother. She is dark brown with some white spots, the prettiest of which is the heart-shaped one on her chest. She has three white socks and one brown one.

Having been through several births, I am much more relaxed about it. I let the girls get on with it. My midwifery skills are not required.

She was born at night in the shed which I had filled with hay. When I went in the morning to let the animals out, there she was half hidden in the hay.

Ma Vache had already dealt with the placenta.

When I came in, Ma Vache made a gentle lowing sound as if to say: Look what I did.

I congratulated her on her achievement.

When I opened the door to let them all out, the goats and Mon Veau happily trotted off to start their day, but Ma Vache stayed with Jenny. I sat in the hay close to her and she sniffed at me warily. I reached over and began stroking her gently. Ma Vache didn't mind at all. Now and then she would make those comforting lowing sounds.

I think we will become very good friends, Jenny and I.

My wrist is almost one hundred percent back to normal. I get twinges of pain every now and then, but mostly I can do everything I need. My face has some scarring that I think I might to live with for the duration of this incarnation. Clo would be horrified.

I am beginning to look more and more like a caveman, or one of the locals of this region ten thousand years ago.

We know they did live here because they left their art work on the walls of caves. Some of them were quite close to here.

Maybe I was one of them.

Ever since I discovered the meditative potential of the swing, I have done it every day, except when it rains. It has become like entering another world. I get on, push myself away, work up the swing and then I begin to go into its hidden moments. I always come away feeling like I just gave myself a recharge.

Then one day I had a very sweet revelation. I was meditating in the chapel and concentrating on my breathing, when I suddenly recognised that it was like the swing. When I breathe in, there is a moment when the breath stops, before it reverses direction and goes out again.

Then the same on the outside. You breathe out and there is a moment when there is nothing, a stillness, the body has no air in it, you have expelled everything, before the new breath begins to come in.

I began to concentrate on these two places, one on the inside where the breath stops and I could feel the energy of the new breath spread out through the body, and then the other one where the breath stops on the outside, having taken away the stale and spent air.

As I did this, the moments of stillness at each place got longer and longer.

I could enter into them and be there, in that stillness, for what seemed like ages, before the impulse to breathe came back.

I began to love these meditations and very often, after I did it for a while, the technique of focussing on the breath disappeared and I was just there, still, peaceful and unbodied.

Sometimes I would focus on the moment inside, and then I would plunge into the body with the newly indrawn breath and spread out with it through my blood and my nerves and my limbs. It was exquisite and made me treasure the body I was experiencing all this in.

At other times it would be the outbreath that drew me into its other world. Here it was as if I were released from the body with the outgoing air. No longer was I trapped in the heaviness of flesh and bone, I had been released and I could float out and away for what seemed like hours, but in fact must have been maybe no more than one minute.

So if nothing else, at least my confinement on this hilltop had taught me some good meditation.

When I did finally pluck up the courage to return to Saint Fé, it was getting quite cold. The sun was getting lower and lower across the southern horizon and the days were noticeably shorter. Most likely I was past the equinox.

My wrist was strong enough to hold the handle bars of the bike but there were twinges of pain every now and then. The bike would hit a bump and that would hurt.

Because Saint Fé is in a valley with hills on three sides, it does not get much sun and it was beginning to feel damp there.

I propped the bike by the church, checked to see if Adèle's plaque was free of insect dwellers and went inside the church. Another pigeon had died there. What is it about pigeons dying in churches?

I did a rapid pigeon burial and went back in.

I gave the Virgin Mary a clean, eliminating the spider webs and grime and then I spent a moment sitting in front of her. She radiates calm and I was pulled inward, closed my eyes and dropped into a serene meditation.

There was a presence but nothing coherent, rather like subtle incense in the air. I accepted that she was there and that I was with her.

I ascended after a while, mostly prompted by the cold.

I gave the other two saints a bit of a polish too, wished them well and then had a thought. If this church is named after Saint Fé, then she should have a statue or at least a painting of her. I went searching which wasn't difficult. It is a very simple one- room building but then tucked into a corner I had not noticed before, there she was.

It was a faded painting of a young woman with the obligatory halo. She wore peasant clothes.

Around her feet were baby goats, which made me smile.

She and I had that in common.

The painting was in a wooden frame that must have been painted with gold leaf but was now mostly brown.

There was a tiny brass plaque on the bottom with Saint Fé and nothing else.

I cleaned the fly specks off her glass and gave her a little polish.

So that was Saint Fé.

Maybe she is the patron saint of goats.

I thought about taking the portrait of Saint Fé back to the château but I decided that, as she had been living in the church named after her, she should stay there.

I headed for the cemetery.

Nothing had changed much there, except the weeds maybe a bit more dominant, the creepers a bit further advanced. Certainly there was no sign of any human activity. Plenty of small animals had left their calling cards, squirrels, rabbits, foxes maybe.

The family vault had been re-invaded somewhat, and I cleaned off the ivy and pulled out the weeds from around the doorway. I cleaned up the four angel statues.

Inside, nothing had changed. I said Bonjour to my ancestors but felt no need to do anything else.

It felt like a dead spot and that's what it is.

I began to wonder if I needed to come back any more.

Maybe I had learned all I needed to know.

I ignored the de Beaurepaires. Their weeds could take care of themselves.

Then I turned to the houses.

At some point I would explore the Mairie too.

The residents' houses were all the same style, typical of so many Lotois villages. Each house was square to the road, which is narrow as it passes between them.

Each house is made of stone with slate or tiled roofing.

They all had shutters made of wood and on all of them ivy or honeysuckle climbed the walls.

The only way to intrude was going to be to break in. I pulled at various shutters to see if they would give but they were solid and tight. Then I got lucky. At the back of one of the houses a tree had fallen and smashed against the back of the house. A solid branch had hit the corner of the house, brought down some of the roof and cracked a door.

With some extra help from an axe, found in a shed, the door fell inward. I climbed over it and went into the darkness beyond. I had brought candles and matches to use in the shuttered darkness.

I passed from room to room and everything had the look of being cleaned up and put away. I opened the shutters to let the light in for the first time in something like eight months.

The house was a basic square with a parlour on one side of the front door and a dining room on the other. The kitchen was at the back. Upstairs were four small bedrooms and a very basic bathroom. It felt like the residence of an older couple just like all the other houses I had been into.

There was a sadness in the house, a sense of lifelessness that existed, I suspect, even before they evacuated.

I opened cupboards and closets and began making a pile of useful stuff. There were some warm clothes, a good coat and some scarves. I found a pair of unused sheepskin gloves still in the packet. They were going to be useful when it snowed.

In the kitchen I found some useful tins of food. They clearly had a fondness for Foie de Morue Fumé. I found a dozen tins of it, smoked cod liver. Good for protein and vitamin E. Maybe it had been on special at the supermarket so they bought lots, but in fact they didn't like it all that much, so they left it behind when they evacuated. You could concoct a whole story about smoked cod liver.

Sadly there was no coffee but I did score some more toilet paper.

As I wandered through the house I felt again like I was in a museum.

I studied the photos on the walls, but I didn't recognise anyone. I looked for mail to see who owned this house. I found some old electricity bills in a drawer, addressed to Monsieur et Madame Mercier.

I had no desire to stay there very long, so I piled up what was useful by the broken-in door ready for transporting home. I found some more pens, a small gas bottle attached to a one-ring cooker, and a big torch plus a supply of batteries. I was going to have to make a few trips or persuade Mon Veau to walk this far with the cart.

Then I attacked the next house.

Now I had the axe, I simply demolished the back door. I was becoming an expert at breaking and entering.

It was much the same as the first one, except when I discovered I had broken into the Mayor's house.

This was Madame Chauvin.

She had a whole wall of photos of herself draped in the Mayoral sash officiating at weddings and openings or closings of buildings. Her photo with President Jacques Chirac was obviously her favourite, in a gold frame above her mayoral desk.

I worked out who Monsieur Chauvin was by reading some of the captions. I felt a bit sorry for him, as he seemed to be always slightly in the background. Where Madame la Maire was a solid lady, broad of hip, her husband was narrow to the point of thinness and seemed over-shadowed by his surroundings.

I wonder where they are now?

I was not drawn to taking anything mayoral, although in a way I am sure I was now the best candidate available for the rôle, being the only one. Seeing what she had amassed in her home office I wondered what she had in the Mairie across the road, but that would be for another day.

I rummaged about in the rest of the house and found a few things. They were keen on Cognac and Armagnac and I put together a good stack. This would need the cart for sure.

Then I found the basement.

They had cheese!

They had wine!

They had hams!

Obviously the mayor was what the French call admiringly une gourmande , a lover of good food. Their basement was really well insulated and naturally cold. I imagine when they evacuated they took what they could, hoping to be back pretty soon. There were full rounds of cheese uncut, a rich yellow cheese from the Pyrenees and several local white ones.

They knew their wines. They had all sorts of wine right across the spectrum from all the best appellations. Madame Chauvin must have come into some money somewhere, or she had excellent connections.

The prize find was the two smoked hams hanging in hessian bags.

I sent them a very strong silent thank you. Dear Monsieur and Madame Chauvin, wherever you are now, please foregive me but I am going to consume your treasures. Thank you for preparing them for me.

Having found so much in just two houses, I decided it was enough for one day. I took what I could in the backpack. One smoked ham took up a lot of room.

I closed up the two houses as best I could, and as I pedalled home I was filled with gratitude.

Life is good.

Ah, the taste of smoked ham with roast potatoes.

The nights are cold now so I keep the fire going in the kitchen. The fireplace is so big you can sit in it which I am sure many generations of Dieulefaits have done.

I sit in there with a hot plate of really fine food with the fire crackling at my feet.

Heaven.

Mon Veau is a champion.

He pulled the cart all the way to Saint Fé, let me load it up with the spoils of the two houses I had plundered, and carried it all the way back as if he had been a cart horse all his life. He is such a placid boy.

Usually, if I recall properly, bulls do not pull carts because they have too much testosterone. Most of the male cattle that pull carts have been knackered. De-sexing anything has not been part of my life experience and I am not starting now. Anyway it's probably too late. He has a fine piece of equipment back there and I will not be applying the shears to them.

So now I have more wine, rounds of cheese, some good winter men's clothes and lots of useful tools.

Providence has been kind to me!

Certainly the menu has improved.

I have been thinking of the women in my life.

I have never really enjoyed the company of men.

I have worked with men, directed men, spent time with them, but none of them, I don't think, had much impact on my life.

The women on the other hand did.

My mother, God bless her, did her best to understand me, nurture me and tell me I was a good person. My father was rather reticent about all that and I always felt he was harbouring a set of basic criticisms that amounted to disappointment in his only child. If I only I had been more normal, got a proper job and fallen in love with a plain but dutiful woman and bred the next generation, he would have been proud. He never said that of course, but that is the image I carry.

Deidre was probably the first woman who reallly changed my life. She believed in me, and pushed me to do things that I wouldn't have done on my own. She had her motives for doing that but I am eternally grateful for her friendship, her coaching and her love. I think she loved me.

And then Clo. She has been so good for me, so good to me. She brought out the best in me, she shaved off the rough edges and she made me feel whole and good. I thank her every day, even as I crave her presence and miss her terribly.

And now Adèle. This is something else but I cannot deny it. She is as real for me now as if she and I had been lovers for years. And yet not lovers. That's not how it is. What she is to me is something of a mystery.

She guides me from wherever she is, in whatever forms she decides to appear.

I don't know what she is to me, but she is the most powerful woman I have ever known. There is a part of me that is terrified of her. There is another part that is desperately in love with her.

Then there is a huge part that is lost in the unknowable.

And now, even the Virgin Mary has appeared.

And the local village is named after a female saint.

And I mustn't forget Ma Vache and Betty whose milks have sustained me.

And the young ones, too.

So I salute all the women, all the females in my life.

This thought about the women in my life became a thread in my meditation.

I didn't mean it to be, but several days in a row, when I sat there in the chapel, this thought about all the women in my life would come up.

I would be filled with love and gratitude for them all and that would lead me into a very sweet inner loving place.

Sometimes I would see them and at other times they would merge one into another, as if they were becoming the archetype of woman.

Then in one incredible meditation, I began to feel as if the archetype was actually a force.

The great feminine power.

It was as if I could see, just for a brief moment, that everything that moves in the universe is motivated by this feminine force.

She does it.

I felt a deep reverence, not just for the forms she has taken, but for that force herself.

In the very deepest moment that was great stillness inside.

I had become that force.

It had no form or words to it, just a deep knowingness.

I am you .

I came out of it full of awe and with a new awareness.

That femaleness is everywhere including in me.

When I went outside the wind was blowing, the feminine force.

Clouds raced across the sky, the feminine force.

I looked over at the garden that had produced so much all summer, the feminine force.

Out of her womb has come everything.

And then I felt my own heartbeat, that too, is the feminine force.

I went back to Saint Fé and Mon Veau came too.

I broke into the Mairie, which was not hard, the back door being surprisingly flimsy. Apart from a lot of photos on the wall and locked filing cabintes it had nothing much to offer. I imagined Gervais sitting at the desk or conducting the occasional wedding.

I did find a small, rather tattered pamphlet that was a pitiful attempt at a tourist brochure, promoting this inconspicuous little hamlet.

It outlined the history and had a couple of grainy photos.

People had occupied the little valley in which it sits since neolithic times, according to this pamphlet. There are remnants of cave art close by. I wondered if the first draft of this small work of literature was started by Gervais, but it did not acknowledge the writer. Maybe his book was used as a reference.

The name Saint Fé is reported to be the name of a young girl saint who lived in the area around the fifth or the sixth century. Her name could have been Saint Faith of Conques but no-one seems too certain about that. What she did to become saint and why this little town was named after her remains a mystery.

The brochure does have one important claim to fame and that is Adèle. This brochure has a small picture of the plaque on the wall of the church and a description of her heroism during the second world war.

I took the brochure home to add to my collection of relics.

The other houses were all much the same. I broke into them all, becoming very adept at the art of breaking and entering, and in the end I had plundered the whole little village. I had another cart load of stuff. More tins of food that the residents decided not to take, but nothing as high end as the treasure trove from the Mayor's cellar, no more ham and cheese.

I got to the point where I looked at all the sad belongings in the houses and shook my head. The stuff that wasn't valuable enough or meaningful enough for them to take when they evacuated, why would I want any of it?

We wandered back, my trusty bull and I, with a cartload of things that I really did not need. Well the toilet paper was valuable.

As we headed home, I thought that other than checking out the cemetery and the church now and then, I had had the best of Saint Fé.

As we climbed back up our hill, I had the happy feeling of coming home with no real need to go anywhere any more.

Winter is coming and I will imitate the shy squirrels who have disappeared.

I will stay in my hole and stay warm.

That evening I sat for meditation and I had a glimpse of Saint Fé.

It was fleeting.

The image of her from the church appeared, vague at first but becoming more focused as I watched it. She began to move and the goats around her began to move too.

She smiled and raised her hand in a greeting.

She felt calmly benign, just a simple young girl saint with her goats.

And then she began to fade again.

I wanted to ask her what she had done to be called a saint but she wasn't willing to wait for that.

I am guessing we are in November.

It is really cold.

The animals venture out of their sheds for a while but they don't stay long. I have opened up the garden to them and they can go in and eat whatever they like. I have taken in so much I could feed a company of Dragoons for years, so what is left is beyond what I can use. It will be good for the animals and good for the garden. They will eat everyting down, get good nourishment and leave good manure.

I hang out by the fire and I am ploughing through books.

I alternate between English and French, which means I alternate between frivolous holiday piffle and serious literature, which also means I alternate between escapism and study.

Actually I like both experiences, as if I am exercising different parts of myself.

I have given up on my afternoon mint teas and contemplation in the turret, the wind drove me out of there weeks ago

Now I am writing by the fire.

I do exercise my body too.

I have to.

If I didn't get out and do something physical, I think I would go nuts in a day.

Every day I make myself walk the bounds. I found a terrific thick military greatcoat in one of the Saint Fé houses and it fits me very well and is warm as toast. I have a beany made of alpaca that someone left in the Mayor's house. It's pink but no-one is going to see it.

Mon Veau is still my faithful companion although he is bigger than me now, at least in body mass. Sometimes little Jenny will come too. She likes to skip, the way calves do, every now and then suddenly bopping up and down as she runs. She is a very happy calf.

The goats are home bodies and they have no interest in long walks. Adèle used to come, but not any more. She watches me go, I invite her to come, but she gives it a miss. She is a bit like her namesake, very independent, not to be commanded.

The leaves have dropped off the deciduous trees and there is a greyness and a brown-ness about the landscape, except where the white outcrops of limestone protrude. It is a hardscrabble landscape where those who lived here had to be tough and resilient. They had to carve out their livelihoods by hand and wrestle with the constraints of nature and topography.

I sense, as I walk in winter, you would have to be tough to live here.

Am I tough enough?

I visit the safe house and keep it tidy.

Even in the cold of winter I like to stay there for a little while and just be still. I always remember those who finished their lives in that house. The creek gurgles behind it and the occasional cynical crow will make a comment from a bare tree branch.

I go to the little cemetery at the bottom of the hill and keep the weeds down. Now they are hibernating it doesn't need much. The little spring is gushing as it threads its way between the tombstones.

I honour those whose bodies lie there too.

Sometimes I stop and root around in the sheds of Jean-Claude.

I always find something useful.

I think of him and Eveline and send up a little thank you to wherever they are now.

So that's my day as winter closes in.

The tough part is that winter is dark and the nights are long and cold.

I use a hotwater bottle to keep me company and many blankets.

Chloé had the heating installed but if there is no power, nothing works.

The only source of heat now is the fire.

Washing requires a big prep. Water has to be boiled on the fire, with a bucket and a pourer ready to go and a big tub to sit in to catch the run off.

I used to wash like this in Malaysia and in Thailand, but there the water was naturally warm. Here I have to be quick and careful, not to scald myself and not to let the water get cold. With practice I am sure I will get better at it. After all, except for the last however many years when there was electricity, this was how the whole world washed.

In the cold and the dark of winter there is a sadness in the air.

I suppose it is normal as the dark nights get longer and longer and the wind howls achingly across the hilltop.

It is sad.

I am sad.

The afternoons are the hardest when it gets dark so soon and the air feels damp. The light is going. It was with me for such a short time, now it is going and the endless night is coming back

It feels sad.

I wonder why I am still doing this.

Why I am still persevering?

What am I waiting for?

It's the same old question: What's the point?

My world has shrunk.

I have moved into the kitchen.

I tried to be a rugged country boy and sleep between freezing sheets, even with the hotwater bottle and a mound of blankets, but I am too much of a softy.

I have built myself a very nice warm cosy spot near the fire in the kitchen and this is where I will live out the winter.

If I live that long.

I have even let the goats come in. The older goats explored a bit but then went out again, but the two kids, the girls, Glove and Adèle, seem to like it.

So far no-one has disgraced themselves inside.

The chapel is freezing.

Even if the electricity were still on, the chapel would be cold. Chloé regarded it as storage space, so why put heat in it.

I make myself go there every day.

It's my austerity.

It is the one part of the house I will not neglect. I clean it, even the windows. I carefully dust each item that I have come to treasure.

I chant the Buddhist prayer and I wrap myself up in layers for meditation.

Meditation has its days.

Sometimes I labour to keep repeating the mantra.

Somedays I fall asleep sittting up and have a horrible crick in my neck when I come to.

Sometimes I have journeys to take inside, where I will find myself in places I do not know, or revisiting places I know but are different from what I knew before. Sometimes Adèle will be there, when she is, she is mostly still and benign.

We sit together and we meditate and I am filled with warmth and contentment.

Sometimes others will come. I have seen my parents as vague figures far off, but seemingly friendly.

The saints have shown up.

I do love being in the company of the Virgin Mary. I can see why she is loved all over the world.

And every now and then, a surprise visit from people I have never met, that I know of, but who seem to know me. Some appear to be out of the past. Maybe they were me back then, coming down to say hello to the me I am now.

Meditation is never the same twice.

Although winter is sad and dark, cold and long, meditation is my saviour.

Meaningful meditation or non-event meditation, I come out feeling that I have been transported to a place that nurtures me.

And every day, even if it is just for a moment, in that freezing chapel, I feel warm.

She came on her birthday.

I had no idea what day it was but in meditation she came in fast and powerfully. Adèle was as she appeared in the first photo I found, which is how she appears in most of her visitations.

I had lit the candles in the chapel, chanted the hymn, and then sat back for a moment looking at my collected relics, when I began to feel her presence. I quickly layered myself in blankets for meditation, closed my eyes, and there she was.

"November the 12th" she said.

She seemed to glow, there was so much light around her.

Inside my meditative state I willed myself to bow forward in reverence. By now she was not just the girl in the photo, she was the manifestation of the knowledge that was beginning to emerge inside me. She was both the incarnations I had seen and she was the universal feminine force.

Both at once.

"I was born, in my last life, the last of all my lives, on November 12th."

"Is that today?"

Did I say it aloud or was it just a thought?

In the temporal world, everything is measured, she said, as if this was something I should have known. Having lost my solar watch, temporality was no longer part of my awareness.

"So is it *Bonne Anniversaire?*" I asked.

I don't even know what language we were speaking in. French I think.

Then I added:" Why does it matter, if you are not in that body any more?"

"The soul takes its form according to its destiny. The form appears at the right moment in the right place."

"So what is it about November the 12th 1918?"

I thought I knew, but I wanted to hear it from her.

"Armistice."

That's what I had thought.

"But that was on the 11th."

"I was born on the first full day of peace."

"But you died in war."

"Fighting for peace."

It was the longest and most coherent conversation we had ever had.

"How shall we celebrate?" I asked.

"I will show you." she said.

Suddenly there was a great flash of light and she seemed to explode.

In her place there was a luminous tunnel full of bright light and moving shapes, and I was hurtling through it like a gigantic waterslide with a thunderous roaring. I was terrified, ecstatic, and at the same time strangely detached. I had no control over this wild ride.

And then it threw me out into a garden, a paradise of a garden with lush greenery, and vibrant flowers, trees heavy with fruit and multicoloured birds.

It was full of fragrance and light.

Birds sang in trees.

I landed on my feet, as if I had simply walked in.

I looked around for Adèle, expecting that she would be my guide.

Instead, I was amazed to see Ma Vache, Mon Veau, Jenny and all the goats, including Billy. Boris the rooster was there and the hens.

And then weirdest of all they began talking to me. They wanted to say thank you for looking after them. They spoke perfect french.

Ma Vache was the leader of the group and she had a lovely velvety voice. She spoke on behalf of them all, that as the world of humans was finishing and they had been abandoned, left behind, they were grateful that the last of the humans was kind to them.

I wanted to ask her what she meant about the world of humans finishing, but they all turned to lead me further into the garden.

I did get to tell Boris that I was sorry that I had eaten some of his children. He cocked his head on one side and said:

"You feed us, we feed you."

Did he have a Russian accent?

The lady goats were very sweet and told me that they loved me.

Mon Veau led the way through an archway of bougainvillea into a wide open, wonderfully manicured garden with topiaried hedges like in the palace of Versailles.

And there was Adèle. She was dressed in a long white robe without jewelry, sitting on a throne made of dark wood surrounded by massive vases of flowers. Her hair was piled high above her head and she wore no shoes. She was more like a priestess than anything regal.

She had a gentle smile.

Around her throne was a large group of people and as I approached, they all turned to look at me with the warmest smiles.

I knew every one of them.

I really think my heart stopped.

They were people I have known in this life, my parents and Diedre, the girls in Malaysia and Daud, Tante and Chloé. Then there were others whose lives had passed by mine almost without me noticing, but with each of them I knew we had some kind of important connection. Lydia from the Ukraine was there, but she no longer had that lustful look about her. Arturo was there and he saluted me with the Buddhist hand greeting. Olga and Ramanuja from Varanasi and then Indira. She was in her finest sari and had the air of a princess not a sex goddess. There were others who I had given no thought to for years, students from Drama School and several girls I had slept with perhaps just once and had thought there was nothing to it.

Jean-Claude was there with Eveline. He waved and then brought over an old couple who smiled and nodded. They were the Dupuys and they thanked me for taking care of their passage out of the physical world.

And then Clo.

I so wanted to hug her and tell her how much I missed her and yet she seemed serene and detached. She stood just a little way from me, but her eyes were full of love and I knew that was enough.

And there were others and somehow I knew who they were.

They were Dieulefaits and Teagues.

Gervais, who I instantly recognised, looked quite regal in his mayoral outfit, introducing me to our lineage, telling me who each one was, but I felt that I already knew them.

I had been several of them.

Adèle watched all this from her throne and then she stood up and came down. She brought forward a man I immediately knew.

"My Jacques," she said.

He was me.

He looked at me with a calm face, studying me, much as I was studying him.

Then he dropped his head in the subtlest of acknowledgments.

Adèle took my hand with the ring on it and slipped it off effortlessly.

Jacques looked at me with a gentle smile as Adèle slipped the ring onto his ring finger.

Then he held his hand for me to see the ring and nodded again.

I felt he was thanking me for keeping the ring safe for him.

I so wanted to ask Adèle to explain all this.

I could feel the boiling cauldron of questions inside me, but somehow in this state I could not speak to her.

I wanted to ask her what was I supposed to understand?

Then my mind kicked in.

Is this real?

In a flash they were all gone.

I was shot back up the tunnel in reverse.

It grew darker as I went, until I crashed back into my physical body all bent over in the cold chapel.

I looked down at my hand. The ring was gone.

Then I started to cry, deep desperate grief pouring out of me.

I was back in the château, alone and cold and I did not understand anything.

I was a different person, but I didn't understand yet what I had become.

Something had shifted.

Something big and heavy had been moved.

I did not know what it was, except that it had been a weight that I no longer carried.

I go back to that meditation again and again.

I try to recreate it when I sit for meditation.

I try to bring back at least the feeling of being there.

I ask for help in understanding what I am supposed to know.

By now of course I know that trying to create anything in meditation is a fool's endeavour.

When I try too hard it leaves me feeling wretched.

I need my own Armistice.

I need my own peace.

And now it is snowing.

I woke up to a strange silence.

Before I opened my eyes I wondered why I couldn't hear anything, not even Boris.

Then when I got up and looked out, the landscape was entirely different, softened and blanketed.

Nothing moved.

Tree branches held delicate snowflake sculpures and little cones of fallen snow sat on top of the fence posts.

Nothing moved.

I put on a coat and hat and went out to let the cows and Mon Veau out.

They seemed reluctant to leave the warmth of their hay-insulated sheds, but one by one out they came.

The goats came out from the warmth of the kitchen and all dutifuly relieved themselves.

Once she had got used to the cold substance under feet, Jenny began to skip and jump in it. The others showed less enthusiasm.

I spread out some fresh hay for them all and chicken feed for Boris and his harem, then I retreated inside.

After breakfast however I decided to walk the bounds and see how it looked under snow.

It was a superb transformation. Everything was rounded and softened out by the fabric of snowflakes. They laid out a monochromatic sheet that veiled all that I saw.

I had the sensation that it was like a burial shroud. Everything covered in a white cloth, to hide the death that lay underneath.

It was hard to shake that feeling.

Although it was very beautiful it was also terrifying.

Mon Veau walked with me and we left our six footprints behind us, as the only evidence of life.

It was only when I arrived at the safe house and gently cleaned the snow from the altar that the dread of death began to lift.

As I stood in front of it, I began to feel a warmth.

And then her presence, very subtle but unmistakable.

Whatever time is left, I felt her say, rather than heard her say. Whatever time is left, be well, take care of what has been given into your care. Be at peace.

Even though it meant getting a bit wet, I knelt in the snow and bowed to the altar.

Thank you.

Walking back to the château I felt a great sense of relief.

I did feel at peace.

Whatever time is left.

Although that was not very specific, it stayed with me.

At least I understood that much.

Soon all this will end, one way or the other.

When I sat for meditation that afternoon, I felt at peace with it all.

If there is not much time left, so be it.

I sank deep inside and felt the inner warmth.

And there was Gervais.

I could see him quite clearly. He was dressed in very dapper clothes and he wore a beige beret. Across his chest he wore the sash of the Mayor.

"You ask why we gathered to greet you?"

I couldn't remember asking such a question but it was a good one.

"We exist inside you. We are in your thoughts, so we exist. You hold us there. Some of us you have almost forgotten, but here we are."

Behind him some of the faces from the vision floated in the air.

"When you let us go, then we will be free."

And then he faded off into blue light and I went deeper inside to an unconsciousness that was like a living death.

I had no body, no thoughts, no sense of self-ness, but I was me.

How long I stayed like that, I have no idea, but rising ever so slowly from it, I was wrapped in benevolence.

This is the peace I was craving all along.

I can live anywhere and do anything if I have this kind of peace.

I thought about what Gervais had said.

If I could hold this kind of peace then I could let all those souls go.

I thought about consciously letting them go.

How would I do that?

I might try to invoke Gervais back and we could discuss it.

If I did that then he would still be stuck with me.

Am I holding Adèle back?

Maybe, because I do not want to let her go.

And there it was. I could see the power of my attachment.

If I am thinking of any of them, then I am holding them back.

It is hard to understand what to do about that.

When I went outside again, the sun was setting low in the south and west, darkly red through a slit in the grey clouds.

I closed up the sheds with the animals and poultry and I talked to them all. Now that they had talked to me in the birthday party meditation, I felt even more comfortable chatting away with them, assuming that although they cannot talk to me on this physical plane, I knew that they could understand. Maybe if I was attentive enough I would begin to intuit what they were saying to me.

There was a pinkish glow to the snow as the sun disappeared and then the night came in, dark and monochromatic.

I retreated inside and built up the fire. I made a lusty veggie soup with chunks of smoked ham in it and opened a bottle of Saint Emilion from probably a very good year, thanks to the lady Mayor of Saint Fé.

I was in a good state.

I was warm, comforted with some new inner contentment and outer contentment.

I could not wish for more.

After dinner and several glasses of the excellent red, I dozed off in front of the fire.

Adéle walked in.

Was it in my dream, or was it in reality?

Was it the result of the wine?

Did I invoke her?

She was her eighteen year old self, childlike and sweet. She cuddled up to me and I held her. I had such a physical sense of her.

"She can't breathe", she said softly.

I looked at her young glowing face, her clear eyes.

"Who can't breathe?"

Mother Earth. She needs a break. We have despoiled her, we have filled her body and her lungs with toxic poison."

"Pollution."

"Everything. What man has made, it suffocates her. The way man thinks, it depletes her joy to extinction. She cannot bear it."

"So we have to leave?" Was that what she was telling me?

"We do."

"Then what?"

"She will be reborn. She will breathe again and a new life will emerge."

"Will we be here?"

"We will. There will be a new opportunity to learn how to live in harmony. It is a cycle. We have done this before, many times."

Then she lay quietly

"She has to breathe." she said.

I woke up the next morning with such peace inside me.

I have a rôle to play, just for a little while, till it is time for me to go.

I know what to do and I know why.

There was no fear, no sadness, no worry.

I would do whatever I had to do, till I did not have to do it any more.

And then I would go.

It was deeply satisfying.

Is that why no planes fly?
Is that why nothing has moved on the freeway below the château ever since I got here?
Am I, in reality, the only human left?
It is beginning to seem like that.

Other questions float through my mind but they are fading.
I don't need to know why there was an evacuation ordered and all the residents of Saint Fé left.
I don't need to know where they went, but maybe there are camps of refugees somewhere.
Even if there are, I wouldn't want to go there.
I have seen what refugee camps look like and I don't want to go near one.
I am a refugee already, but at least I am living in an idyllic situation.
I have food and fire, I have ham and wine.
I have meditations and the visitations of beings who are guiding me.
What more would I want?

The snow melts and winter sun dapples the fields.
The grass has turned brown and I feed the animals every day.
They root around in the garden but there is not much left.
What I feed them keeps them happy.
On sunny days like this we all venture out and enjoy what warmth there is.
The safe house gets a good clean after the snowmelt.
A few deer had visited and left me something to clean.

At the end of the day, spent outside and breathing the fresh air of winter, I wonder about Mother Earth.

Although the air is fresh right now, I do know what she meant.

Suddenly, maybe two hundred years ago, we started to pour dirt particles into the air, coal smoke and petroleum fumes, chemicals and methane.

We flooded the rivers and the ocean with plastic.

We tore down the trees who recycle the air.

We lived in cities that produced heat and filth.

We filled the skies with aircraft and microwaves.

Electric currents disrupted the natural rhythms of life.

Animal species died away.

And we harboured thoughts of greed and enmity towards others.

No wonder she can't breathe.

She does need a break.

I am beginning to have the experience of approaching death.

Sometimes, when I am asleep in the kitchen by the fire, I feel my body is dropping away and that my mind is gently shutting down and that I can leave.

There is no fear.

It is as if I am practising to leave.

It feels incredibly normal, natural.

But it is not yet time to do that.

I am still here.

I wake up and rediscover that I have a functioning mind and a working body.

It feels a bit disappointing in a way.

The body is heavy.

The contents of the mind are a burden.

I was quite happy to go.

It's not time yet.

OK, it's another day.

I will trundle around inside this body for another day.

My mind will conjure up all its usual unnecessary nonsense for another day.

Maybe this will be the last one.

Whether it is or maybe not, I will get up and go about my day.

I will make the most of it.

I vaguely remember some new age slogan somewhere that said: 'Approach each day as if it will be your last.'

So I will do that because it could well be the truth.

I am thinking about how to leave everything if I go.

What will happen to the animals?

Do I leave this exercise book in a place where the new occupants of the earth will find it?

What will happen to my body?

Does it matter?

It's just the vehicle I am driving around in.

At a certain point we all turn our bodies in and head off unencumbered, and then most often, as I have now discovered, we take on a new model and drive into another life one more time.

I read about how the Parsi people in India leave their dead bodies on the roofs of their houses so the buzzards can eat them and distribute their bones.

Good recycling.

Better than the tombs in the Saint Fé cemetery.

Where will I die?

I have a couple of cemeteries to choose from, or do I go like Jean-Claude and the Dupuys?

Will I have a choice?

At the same time it is such a pleasure to be living.

Now I seem to relish every day as a great blessing.

Oh great, I say to myself, I have another day, what will I do to make the most of it?

More ham, more cheese, more wine for sure.

Spend time with my four-footed and feathered fellow travellers.

Go to the sacred places and take care of them.

Life is good.

The dogs came back.

There was the same screaming and I knew what it was.

This time I was ready and grabbed the gun.

When I flew out the door I instantly saw that they had Glove. George was courageously trying to fight them off. I ran towards them shouting.

They backed off, but one still held Glove by the throat.

I pointed the gun and pulled the trigger. The shock of it made me stagger back, but when I looked I had hit one of the dogs. The others ran and the one I hit limped off yelping after them. Obviously I had hit it somewhere less than fatal.

I went over to Glove and she was on her feet. I held her gently and felt to see what kind of wound she had. Luckily it seemed like the dog had her mostly by her skin rather than the throat itself. She was bleeding a little bit, but not too badly.

I congratulated George on his heroics and carried Glove back inside. George trotted along behind me, like my security detail.

I put the gun back in its place and replaced the bullet. I thanked it for its good service.

I have never liked guns but now I was grateful I had one.

If those dogs came back I would be ready.

Anything can happen in a day.

I put some ointment on Glove's throat but the wound seemed superficial.

As I gently rubbed it on, she gazed at me with her mysterious goaty eyes.

I felt such trust coming from her.

I was her Saint Fé.

I told her she was going to be fine, and that her Dad was a great warrior.

Life and death.
Anything can happen in a day.
This could have been her last day.
This could have been my last day.
Maybe it's the last day of the dog that I shot.
Anything can happen in a day.

At the end of the day when I sat in the chapel I felt vey content.

No matter who or what I am, all is good.

I could be God, as Adèle suggested.

I could be just the last human about ready to retire from the earth so she can breathe.

I could be the last incarnation of the Dieulefaits.

I could be all of the above.

And in the end it doesn't really matter.

Meditation was deep and still.
Sometimes the best meditation has no content.

And then there was another day.

I suppose I am just like everyone else, even people who get up every morning and go to work in some anonymous office doing mindless repetitive paper work for a pitiful salary, who ask themselves, Why I am doing this?

They could quit. But then what?

Can I quit?

I could.

I could get on the bike and ride and ride till I discovered what was beyond my current known world.

I could be the Columbus of the Lot and sail out to discover what's over the horizon.

But I don't.

Most people never really have the courage to do that, so they settle for a humdrum life in a boring suburb, doing nothing significant till they die of boredom.

Is it that I lack the courage to venture beyond Saint Fé?

Probably.

It could be that I find total destruction and chaos, dead bodies everywhere and marauding packs of dogs, chewing on human carcasses.

Or I could find out that I have been living in delusion and that the world outside is functioning perfectly well, but I couldn't see it.

Empty skies and the utterly silent freeway say otherwise.

I let the whole question fade away and try to find a purpose for living out the rest of this one day.

Just this one day.

I can focus on what gives satisfaction and go from there.

Cow's milk.

Goat's milk.

Mon Veau walking with me in crunchy patches of old snow to the safe house.

The way Glove looks at me with such devotion. Goat love.

The warmth of the fire and clever French writers from the 19th century.

Meditation with the occasional visitation from beings who offer me interesting insights into the nature of existence.

A warm bed by the fire.

And that's enough.
So there goes another day.

How will I die?
I am healthy, totally healthy.
And yet, given what seems to be the message, my days are numbered.
Our days are always numbered.
In the meantime, every morning I wake up and I say to myself : I'm still here.

I suppose it must be December by now.
No need to do any Christmas shopping.
I don't think I will put up a Christmas tree.
We could do a nativity enactment with cows and goats.
I could bring the Virgin Mary from the church in Saint Fé.
I have lots of hay for a manger and I have a stable.
I could be Joseph. Remembering all those exercises we did in first year at drama school, I would have to explore what my motivation is, as the character, what is the hidden agenda. Maybe he secretly disbelieves all that story about immaculate conception. If he didn't sleep with her, then who did? Maybe it was that rascal Archangel Gabriel.
I wonder if angels or even archangels can have sex.
The Cathars believed everyone is an angel, so maybe they can.
Anyway, there's not much point in playing Joseph, there's no audience.
Forget the play for Christmas.

Now I am thinking about Christmas, I start singing Christmas carols. Though the frost was cru-el . I can pretend to be Good King Wenceslas on the feast of Stephen, when the snow lay crisp and even .

Actually the snow is melting, because we are having sunny days. There are only a few patches under trees.

I have lived through forty Christmases, most of them thoroughly unmemorable.

As a kid we went to church as a family, dutifully but without any devotion that I recall. My Mum made the Christmas dinner, hot roast dinner with brandy-laced Christmas pudding in the middle of a blazing Australian summer.

As an adult I tried to skip the family ritual as best I could.

The first time I really got a sense of what Christmas was supposed to be was in the monastery in Chiang Rai. The monks acknowledged the day as a commemoration of the birth of a great soul. They were quite eclectic about great souls.

They did their regular daily schedule of spiritual practices, but they referenced the significance of the day in each one.

Arturo the Italian Franciscan monk was there then and he was in tears all day. He said he had never had such a moving experience of Christmas. He told me that these monks were more in tune with what Christ represented than any of his Franciscan brothers.

The monks in the temple asked me to describe how I was celebrating it and I had to admit that I didn't really pay it much attention.

They scolded me, in their very good-natured way. If you follow the teachings of Christ, you should honour his birth, they told me.

It did make me think.

Was I a Christian?

Did I follow the teachings of Christ?

Clo is not religious, but the year we lived in Versailles she decided we should go to Midnight Mass. The Cathedral Saint Louis de Versailles, built in the eighteenth century, is huge and lofty. The pews were packed with families and the vaulted ceiling glowed with a thousand candles. The choir was really good and I held Clo's hand and felt quite happy to be there.

Was I celebrating the birth of Christ?

Maybe I should choose a day and say it is Christmas Day and go to the church in Saint Fé and celebrate.

I could do a one man Mass.

I could invite the goats.

Nah.

Too far for goats.

I have no intention of becoming a lonely goatherd.

Yodel lady yodel lady yo he who.

Weird where the mind goes.

The idea of Christmas was just a whim, but someone on the other side took it seriously.

In meditation, Saint Fé appeared with the Virgin Mary, both with halos.

They said they were looking forward to the Mass and said it was in two days' time.

Be careful what you invite into your consciousness.

Now I have to go.

I have been commanded and I will have company.

At least I knew what day it was.

I hunted up an old calendar on which the saint of each day is listed.

Every day of the French year is dedicated to someone.

Children get to receive gifts on their saints day.

I had wondered if the calendar actually said that the the 25th of December was Jesus's day.

It said Noël instead, which amounts to the same thing.

However, what shocked me was what happened the day before.

December 24ᵗʰ is Saint Adèle's Day.

I stared at it.

Then I had to laugh.

We could have a Saint Adéle's Day and then the day after that we could have a Christmas Mass.

I was going to be busy.

The next morning she woke me.

I was all cuddled up in the warmth of my blankets in the kitchen.

I had got up during the night to keep the fire going, so now I lay there looking at the glowing embers and thinking I should probably put another log on when she seemed to waft out of the glowing fire.

She came and lay down with me in front of the fire.

Was it a dream?

I couldn't tell.

It was very physical though. I could feel her warmth. She was not just a vision but seemed to be a living breathing person with a body.

I put my arms round this body.

At last she whispered: "Today is the day of Saint Adèle .

"Who was she?" I whispered back.

"She was a German Saint from a very long time ago."

"She was German?"

"Mmm."

I had a strange thought." It seems ironic that you died at the hands of Germans."

"You think so?"

There was a long silence as the fire crackled.

"She was not German".

"Saint Adèle?"

"The woman who ordered my death".

"She? It was a woman?"

"When I was taken from the safe house, they held me in the prison in Gourdon. I was tortured there. The person who did it was a woman. The men watched. They wanted to know who my fellow Maqui were. I would not tell them."

"She was French"?

"From Alsace."

"You must hate her."

"Not now. We have made our peace."

We lay again in silence and then she began to fade, literally fade away, even as I felt her body weight lighten and the warmth of her dissipate.

Don't go, I whispered.

"*À demain*", she said, "see you tomorrow."

I said:" Happy Saint Adèle's Day ".

"*Merci*", she said, and was gone.

The rest of the day felt very peaceful.

The physicality of her presence stayed with me.

I gave the little goat Adèle some extra sweet little carrots to celebrate her saint name day.

In the later afternoon when I sat for meditation in the chapel, I wondered if Adèle might reappear but it was a very still and quiet meditation.

I began by invoking her, both the Adèle that I had come to know, and the saint after whom she was named.

As I came out of the meditation, I felt a warmth in the room and accepted that they were subtly present.

And that was Christmas Eve.

As soon as I awoke the next morning and remembered it was Christmas, I felt as excited as a little kid about to rush downstairs to see what Santa had left under the tree.

For once I knew what day it was.

And I knew what I was going to do about it.

I was going to celebrate Christmas.

As I had breakfast I thought about how I would celebrate.

We would have a Mass.

I decided I would take the goats.

I found a good shirt and a tie and jacket coat in a closet.

I also dug out the bible.

I took lots of candles and matches.

I put Glove and Adèle in the cart and hooked up Mon Veau.

Ma Vache, Jenny, George and Betty all watched us go and they must have wondered what it was all about.

Then I had a thought.

I turned to them and I said: We are going to the church in Saint Fé, if you want to come you are welcome.

And they did.

So now I was leading a whole troop of animals *en masse* to Mass.

We trundled along at a slow pace and I had no inclination to hurry anyone or even to make sure they kept up.

Mass would happen in God's time.

If they wanted to go off, they could, if they wanted to go home, they could, if they wanted to go to church they could.

It was a cloudless morning with just enough sun to take the chill off.

I walked along beside Mon Veau and I felt very happy about the whole adventure.

Every now and then George or Betty would sample something delicious off to the side of the road but then they would trot to catch up.

The two kids in the cart seemed very content to ride along and made no efforts to jump out.

When we got there, everyone was still with us.

I uncoupled Mon Veau and lifted the kids out of the cart.

Adèle's plaque needed a bit of a clean before we went in.

I pulled the door of the church wide open and we all trooped in.

It was freezing cold.

This was going to be a short Mass.

The animals wandered about sniffing here and there.

I found a store of long white tapered candles in a rack with a sign saying that they were one euro each and there was a box with a slot in the top for the donations.

I was sure Jesus wouldn't mind if I didn't pay for the candles for his Mass.

Money was no longer relevant.

I lit all of them and the church began to glow.

Was it just a little warmer?

I gave the Virgin Mary and the other statues a bit of a polish.

I gently took the portrait of Saint Fé off the wall, gave it a clean and brought it over to sit next to the statue of the Virgin Mary.

There the two of them, surrounded by candles, were my focus.

I sang my Buddhist hymn and as I did, all the animals became still and quiet.

As I sang, Glove came over and gently rubbed her muzzle against my leg.

Then I opened the bible and read aloud the first verse of the Gospel of Matthew. I had never read much of the bible in French, but it all resonated nicely back from the wooden ceiling of the church.

At one point Ma Vache gently mooed as if she was commenting on the reading.

I said a little prayer and I thanked Jesus for appearing now and then, always a bit vaguely, but recognisable, in my meditations.

I wished him Happy Birthday.

After that I ran out of things to do by way of a Mass.

I should have brought food and wine but as that was never part of the Methodist ceremonies, I totally forgot.

I finished up telling the Virgin Mary and Saint Fé that I was grateful that they had reminded me about the right day, I hoped they had enjoyed the Mass and I wished them a Merry Christmas.

I left all the candles burning.

There was a warmth to the church that it probably had not had in years.

I felt the good will of the Saints.

Although Adèle had said *À demain* she did not appear, but I was sure she was hovering about.

Standing at the door of the church as the goats and the cows came out I thanked them for coming, like our minister used to do in the Methodist church when I was a kid.

Not one of them had left any unfortunate mess on the floor.

What a well behaved congregation.

As I was about to close the door, I decided to give myself a Christmas present.

I would take the portrait of Saint Fé back to the château.

I hooked Mon Veau up to the cart and lifted Glove and Adèle back in and off we went.

The other animals wandered along at their own pace, but we more or less stayed together..

I felt so much love for them all as we slowly walked out of Saint Fé.

I think it was the best Christmas of my life.

When I got back, I made myself a Christmas dinner of roast veggies, smoked ham and cheese, and opened a fine Pomerol red.

I gave the animals their Christmas dinner of carrots, and each one got a cube of sugar from my small supply.

The final part of Christmas Day was installing Saint Fé in the chapel.

I had to rearrange all my relics to make a space for her.

I was getting quite a collection.

Now she sits in the middle of them all with Adèle.

I lit my own candle and sat back for meditation.

It was deep and full of love.

Nobody appeared but there was no need.

I was deeply content.

So now it is the feast of Stephen, the day after Christmas. Saint Étienne in French.

In Australia it is Boxing Day and the big focus is usually cricket.

You can't play cricket by yourself.

I doubt very much if I will bother to keep track of the days after this.

Maybe if I need to be reminded of something, a saint will turn up and let me know.

Now it is quiet again after all the festive celebrations.

The weak winter sun is doing its best to keep shining, the snow has melted, and a gentle breeze is whispering in the bare branches of the leafless trees.

It is getting close to New Year.

Whatever that means.

I doubt any saints are terribly interested in New Year, it's such a fake human creation.

Will I have a new year?

Not really.

I think I will just go on having my timeless time except when I am informed otherwise.

In the meantime, life goes on.

George is sick.

My heroic and stoic goat saviour is really weak and doesn't like standing up.

When I woke up and the other goats began to move, he stayed put.

He gave me a miserable bleat and just sat there.

I crouched down beside him and felt along his body but I couldn't tell what was ailing him.

Then I had a strange idea.

I dug out a bottle of brandy. He was going to get best quality Armagnac.

Long ago brandy was considered to be somthing of a medieval medical panacea, so maybe that should fix him.

He let me open his mouth and I poured a little in. How much went down I am not sure but he didn't seem to be worried by it.

He trusted me, I think.

I poured some more and after a while I saw him begin to move a bit.

Maybe he is getting arthritic and needs a bit of a push.

In the end I gave him maybe five doses and then, sure enough, he staggered to his feet.

He seemed to be trying out his legs.

He took a few tentative steps and then a few more and out he went.

I walked with him and he seemed OK for a while.

He had a long piss, nibbled at some hay that I had put out, and a couple of carrots, then took himself back inside.

Later in the day I gave him another dose and he ventured out for a short while.

I doubt that I have cured him, but I have helped to hide whatever is giving him trouble.

The next morning when I woke up, he was gone.

It was the other goats calling that woke me. I knew it was George.

He was lying in the hay with the three girls who were standing over him gently bleating.

He looked very peaceful.

I was happy that at least I helped him to pass his last day without too much pain.

Yet again I officiated at a funeral.

I was getting quite good at them.

The ground was hard from the cold, but I managed to dig him a decent grave next to his son.

The girls hung around as I did, and then when I carried him out wrapped in another sheet and laid him to rest, they stood there close to me.

I sang the Buddhist hymn and thanked George for all his good company and good service.

He had been a very loyal goat.

Well girls, I said, after I had heaped the earth onto the body of the last male goat of the herd, it's a celibate life for you all now.

Having been in that state myself for quite a while I felt a bit sorry for them. No more babies, no more kids.

We had a kind of wake with some sweet little carrots and some other veggies that I had harvested.

We were all in the kitchen, goat girls and me.

On their behalf I drank quite a lot of a very mellow Saint Julien red from the Médoc and I did not get to meditate.

I fell asleep at the kitchen table and had a nasty head in the morning.

The kitchen was freezing as the fire had gone out. I had left the door open, and not shut the cattle into their shed.

I wrapped myself in layers and went out to see how they were doing. They were all there and seemed happy enough.

I felt miserable.

Goodbye, George.

It's snowing again with howling winds.

Sound track from a horror film.

I braced myself against the slashing diagonals of white flakes to open the sheds, but no-one seemed very interested in venturing out. Mon Veau came out for a few minutes, but even he didn't like the look of the weather and went back in.

I soon went back in myself and banked up the fire.

The goats stayed close.

The Lotois had to be tough to live through winters like this.

I wonder what they did all winter, my predecessors.

Knitting and playing chess I suppose.

Are you ready? she asks.

In meditation I hear her voice.

I know what she is referring to.

Inside there is a solid sense of acceptance.

I am ready.

You have to let everything go.

I am ready to do that.

I am at peace with that.

I have done what I could.

I kept myself cheerful.

I found things to do.

I am OK about leaving it all.

Then she begins to appear and it is not who I expected.

I have not seen Clo in meditation, except when everyone was there.

Now here she is looking very calm and happy.

There is a very sweet upswelling of love for her.

Will you be there? I find myself asking.

Je t'attends, she says I am waiting for you.

She begins to fade.

A bientôt, she says, see you soon, and is gone.

I miss her.

The feeling of her company stays and it is very comforting.

I wanted to ask what happened, how did she die, what happened to everyone else?

The meditation left me both very calm about leaving soon, but also sad that I could not keep contact with her just a little bit longer.

She said I have to let everything go.

That means her too.

I remember Gervais telling me the same thing.

To have the feeling of missing her is to not let her go.

She has gone.

I am sure of that.

I am sure now that she is no longer alive.

I am pretty sure no-one else is either.

I will see her soon.

She is waiting for me.

I am letting things go in more ways than one.

Mon Veau has gone.

He just walked off.

My friend and companion since he was born has walked away.

Where did he go, in the middle of all this snow?

What called him?

I have to let him go, just like everything else.

I will miss him.

He was my walking companion, my cart puller, the only male left of our company.

Maybe he will come back.

Maybe like George or Ma Vache he has gone off to mate.

Maybe there is some sexy young heifer somewhere, calling him.

He's a handsome boy, he will make a good progenitor.

So now it's just me and the ladies.

Once again I am in female company, unless you count Boris.

I checked on Boris, just in case he was planning to leave, one way or the other, but there he was, cocksure of himself as always.

The storm has gone and it is eerily still now.

The sky is crystal clear and it's freezing outside.

The snow is crunchy underfoot.

I keep the fire banked up high.

If I am going soon, I look around and feel the château is good.

I will leave it in good shape.

I will leave the chapel just as it is with all its relics.

I have left the safe house and the family cemetery clean and neat.

I will leave the shed doors unlocked so they can be pushed open whenever the girls want to venture out.

I will open all the sheds that have hay so they can help themselves.

I have put out some of the stored veggies that they like, especially the carrots.

I cannot know what will happen to them but I will provide for them, at least for a little while.

I prepare myself.

I sit for meditation thinking it might be my last.

Now I have good discipline, knowing it might be the final one.

I focus on the mantra and breathe deeply and go inside.

When I come out, I feel very peaceful and a bit disappointed. That wasn't it.

I realise I have expectations about going.

It's ridiculous I know.

I have to tell myself : Not today.

I almost envy prisoners on death row or the saints who were put to death for their faith. They knew what was coming and could make themselves ready.

I make myself as ready as I can, but I am still here.

When Adèle finished her last life, she knew how and when she would die.

I can imagine her standing up against the wall of the church of Saint Fé.

I imagine she stood erect and proud.

What were her last thoughts?

Most likely the torture had been terrible and she was in great pain, but she would not want to show that.

I can see the German soldiers with their rifles ready.

She can see them.

Do they blindfold her?

What do they say to her before they fire?

Maybe they don't say anything. Maybe these executioners are just poor dumb German soldiers, maybe just kids, maybe teenagers.

Is it the Alsatian woman who gives the order?

I can imagine the sound of the shots ringing out through the valley of Saint Fé.

The silence that follows.

I almost envy her.

She had courage.

She had conviction.

She had faith.

I look forward to asking her about all this.

I go to sleep with the same idea.

This could be the last one.

Then I wake up in the morning and I say: Oh well, still here.

And I get to enjoy another day of life on earth.

I keep expecting.

I have to stop doing that.

I expect Mon Veau to turn up looking frisky.

I expect someone to come in my meditation and tell me things. I don't really mind who it might be.

Anyone would do.

I expect not to be here after I go to sleep.

I expect......

I have to get rid of all that.

No expectations.

I woke up today with a shock.

A sudden powerful thought had shot me out of sleep.

Am I completely deluding myself?

I am forty-one years old.

My birthday floated by in June and I totally missed it.

Why am I thinking of dying?

Do I want to die?

Not really.

I am a healthy person with a strong body, no health problems and a healthy, I think, mind.

My parents, lived into their seventies at least. Last time I spoke to them they had both just made it into their eighth decade and were planning their next holiday to the Gold Coast.

My grandparents, all four of them, lived to a ripe old age.

I have longevity in my genes.

So why should I cut it short?

I woke up with a fresh zest for life.

Life is there to be lived.

It has its own purpose and its own trajectory.

I was happy to wake up, go into the chapel and have a good meditation, then a hot breakfast, and then go out to see the girls and milk myself a blend of goat and cow juice.

Life is good.

I have a cellar full of great wine, a year's supply at least of smoked ham, fabulous cheeses, and enough jam to last several lifetimes.

Why waste it all?

I could not believe how happy I was with this new idea.

I was as happy as I have been for a long time.

The sun came out, low and white on the southern horizon, but there was a definite warmth in it.

The girls came out, the cows from their shed and the goats from the kitchen, and I loved watching them as they grazed in the freshly unsnowed pasture.

They seemed happy.

Boris and his harem clucked and pecked their way round the sleeping veggie garden.

They were happy.

Maybe what had made me think of death was the greyness of winter, the shortness of the days, being shut in by the snow.

Maybe all that made me depressed.

Was that it?

Anyway right now I am feeling like I can go on with my simple rustic life.

I put some work into sprucing up the safe house memorial, because the snow had messed it up a bit.

There is something majestically austere about it in the winter. There are no flowers, but there is a quietness there, and the simplicity of the altar and bare stone floor that seems to be just the right thing to honour those who died there.

I visited the family cemetery, but everything was fine there too.

Nobody stirred.

I did miss Mon Veau on my walk.

I do hope he comes back.

Now it's the end of a very good day.

I have opened a fine bottle of Saint Etienne.

It has depth and leaves such an agreeable blackcurrent afterglow on the palate. I am most grateful to the tastes of the mayor of Saint Fé.

Life is good.

You are fooling yourself, they tell me.

After a day of joyful entertainment and *joie de vivre*, those souls who I suppose have my best interests at heart came to let me know I had strayed from the path.

They littered my dreams in different forms.

Gervais came and wagged a finger at me.

Female figures morphed from the Virgin to Clo, Adèle to Saint Fé.

They were all expecting me to be with them shortly.

They had expectations!

I woke up feeling totally confused.

I didn't know what was right.

Should I embrace living, or to get ready to die?

The whole question of dying is weird.

How am I going to die?

I am not sick.

I am certainly not about to commit suicide.

I don't climb trees or drive a quad bike.

Will I just stop breathing and that's it?

Or is this a completely idle question that I get no answer to until I actually do die, then it will be completely irrelevant.

It is better to think about how I will live.

How I die can take care of itself.

The problem with all this is it leaves me in limbo.

I drift back and forth between accepting that I will die soon and wanting to go on living.

Sometimes in meditation I am deeply content to die, I almost feel as if in that moment I have already died.

And then there are times when I am with the animals enjoying the winter sun outside or sitting snug and warm by the fire with wine and a book where I feel idyllic.

Back and forth.

Back and forth.

You have died so many times, he says. What holds you back?

Who is this?

It is a male presence but not one that I recognise.

You died by fire, by plague, by your own hand, by the sword, by despair, by the gentle portal of destiny. And every time, you had to let go. That's how you die.

I found myself calling out : When? Is it now? Is it soon? How can I know?

You will know.

But I am stuck in the middle.

Let go.

How?

If you held a snake in your hand that threatens to bite you, you would drop it. Simple as that.

No it's not.

Learn how to let go

And then whoever it was said nothing more which did not help much.

I sat there in the chapel, as confused and unsure as I had ever been.

Whoever that was did not clear up anything.

I really need a spiritual counsellor.

The beings who are hovering around me are way too enigmatic.

I need straight up and down answers to the basic questions.

If, for example, I have died many times by all those different methods, then who am I that keeps dying like that?

Who is the I that comes and goes?

Adèle said that I was God, but that raised more questions than it answered.

If I am God, then who is everyone else?

And how come God can keep dying all the time?

It really is quite a burden carrying round all these questions with no reliable source of information.

I wonder what would happen if I could Google God?

So here I am writing down my questions and spending all day agonising about when and how I am going to die.

What kind of life is that?

It might be a great relief to die, just to stop the incessant self-questioning.

That voice suggested I had died by my own hand, at some point, would I be willing to do that again?

Don't think so.

The only relief from this is to do things, practical and tangible things.

I am almost frantically looking for things to do.

I cook concoctions to keep myself amused. I have not poisoned myself yet.

That would be one way of going I suppose.

Clo and I saw a film once made by French anarchists, called La Grande Bouffe where four men decide to eat themselves to death and spend a weekend of gourmet cooking and other sense pleasures, then one by one they die.

I don't have the stomach for that.

Instead I fix shed doors and feed the animals and go on living.

I root around in the cellar and find boxes of junk.

I sort it all out, deciding what might be valuable and what is junk.

Who am I saving the good stuff for?

I read books and enjoy the diversion of living in vicarious worlds for a while.

I float in English flim flam or grapple with French philosophy.

Anything to keep my mind away from the to die or not to die question.

I never got to play Hamlet but I did have to study it. That speech is pretty good in terms of describing what I am wrestling with.

Do I shuffle off this mortal coil?

To sleep, to dream. For in that sleep of death what dreams may come....

Makes me pause.

Funny to think of Shakespeare, because if I remember correctly, he wrote most of his plays in the middle of a pandemic. He was probably as isolated as me and stopped going bananas by writing plays.

He did have Anne Hathaway for company.

All I have is ghostly visitors and an exercise book that is nearly full

I don't think I am quite up to his standard.

The image of all those people who appeared in the celebration of Adèle's birthday is constantly with me.

I assume now that they are all dead, physically no longer in this world and are on some other plane of consciousness. I also assume that as soon as I do get rid of this body, I will end up like them.

They all seemed to be perfectly happy wherever they were.

They had a nice place to hang out.

It also bothers me a bit that according to Gervais I am holding them back from something because I am still here. Does that mean that when I die, and I stop holding them back, they can get promoted to a higher level or something?

Do they get to move upstairs?

Am I responsible for preventing that?

That's a very heavy burden to carry.

Are they laying a guilt trip on me?

Or it could well be that I've got the whole thing wrong.

The whole thing could just be imagery.

No more real than dreams.

I could just die and end up like the corpses in the family cemetery at the bottom of the hill.

Only there won't be anyone round to bury the body there, or to set fire to the château.

When and where I do drop dead, my corpse will just rot right where it dropped.

It's all so completely unanswerable that I really have to stop thinking about this.

The best solution comes on days when I wake up feeling good, have a peaceful meditation, enjoy breakfast, be happy to see the girls come trooping out for the day, draw myself some fresh milk and have a good walk. Glove has started to come with me now and then and sometimes Jenny, so I have occasional companion replacements for Mon Veau.

At the end of a day like this, I feel good.

I can keep going for a while.

They, those folk from beyond, left me in peace for a while, letting me lull myself into a false sense of wellbeing.

Until : We are waiting for you.

Oh no , I thought, in the depths of an otherwise wonderfully warm meditation.

For the last few days my meditations had been very quiet, dropping into a deep space with little content.

I would come out feeling at peace with myself, happy to go on with life.

Then there they were.

It was a floating parade of faces.

Parades have floats, so why not.

Adèle seemed to be the overall supervising presence, but Clo was in there and Gervais.

I wonder if they have committee meetings to discuss how to get me to see the error of my ways.

Do they have the means to just make it happen?

I doubt it.

If they did, I would have gone long ago.

I think it is up to me.

I have to decide.

But I can't just decide to die, unless I choose to knock myself off and I have no inclination to do that.

With my lack of skill with the gun for example, I would probably just blow off an ear and spend the rest of my life looking like Vincent van Gogh.

Bu there's no denying, there they are.

They want me to come and join them.

Maybe it is, as Gervais told me, that I really am holding them back.

Am I going to have to leave the earth so they can go on holidays in heaven?

I can't ask, because they are not open to conversations about this, they just keep nudging.

They float in and out and tell me to get on with it.

So I tried an experiment.

I sat in meditation and I said to the universe: OK, if I am supposed to die so that the earth can breathe again, I am ready, take me out.

Then I sat there.

And sat there.

And sat there.

Absolutely nothing.

I got up feeling dejected.

On the one hand I am still alive, healthy and quite willing to do my daily routine.

On the other hand, there is pressure from above.

Either way, I would really like some kind of resolution.

I love having the goats live with me in the kitchen.

They have their own corner where I put fresh hay every couple of days.

They like it in the kitchen.

I leave the door open all day and they come and go.

The two cows not so much, although Jenny ventures in now and then. Ma Vache is much more of an outdoors girl.

At night by the glow of the fire and with candles burning I have company.

The goats settle in together all three of them in their hay bed and it makes me very happy.

Glove is particularly loving. She will often come up to me and rub herself against my leg and look up at me with her curious goaty eyes.

I have never had much experience with goats but I have come to really appreciate them.

Most of the time they seem to know not to poo inside, but every now and then I have to clean up.

I don't mind.

It is getting beyond a joke.

They are beginning to really annoy me, not the goats, the beings who are insisting on turning up in meditation and urging me to die.

Today I yelled back.

For God's sake, stop bugging me. I don't know how to die and you are not helping. If you could tell me how to do it, in the right way, not just shoot my head off with a gun, I would give it a try.

That was pretty weird.

I have never yelled in meditation but it was heartfelt and rather satisfying.

They were driving me to distraction, and they had begun to seem almost selfish about it.

It's what they want.

They want me to join them, free them up from being yoked to my earthly existence.

I was beginning to not like them at all.

Even Adèle.

It's all been lovey lovey for so long, but now I am fed up.

So when she appeared, looking quite angelic, I wasn't having it.

You are an illusion, I yelled at her.

She just looked calmly at me for a long minute and then she smiled.

So are you, she said, and faded away.

I was so pissed with that I jumped up and charged out of the chapel in a rage.

I put on a coat and boots and went down to the safe house.

It was cold but not freezing. I stood there looking at the altar and thinking about the people who died in the house.

They died.

They ceased to have a body.

I will do the same, but I don't know how.

Then there was a rush of wind and I felt a presence.

I couldn't tell who or what it was but then a big male deer, a buck with mature horns walked out of the underbrush by the creek.

He stood watching me for a long minute.

You want to know how to die?

Did I hear this in my head or was it the deer?

It took several steps towards me and then stopped.

Like this, I heard.

It crashed in a heap across the stone of the floor of the safe house with its horns up against the altar.

I was so stunned that I stood there for a long time staring at it.

At last I went over and touched it.

It was warm but didn't move.

I felt round its neck to see if I could feel a pulse.

Nothing.

He was dead.

I jumped back and raced out of the safe house.

Now I was beginning to freak out.

I rushed back up to the château and built up the fire and cooked some veggies and tried to get my mind calm.

What is all this?

What I am supposed to do?

If nothing else I have to get rid of a deer carcass from the safe house.

A weird idea crossed my mind: Was it a sacrifice?

Like in some ancient temple, like the bulls in the temple to Jupiter or offering virgins to the Mayan Gods?

Is this what it was?

I had no way of knowing, and even if it was some kind of sacrifice what did it signify?

Who was sacrificing to whom, and why?

It didn't seem to have changed anything.

In the afternoon, I felt brave enough to venture back into the chapel.

I lit the candles and I looked at all the relics.

I sent up a prayer.

I am sorry I yelled at you all, but I need some decent guidance.

Then I sat, wrapped in blankets and closed my eyes.

Nothing.

Nothing.
Are they playing with me?
Have they taken compassion on me and backed off?
Are they pissed with me?
Just nothing.
I eventually got up and made mint tea and tried to make sense of it.
I am trying to make sense of it.
It is making no sense.

The next morning I went back to the safe house with the tools to bury the deer.
There was no way I was going to try to extract some venison.
I am no butcher.
I just wanted to get rid of it.

It was gone.
Of course it was gone.
The whole thing was probably another illusion.
I was so pissed off.
I stood in the middle of the safe house and yelled and yelled till I was hoarse.
I ended up on my knees in front of the altar.
I was the most wretched I had ever been.

Then all the goats appeared, all three.
They must have heard me.
Glove rubbed herself against me and Adèle came close and bleated, looking up at me with her head on one side.
Even Betty seemed concerned.
I fondled them for a while, just trying to get a sense of calm.
Their warmth and their lovely faces were exactly what I needed.
At last I got to my feet.

They walked beside me as I slowly went back, carrying my unused shovel and superfluous pick, feeling like a lost soul.

The goats were keeping me company.

Thank God for goats.

I think they saved my sanity.

I dreamed I was dead.

It was such a relief.

It felt incredibly light and free.

I didn't go off to some other plane of consciousness though.

I didn't go anywhere.

I didn't see any of those who have been waiting for me.

There was no-one there.

Instead I floated up above the kitchen where I could see my body lying by the fire, and I could see the goats asleep in their hay bed.

I knew I was dead.

It was not a thought.

I had the sensation of having dropped the weight of that body.

It didn't bother me at all to be dead.

I just was.

But nothing else.

I simply floated there, in mid-air, disembodied, dead.

I didn't go anywhere, didn't see anyone, no blue lights, no angels, nothing.

Then I woke up.

I wasn't dead.

It was a nasty tease.

But something is happening.

Or rather not happening.

Somehow I think it is connected to the moon.

I can feel my energy dropping off.

I get up in the morning and I see the moon which is quite full, and it makes me feel very quiet. I spend a lot of time staring at it without thoughts.

I watch it set before I start anything else.

I do what I normally do but I am dragging myself along.

No energy.

I quite like this state.

It is peaceful, still and warm.

I find myself sitting somewhere, vacant, no thought, no action.

I just sit.

I watch the goats and the two cows doing their animal things, and I can sit there for ages.

The moon is waning.

I am becoming very aware of its trajectory each day.

I now get up in the night to look at it.

The moon is waning.

I am waning.

We are diminishing together.

My days get simpler and simpler.

I don't bother to milk Ma Vache or Betty any more.

I feel no need.

I eat almost nothing.

I walk around, but slowly.

It takes ages to make it down to the safe house or the cemetery.

I walk gently, almost as if I am walking in meditation.

The goats come and they have more energy than I do.

The moon is down to less than half.

High and still in the middle of the night.

The moon and I fading together.

The moon is my companion.
I am fading away.
I can feel it.

The moon is now just a sliver of curved light.
It has appeared earlier and earlier in the night, and I have watched the gradual diminution.
At first it rose in the evening, and I would wait for it before going to bed.
Now it is rising almost at dawn.
I watch it appear before meditation.
I have the image of its crescent very clearly as I close m eyes in the chapel.
In the same way, little by little I am fading.
Every day there is a little less.
While the days are getting longer and the hints of spring are appearing, I am in my personal autumn.
I can feel it.
Fading.

Just a fingernail of a moon left.
A tiny shining filigree ring under a dark circle.
Such quietness in the chapel.
Such peace in the air.
I am going.

Barely make it to open the book.
Nothing to record.

I did not see the moon.
Clouds.
Fading.
Every day less.
Less.

Fading.
No moon.
I am coming.
I feel it.

Barely move my fingers to write.
Barely open my eyes.
No-one needs to tell me to go.
Letting go.

I am ready.
Coming.

Fading.
Goodbye girls, take care of yourselves.

Such peace.

Gone.

Note attached to an exhibit at the Museum
of Post Corona Extinction.
Mullumbimbi
Australia
Document discovered July 2092
Found near Gourdon in the Lot
France.

While the only countries to survive the near global human extinction of 2020, Australia and New Zealand remained isolated and self-sufficient for the following fifty years, the first explorations of the rest of the planet were robotic drones.

This document was discovered during the later explorations of rural Europe after it was deemed safe for humans to travel there.

The earlier exploration by robots and drones had determined that there may have been isolated examples of humans able to survive for longer after the mass extinction of Europeans, as a result of the catastrophic combination of Corona virus and 5G radiation.

While whole cities were simply emptied of human life, here and there small groups or even single individuals seemed to manage to survive for a short period afterwards. This document, discoverd in a château in the Lot, is a very detailed account of the person concerned and how he lived for nearly a year after the extinction.

So far this is the only documentation discovered of an Australian who survived the initial extinction.

AUTHOR'S NOTE

The writing of this work took place as the world wrestled with its Covid 19 onslaught. My confinement was the writing of this work using the thoughts and ideas that were alive during the pandemic. I felt I was living two lives at once, equally absorbing, my own and that of Simon Teague. In one sense quite a bit of what he thinks about it what I found myself thinking about.

My thanks to all the women in my life. That thought is mine. And it includes dear Susie Langley who diligently proofread the text, which having been written fast contained all sorts of ineptitudes.

August 2020